A CRY

IN THE

CITY

Also by Pauline Glen Winslow

Judgment Day
The Windsor Plot
The Rockefeller Gift
I, Martha Adams
The Counsellor Heart
Coppergold
The Witch Hill Murder
The Brandenberg Hotel
Death of an Angel
Gallows Child

A CRY
IN THE
CITY

Pauline
Glen
Winslow

ST. MARTIN'S PRESS
NEW YORK

Library of Congress Cataloging-in-Publication Data

Winslow, Pauline Glen.
      A cry in the city / Pauline Glen Winslow.
          p.   cm.
      "A Thomas Dunne Book."
      ISBN 0-312-04289-2
      I. Title.
    PR6073.I553C78   1990
    823'.914—dc20   89-77682
                                                                   CIP

First Edition

10 9 8 7 6 5 4 3 2 1

For Ray, with love

Acknowledgments

With warmest thanks to the Special Frauds Squad, Missing Persons Squad, and the First Precinct of the NYPD, and Troop K of the NYSP, for all the help that they have given.

PART I

1

The tree on the front porch was still lit up. The old colored lights shone on the ornaments hanging from the branches—the little houses, the snowmen, the angels, the bells—and they cast a glow on the children, huddled over their new jigsaw puzzle. Tom Christopher's dark head was bent, concentrated on his task, but four-year-old Linda heard her mother approaching the doorway to the living room and looked up, pouting a little to see her dressed in coat and scarf and carrying her overnight bag.

"Mommy!"

"I have to be off, darling; Grandma will be here in a couple of minutes. You would insist on staying, you two, so behave yourselves now. You mustn't annoy Grandma; it's very good of her to let you stay. Mind your manners. Tom, you'll look after Linda. I'll see you on Thursday."

"Okay," Tom muttered. He was still absorbed in trying to find a place for the piece in his hand. But Mary knew he was pleased to be appealed to as the elder child. For the last year or two he had been helpful with Linda, the early storms forgotten. And both of them had wanted to stay; tomorrow's children's party with all their cousins at Susan's house was a highlight of the holiday. For the hundredth time she felt sorry she had to go; for the hundredth time she told herself that her engagement was important and that Alice could manage for a couple of days.

The children could stay on the porch until she came. It was

warm; the Thermopane glass held in all the heat that came from the living room. They were quiet— Then Linda jumped up to give her a kiss and a hug, and her flailing little arms knocked a shiny ball off a low-hanging branch. Fortunately, it fell on the rug—the ornaments had been brought from Germany by a traveling Christopher over sixty years ago and were very fragile. Alice cherished them, and Alice, though a kind, warm grandmother, believed firmly that children should be raised to be civilized indoors. "They can go out to the orchard and raise hell when they feel like it," she would say. Mary knew, with a feeling of guilt, that her mother-in-law was more strict than she was. Often she felt anxious about the children let loose among the antiques in daily use in that house. Deftly, she replaced the gleaming ball on the branch.

"Now, be *careful* with the tree, Linda."

The rain was beating down hard against the glass. She checked the time on her watch; she was cutting it very fine. Because of the weather, Mary had decided to leave her car at Hastings Wood station, go by train down to New York, and pick the car up again on Thursday. It would save her a long night drive. But Alice was late coming back.

"Who's going to put me to bed?" Linda demanded suddenly.

"Grandma will."

"When is she coming?"

Linda had got to the questioning stage.

"Any moment now."

Alice was coming from the nearby town of Burgoyne, where a concert had been held that afternoon in the big, beautiful, historic house of Boy Burgoyne, her special friend. He had sent a car for her.

Mary looked up the lane, but it was totally dark. If there was any delay in parking the car, she would miss the train. And it was the last train from Hastings Wood. After hugging the children, she picked her bag up and went to wait by the door of the back porch, which led to the driveway. She had already brought her little white car out of the garage and it was sitting under the dripping branches of the maple tree a few yards from the house.

Then the corner of the lane brightened in the beam of headlights. Mary went out with her bag onto the steps, slapped by the cold rain. Alice was smiling from the back seat of Boy's new black Cadillac. Boy Burgoyne wasn't driving; it was his handyman, Lesska, whose pale, thin face peered over the wheel. Alice liked to tease Boy about his fancy new possessions, including cars, which Lesska seemed to worship. She leaned out of the window and remarked, "Not as roomy as my old Chevy."

For a moment she looked like her former self, almost girlish as she giggled, the slight look of strain that had become noticeable since her small stroke quite gone. Then she settled herself back in the car.

"Drive me up to the garage, Lesska, please. Mary"—she turned to her daughter-in-law, who was standing by the side of the car—"you should have something on your head." Reaching into her bag, she brought out a plastic hood that was folded into a small sheath and watched while Mary unfolded it. "Boy asked me for some old survey maps of the property that I've got stored in that big box out there; he's doing some project for the town. It's not urgent, but I might as well do it while I think of it; it'll only take a moment. Have Tom and Linda had their supper?"

"Yes," Mary replied, "and they have the new puzzle. That should keep them quiet."

"Well, you'd better hurry. Take good care. I think the rain is freezing."

It was. Mary's fingers were chilled and she fumbled with the plastic strings, trying to tie them under her chin as she went to her car. The keys slithered from her hand and fell in a clump of grass. She was doubled over, groping, when the Cadillac swung around from the garage and shot by her, clearing the drive.

The roads were slippery up here in the Dutchess County hills and she was glad she only had to drive to the station. But soon she was sorry she had decided to make the trip at all. It would have been better if she'd stayed over with the children. Alice, who'd loved having Linda and Tom to stay, had been frank as always as her health declined.

"Take them, Mary," she'd said, the last time she had handed them back. "I'm too old to be mothering again. I can enjoy them much better with you in charge." She had laughed, but it had been true. Then Christmas had come and she had wanted the children to go to Susan's party. From the first year of her marriage, Alice, who had been a Bailey, opened her house in Spenser for the whole Bailey-Christopher clan on Christmas Day; when Mary came into the family she was allowed to help. But after her illness, Alice had had to give it up. "It's the noise, Mary," she had said resignedly, "even more than the work," and Christmas had broken up into small family groups, with one or another of the family giving a party for the grownups on New Year's Eve or meeting each other at the Burgoynes'. The children had complained bitterly that they were left out, so now kind-hearted Susan gave an afternoon party for them, a combined Christmas–New Year's celebration.

"Don't worry, it will be all right," Alice had said. "If I need help, Jane will always come over."

Jane Johnson was her neighbor, a farm wife, almost as old as Alice, but still in good health. It had seemed important to Mary to keep her appointment, for Alice as well as herself. The editor who was helping her with Quentin's book had promised her several uninterrupted hours the next day. Because of the holidays, there would be few people working and they should be able to thrash out a few problems and get a lot done. Alice was eager to see the book appear in print, a memento of her son, her only child. And yet—

Mary was driving down a steep hill by a stream, well away from the Cyclone fence, when she felt the car going into a skid. She wrestled with the wheel; by the time she got the car under control, she was in a heavy sweat. "More luck than judgment," she reproached herself and slowed down. The car was old and had never been good at holding the road. Because it was so small and light, Quentin had enjoyed its convenience in running around the city and its economy in gas, but for the children's sake, she should get something better. As soon as Linda was in school and she got back to work. Of course, then there would be two lots of school fees, and the city wasn't doing much about librarians' salaries.

And the car had cost her a lot of money just six months before. She'd been sideswiped on Seventh Avenue, bringing the children back from the Planetarium. Tom got a bruised elbow, but none of them were seriously hurt. She had worried about Linda being afraid of riding in the car afterward, but the little girl had been composed the next time they went out.

"Don't forget to put your seat belt on, Mommy, and don't break the car." Mary smiled, remembering. Linda, the little grandmother.

Thank heaven she wasn't driving all the way back to New York in this weather. She drove slowly and carefully but the rain was coming down harder. To make matters worse, the wipers weren't doing their job. They seemed to have picked up grease or oil and they were smudging as they wiped. She stopped at the next gas station, but it was jammed with cars. It seemed forever before she could get the attention of one of the men pumping gas and then a long, fidgety wait while he found a pair of wipers.

When she arrived at the train station, the platform was empty. An elderly man, pulling out of the lot in an old Buick, told her the train had gone.

"But if you're going to the city, you might make the connection at Brewster. There's been emergency track work going on and the trains have been running late every day."

Mary had had to make that trip before. Thanking him, she took the two-lane highway. The traffic here was light and it wasn't quite forty minutes later when she drove into the town, congratulating herself. But the streets were busy for such a wet night and she wasted a few minutes poking along. She knew of a place close to the station where she could leave the car, but she never got there. As she came within sight of the tracks, she saw the rear lights of the New York train glowing red for a moment before they disappeared into the dark. For once the 7:15 had been precisely on time.

Well, this was the main line, she told herself. There would be another train in an hour. The rain drummed on the roof. Very likely the next train would be late; it was that kind of day. She had come so far and the driving really hadn't been bad on the highway. Making a quick decision, she turned the car around and headed for New York. In an hour and a half she would be home.

But as soon as she was on her way, she found herself behind a big, slow-moving truck that was spewing a black exhaust. When she finally had a chance to pass, she shot ahead. From somewhere behind her a horn blared angrily, but she felt a sense of relief as she scanned the road for the southbound highway. She was moving along at a decent speed and the entrance had to be coming up at any moment. Farther along she was puzzled; she saw no underpass, no overpass, no brightly lit sign, only the dark, narrow road. Soon she wasn't sure which way she was going, only that she was winding around between stretches of grass and bushes that seemed to lead nowhere.

At last there was a glow of light. About twenty yards off the road a sign announced TONY'S TAVERN. Thankful, Mary drove up to the parking lot and ran inside to ask directions. It was a large, barnlike place with a few customers on stools up at the bar, still bright with Christmas decorations. Two couples were sitting in booths, absorbed in talk.

Mary asked the bartender for directions, but he was washing glasses and two men at the end of the bar were calling impatiently for fresh drinks. A young man with receding blond hair, wearing a bright plaid hunting jacket, had been staring at the television set. He turned and smiled at Mary.

"I can tell you, but it's kind of a hassle. Why don't you sit down, let me get you a drink?"

"Thank you." Mary smiled in return. "But I'm running very late. I really can't stop."

"Okay." He explained, drawing the route with a thick pencil on a paper napkin, and giving a lot of instructions. "It's really hard to spot, if you don't know the area," he ended, and he rose from his stool and stood close to her. He smiled again, an ingratiating smile, and she got a strong whiff of liquor on his breath. "I think I'd better get in your car and show you the way. It's just a couple of minutes to the approach, then you can drop me back and shoot off to the big city."

He tried to take her arm, but Mary backed away. "Oh, please don't trouble. I do understand perfectly—you've made it very clear. And I am in a hurry. Thank you for being so kind."

Outside it seemed darker than ever. As she walked toward her car, her heel caught in a hole in the macadam and she tripped, staggering into the bushes, deep in mud. As she righted herself, the light was shining in the doorway of the bar and she saw the figure of the too helpful man. He was laughing.

She was soon back on the highway. It was a miserable drive but nothing else went wrong until she reached the Hutchinson River Parkway. There she was stalled for about twenty minutes; a three-car pile-up was blocking the lane a mile down the road. By the time she had passed the George Washington Bridge, she was tired and frustrated. Fortunately the West Side Highway was reasonably clear and she got down to the Village with no more difficulty.

It was a pity she hadn't eaten with the children. Five o'clock had seemed too early, but she was too tired to bother now. And there wasn't any cream in the apartment for coffee. She drove straight to the all-night supermarket, miraculously found a parking spot outside the Corner Bar, and dashed across the street. There weren't too many people in the market and she went down the aisles quickly, picking up eggs, bacon, and bread. She was looking doubtfully at the loaf in her hand—there was nothing left that she really liked— when someone called her name.

"Mary!" It was Carol Grafton, an old friend from her working days, also a librarian.

"Lovely to see you," Carol said, "though you look like the orphan of the storm." Mary looked down ruefully. Mud to the ankles—that parking lot in the wilderness. She had lost the plastic hood, too, in the bushes up there, and her hair was damp and mussed.

Carol, blond and bubbly, looking chic in a well-tailored raincoat and a broad-brimmed matching hat, was obviously delighted to see her and eager to talk. "It's been years—I've moved out, you know, to Staten Island. I'm working at a branch there now. Very quiet, but living's so much cheaper than in Manhattan. I'm just here for a couple of days; been staying with my brother and his wife over Christmas. Let's go down to Fanelli's and get a hamburger and a drink and you tell me what's been happening."

Mary disliked bars, but Fanelli's was different. It had been a favorite spot with the whole crew at the Minetta branch and it was always full of Villagers. It seemed as old as Manhattan itself and it was as friendly and cheap as any eating and drinking place could be in the city. And they wouldn't mind her disheveled looks. She tidied up a little in the ladies' room and felt better after a drink and a hamburger with French fries. Only rarely would she eat the bun, let alone French fries; she was inclined to put on weight, but that night it all tasted good. Since the death of Quentin she had hardly seen Carol. They had a lot to talk about.

"You look well, now that you've dried off," Carol said, grinning. "You were pretty down, last time I saw you."

It had been just after the funeral—a memorial service, really, as Quent's body was already interred—which had been held in Spenser. The family had a plot in the cemetery; a grave had been waiting for Quentin, with one for Mary beside him. It was, of course, what Alice wanted and Quentin had liked the idea of their having a place with his family when it had been proposed. But not many of Mary's and Quentin's New York friends could go up to Spenser on a weekday and so some of them had arranged a private memorial. A professor from the Fine Arts Department had lent his spacious loft for the occasion; a minister had said a prayer; and several of Quentin's former colleagues had spoken a few words of reminiscence, honoring his life. Mary had been touched and when someone handed her a rather stiff drink and she saw herself surrounded by friends, she had relaxed for the first time, it seemed, since Quentin had first been stricken. The family at Spenser had been kind and thoughtful, but the people she had known in the day-to-day life of her marriage gave her a special comfort.

Carol, who had always liked Quentin a lot, had come to the memorial. She had never been much of a child lover, but she had held baby Linda and had watched Tom, leaving Mary free to talk to other guests. After that, they had lost touch. Mary felt guilty; she had lost touch with too many people after Quentin died.

"You moved out of University Village," Carol remarked.

Mary explained that her lease at the university-owned building had come to its end and she wasn't entitled to a renewal. "It was really only for the faculty and staff, you know. The people there were very good; they didn't pressure me, but I knew I would have to go and sooner seemed better than later." It had been too painful to sleep in the room that she and Quent had once shared. It had been Quent's sickroom almost to the end.

A young girl and boy were sitting at the next table, very close to Mary. They wore jeans and striped T-shirts, with down jackets bundled up next to them. The two of them were gazing at each other and talking and laughing excitedly while their omelets got cold and their salads warm. For a moment Mary remembered being there with Quentin before they were married. Not so young, a little less noisy, but locked in that same magnetic bond.

She still felt the thrust of sadness, but these days it was bearable. Her wound was healing.

Carol talked of Quent. "Well, you had a good marriage. That's something, even if it was much too short. Not everybody does."

Carol's move to Staten Island, it transpired, had come about because of a marriage. "Well, I don't know if you remember about Steve and me—"

Mary thought she remembered somebody dropping Carol off when she arrived at the memorial. Perhaps that had been Steve.

"The thing is, it's not working out. He's a good guy, a good husband, but— I've been offered a job, in midtown, managing a bookstore for one of the big chains. I'm thinking of taking it. There's a *future*. I mean, not budget cuts every five minutes. Of course, it would be a drag to commute. I can stay with my brother for a while and I figure I can maybe swing a condo—the pay is good and if we sell the house—"

She gulped the remains of her drink. "But what I wanted to ask you about, really, is—well, *what's it like out there?*"

Carol hoped to get up-to-date information about the lives of single women in Manhattan—divorcées and widows.

"I don't suppose it's much different from what it was four years ago." The place was crowded; there were people waiting who would have liked their table and Mary felt tired again. It was time she left, but she couldn't deny an old friend the comfort of a girl-to-girl talk—or woman-to-woman, to be more accurate. They were neither of them young; she was thirty-six and Carol probably close to that. But Carol had asked the wrong person, and Mary tried to explain. After Quent, she had been too much in grief, and there had been the children—"I take them up weekends and holidays to Alice, unless she's on vacation. You've never met my mother-in-law, but she's a wonderful woman. She's been such a help since we lost Quent; it's been a real second home for the children up there, and me, too. It's—an anchor, if you know what I mean."

A happy, peaceful place. On one of the Christmas holidays when Tom was small and Spenser was blanketed with dazzling white snow, Alice had called it "Christmas country." Tom had always confused Christmas and Christopher and from then on upstate had been "Christopher country," one of many family jokes. They had all loved Christopher country.

Carol nodded. "You're lucky. Steve's mother's a bitch and we fight like hell. It'll be a joy to divorce *her*, I can tell you. But you mean you haven't dated in *four years?*"

"I've seen friends but—no, not really. But I do know that people are getting more careful now. About sex, I mean."

"The AIDS thing." Carol looked depressed. "I don't know—I just long to stay here—really, I don't think I can go back to Staten Island. But you know what I mean. I was thirty-four when I married Steve. Now it's thirty-eight. And you hear about all these surplus women."

"Still, now that people *are* being more careful and more choosy, I think it's better for women, really," Mary told her. "With all that quick hopping into bed, and then on to somebody else, there wasn't time to get to know anyone."

She felt silly and pompous after she had spoken, but she meant what she said. In the city, being a faculty wife usually didn't mean much, not nowadays. Most of them had jobs of their own, the students led their separate lives, and the women on the faculty had their own associations. But with Quent it was different. He invited his students to suppers at the apartment, and any professor or instructor that he liked would be asked to dinner. Quent was a good talker and Mary a good listener, and over the ten years of her marriage she had heard a lot—not all intellectual discussion. She had helped dry a lot of tears from students and faculty members, including women of real distinction.

"You were brought up as a Catholic, weren't you? I know you and Quent were very straight."

"I left the church quite young." Mary couldn't stop it; her jaw opened of its own accord in a huge yawn.

"You're tired," Carol said, contrite. "We'd better go. We can talk again. I'll have to go to Staten Island to get everything settled, but I'll come back and forth. The new job opens up in about a month . . . Give my love to the kids."

Outside, a freezing wind was blowing down from the north. Mary checked the parking lot near her building that she had been using recently, but it was full. She wouldn't find another place tonight. One after another, the parking lots were being built over, and to make matters impossible the city had closed down a huge garage nearby for safety reasons. Mary, along with about two thousand other people, had kept her car there; all of them were now parking on the streets. She would have to leave her own car where it was, by the Corner Bar, get up early tomorrow, and move it.

By the time she reached her apartment, she could think of nothing but a hot bath and bed. She fell asleep at once, a deep sleep, dreamless except that sometime before morning Quent came, an apparition that was more like a still shot than a sequence. His face, as it had been in his illness, was ravaged and worn, he looked up at her in all the misery of the helpless. It passed into nothing. She slept until the alarm went off, and she splashed her face, brushed her teeth hurriedly, pulled some clothes on, and got to the car just as the Brownie was approaching.

There still wasn't an empty space in a parking lot or a garage. Even in her usual lot the overnights were still parked and she had to wait for someone to pull out. It was an hour later when she returned to the apartment and put on the coffee. She felt mussed, took a quick shower, and got into a bathrobe. The cream she had gone to the supermarket to buy wasn't in the refrigerator, only the eggs, bacon, and bread. Meeting Carol, she had forgotten to pick it up. She drank the coffee black and before she finished the first cup she wondered if there was any mail—she hadn't looked the night before—and if there were any messages on the answering machine. She was always forgetting to check it. The machine had been Quentin's; he loved gadgets and he had received many calls. She had brought it with her when she moved because she couldn't bear to throw it away, but she got few messages now.

Quentin. The vision from the night came back poignantly. As she passed through the living room, she looked at her favorite snapshot of Quent, from courtship days. Framed, it showed him on the court behind the house in Spenser. He had just won a hotly contested game and he was glowing.

Looking down at the red message indicator on the machine, she saw "22." Impossible—it had gone wrong again. Perhaps, as it had done before, it had been picking up somebody else's calls. She pushed the rewind and the tape whirred back a long way. It was a slow machine and she went and got another cup of coffee before she pushed the forward knob and thought about breakfast. Turning up the volume, she went back to the kitchen, poured the orange juice, and got out the eggs and bacon. Despite her late-night hamburger, she was hungry. Before Quent's illness she had had a great appetite—he had teased her about it. It had begun to come back, this last year or two. The pants she had pulled on had felt tight around the waist.

The first two messages were Christmas calls from friends, people who had known her when Quent was living and who still kept in touch. The next was Alice, sounding unlike herself, upset, asking Mary to call her at once. She seemed to have called several times. Mary was puzzled. Alice rarely telephoned; she preferred to write letters. Then she felt guilty. She should have called to let Alice know she had gotten home all right; obviously she had been worried. But that wasn't like her, either; Alice wasn't a fusser and always assumed her children and grandchildren were well unless she was told they weren't. She had borne Quentin's illness stoically, remaining calm and going about her normal business up in Spenser to the last; on his death she had tried to comfort her daughter-in-law, and suffered her own loss in silence.

While the machine was running, Mary tried her number but it was busy. The machine *had* gone wrong; the last calls, if calls they were, sounded like a lot of squeaks and squawks. As she turned it off, she heard a loud thumping on her front door. Startled, she left the machine and went to answer it, but then she hesitated.

She was still in her bathrobe. Deliverymen and visitors were supposed to buzz from downstairs to be admitted. The only people who came directly to the door were neighbors, but none of them rapped like that. There was a peephole in the door, rarely needed, but that morning she used it. Looking out cautiously she saw a police officer staring back at her. Before she closed the peephole, she saw another officer beside him, a woman. She opened the door, wondering if something had happened to the car in the lot. Fervently, she hoped it wasn't that. It was too old for the insurance company to pay anything, but it was in good enough condition, or had been. If she had to buy another right now, she didn't know where she would lay hands on the money.

"Mrs. Christopher, Mary Christopher?" the male officer asked. "Your mother-in-law's been trying to get you. Your phone's out."

Alice? Calling the *police* to get through?

"Is she ill?" Mary asked with quick alarm. She *knew* she shouldn't have left the children. Alice wasn't well. She would have to go back—

"She's okay," the officer said, "it's—"

His partner interrupted. "She's just worried, that's all. About the kids—"

"I'll go back right away," Mary said. Alice *must* be ill. She wouldn't have sent the police. The appointment would have to be postponed. It wasn't a matter of life or death. "They must have been too much for her. She isn't . . ."

The woman in the uniform didn't look much like a police officer. Her face was plump and troubled; it gave her a resemblance to Mrs. Ferraro, who lived on the second floor. She had looked like that since her husband got sick—

"You didn't bring the children back with you last night?" the policewoman asked.

And that was the beginning.

2

Mary was still holding the front door, one hand clutching her bathrobe, when the two officers had brushed past her and were checking
her telephone. She wished they'd go, both of them. They'd balled
everything up—and frightened her out of her mind. Alice was upset;
she must talk to her. But why would Alice call the police? Probably it
had been the local operator; it must have been her idea, when she
couldn't get through. She would do anything for Alice and since
Alice's stroke the woman had been a mother hen.

"Phone's okay," the man said. He and his partner had introduced
themselves, but the names had gone from Mary's head. "It's switched
through to the recorder."

He was dialing, probably the precinct. They would straighten it
out.

The woman was looking around. The apartment hadn't been
dusted for days; there was a lot of stuff lying all over that Tom had
fussed with, to take or not to take. The breakfast food was sitting
out in the kitchen; the percolator, which had to be watched, was
boiling away. As she went to pull the plug she noticed she'd used
two different cups; there were dregs in both.

She felt unkempt and she saw the eyes of the woman—Billops,
she'd said, Officer Billops—trained on her. A slob; she must think
her a slob. Suddenly Mary noticed a wet patch on the ceiling, over
the radiator. Her upstairs neighbor had a leak again. Mary had only

just had the ceiling painted; she felt a stab of chagrin and wanted to cry.

"Don't get panicked right off, Mrs. Christopher," Officer Billops said, in a kindly way after all. "We'll check it out."

Mary stared, confused. The police could do nothing about the constant leaks. Her upstairs neighbor *would* leave the radiator valve half open. Then Mary snapped back. Of course, the officer meant Alice. She was *very* kind. But—if only they would go. As soon as she got through to Alice she would know what this was all about. Perhaps the children had been *really* naughty. Gone over to the farm without telling Alice. They loved the Johnson farm and Jane's pet cats. With Jane's cooking—pies and cakes, gingerbreads and Christmas logs—it was altogether their idea of paradise. Jane wouldn't have let them stay long; everything was okay now—the little devils. The operator must have called last night.

But the officers seemed to be in no hurry. You wouldn't think there was a mugging or a robbery going on somewhere in the precinct just about every hour of the day—

"Why don't you sit down?" Officer Billops steered her to a chair, as if she were the hostess. She was a big woman, and although she still had a kind look there was something nervous about her; she kept biting her lower lip and her brow was deeply furrowed. "What time did you leave the children last night?"

The other officer, Nunez—she had heard his name again as he telephoned—also wanted to ask her questions. They were polite, but they didn't seem to realize that she just couldn't wait to talk to Alice, to tell Tom what she thought of him . . .

As she answered the questions, it struck her with force what a fool she had been to leave the children before Alice was in the house. Tom was always restless and Linda did what he did. Alice had said she would be only a minute, but Alice hated to leave a task half done. If she hadn't found the surveys where she thought they were in the garage she would have looked further. Her sense of time was not as good as it had been; she must have been absorbed— O God, the rain!

"And Tom is nine, you said, Mrs. Christopher? This is Tom and Linda?" The woman had picked up a snapshot of the children, taken the past summer. Their bathing suits were wet— Mary looked at her blankly. The children must have been soaked, running across to the

Johnsons. Had Tom collected their coats? Jane must have been busy, drying them, getting hot drinks—she wouldn't have had a chance to call Alice, not for a long time.

"Nine in November," she heard her own voice answering. "Look, I must call my mother-in-law. *Right now.*"

Officer Nunez, who had put the telephone down at last, looked harassed. "I'm sorry, lady. I just heard. Your mother-in-law—Alice Christopher, that's right?—she *did* get sick. The ambulance is taking her to the hospital up there."

Mary stared. Alice—another stroke? Oh, God! *And who was with the children?*

Ignoring the officers, she rushed to the telephone and called the Johnsons' number, but there was no reply. Jane could be in her barns looking over her stores; she could be out there for hours. The police were still droning on. It was their job, she supposed. Make-work. What difference did it make what time she got home last night?

She had to get back to the house. Bring the children home—there would be no party now, with Alice ill. The party. They had been so eager to see their cousins; could Tom have tried— He had driven the car up in Spenser once before, her own car. She had given him hell, but— Alice's car had been in the small garage, handy to the house, not the big one, where she had been searching. He could have— Mary's head felt as though it would burst. No. No—not in the rain and dark, not even Tom. There was a house around the corner whose owners had a big, shaggy dog. New people, she didn't know them, but Tom had been there. He had made friends with the owner's children—

At last it seemed as if the police were going.

"Try and relax." Officer Billops sounded like an old friend. "Kids do the craziest stunts; we get it all the time. Go to a friend's house without sayin' nothin'. Or get the idea it's a fun thing to hide. The troopers up there said the area is full of old barns and empty summer houses; the kids could be holed up anywhere. They're searching, don't you worry, up in—what's the name of the place?"

"Spenser is the post office. I don't think there are any police there," Mary said, shepherding them to the door. "Burgoyne is the nearest town."

"I think the sergeant was talking to Burgoyne," Nunez remarked.

"Right, Burgoyne. Well, they're doing everything and extra men have been called in, you bet."

Nunez had just heard that the state troopers were checking the pond near the Johnson farm, but he didn't tell that to Mrs. Christopher. It could wait. The detectives would take over and Missing Persons.

"I'll talk to them when I get there. I'm sure I know where Tom and Linda are—"

"The detectives will want to talk to you, Mrs. Christopher, and the state police will be in touch. You'd probably do better to stay here: we need to know where you are. You can give them all the leads."

Billops spoke without much conviction. Mary, in a rush to get dressed, was trying to show them out. The officers looked at each other. "Let us know where you are, if you leave the city."

Even then they didn't go, not right away. They looked around the place as if they thought Tom and Linda might pop out from a closet, or something. The idiots. Or maybe they were interested in buying apartments in the precinct.

Before they were out of the door she was on the telephone, canceling her appointment. She couldn't reach Gene Meyer, her editor, and had to leave a message. It seemed rude but it couldn't be helped.

At that hour she had no trouble retrieving her car from the parking lot and getting over to the West Side Highway. The day was cold, but bright and clear. Once she left the city, traffic was light. On the Saw Mill River Parkway, on the way to the Taconic, the familiar route, her head was a jumble of snatches of thought. Had Alice panicked? Were the children in the house, hiding in the cellar, or in the old glory hole under the garage? The garage had been a barn once and the lower part a chicken coop. Now it was a storage place, full of old things, a treasure trove for kids—but it would have been cold and dark. Were they shut in? Tears poured down Mary's face, but she knew she was being stupid. If they were there, the police would find them.

A horn blasted behind her; she caught herself veering into the next lane. Perhaps Tom and Linda had gone for a ride with Lesska, over to Boy's house. But Boy wouldn't have kept them and worried Alice. And Lesska would have asked for Alice's permission, which she would never have given. Mary knew that. It had almost been time for bed. And in any event, Lesska had left before she did. No, they couldn't be there.

The attic. Had Alice thought to look in the attic? It wasn't finished; just a place for keeping old mementos, luggage, bits and pieces. But dry at least—

She must have been speeding; already she was driving along the narrow roads of Spenser, and now she turned the corner of the lane and glimpsed the house, yet little more than two hours had passed since she left the city. An image had possessed her mind, hustle and action and police officers searching, but there was nothing happening, no one in sight. The lane was empty except for a cat slipping out from the trees. The house was quiet. Jumping out of the car, she stared through the glass on the front porch. The Christmas tree still stood, but the lights were dark.

"Tom! Linda!" She shouted and heard her own shrieks in the clear air. Abruptly, she stopped, ashamed. What was she doing? She must go inside. Call the police and check with them. Start hunting. And she must call someone and find out which hospital Alice was in. Get some flowers.

Mary went around to the back porch, fumbling for her keys, and pushed the storm door, but it held fast. She stared at it, her brain weary, not wanting to understand. The door was locked. The bunch of keys filled her grasp, nearly all big old keys from the house. Alice had insisted on her having them all. "That's for everything on the property," she had said. "I'll go over them with you, tell you which is which." She never had and Mary had failed to ask, as she had never needed more than the one for the inner entrance door. Painstakingly she tried them all, but none of them fitted the small keyhole.

That door had *never* been locked, unlike the front door, which was always locked and bolted on the inside. She hadn't even noticed that there was a lock on it. *Had* it been there before? Small, a cleanly curved oval, it looked alien on the old door. It was made of bronze and well fitted. She was shut out. Her head was aching in the bright sun. Tears sprang to her eyes and she told herself she was being foolish. Naturally, whoever had taken Alice to the hospital had made certain the place was secure. Perhaps Jane had a key.

She walked over to the Johnson farmhouse. The pond had frozen overnight—a sheet of gray ice glimmering in the sun. The reeds and grass around the edge were trampled, as if men had been working there. But they wouldn't be clearing at this time of year. Children?

There were no children in sight, no children playing with the cats in the Johnsons' barns or feeding scraps to the horses. No children. Neither Jane nor Henry were to be seen outside. She rapped on the porch storm door, but there was no answer and she pushed it again and called, "Jane! It's Mary," but the house was silent. Jane was *always* at home, or so it had seemed. Even when Henry took a vacation, Jane preferred to stay at home. She was so busy. The only time she wasn't there was when she had been in the hospital—had something happened to Jane?

You're still being silly, Mary thought. Even Jane has to go to the doctor, get eyeglasses, buy some things. She would be back. But Mary had to telephone now. There was a lunch counter about half a mile away; it should have a phone booth. She got the car and drove down the main road. The place was almost empty; not many people about at this time of year. Mary had never eaten there and she asked the waitress, apologetically, if she could make a call. The waitress, who looked bored, pointed to a pay phone in an alcove. Mary was going to dial the police, but then hesitated.

Where should she call? In New York the officers had said Burgoyne—did that mean in the town itself? She couldn't remember ever seeing any police there, except in cars. Perhaps they had come from a larger town? In the country, one didn't seem to think about police, except in traffic. So she called the Burgoyne house first. Boy would know, and he would also know, surely, which hospital Alice had been taken to. Someone would have called him.

The telephone rang only twice. But it wasn't Boy who answered; she heard the cool voice of Fiona Derwent, Boy's sister. Breathless, Mary asked about Alice.

"Alice was taken to Slade Memorial. But I'm afraid she can't receive visitors; she's in Intensive Care."

"Oh, but—" Mary said. "What happened? What's the prognosis?"

"There's no way of knowing yet," Fiona said. "She'd been worried to distraction last night and when she heard this morning that the children weren't in your apartment, she collapsed. It seems to be another stroke."

Nothing about the children being found. There was a hard ball in Mary's throat that made it difficult to speak.

"Which—who are the police handling the search?" she asked. "There aren't any—" Her voice came out like a whisper.

"I can hardly hear you," Fiona said. Oddly, she sounded disapproving, like Sister Aloysius at St. Catherine's. The sister had always fussed when Mary mumbled. "All the police are searching. They set up an emergency headquarters on Oak Avenue."

"I'll go over," Mary said, and was ready to hang up. "Oh, Fiona, I should speak to Boy. I can't get in the house, the porch door is locked. There must be a key somewhere—"

Fiona interrupted her. "The place was locked up when Alice went to the hospital. The police, I understand, would prefer that it is not disturbed. They have looked around but they may want to do some more work in there."

Work? Mary thought. What work? Hadn't they searched everywhere? The house had been so quiet. How could her children still have been there?

She drove into Burgoyne on Oak Avenue, looking for the police headquarters. She went all the way to the end of the street, turned and came back, but failed to see it. She should have asked Fiona for the number, but Fiona had rung off. Always so chilly, Fiona. Alice had called her "the icicle." Not like Roaring Boy, that big, amiable lion.

Mary had to stop people and ask. The first man she spoke to told her the headquarters was on the highway. The second didn't know. The third was a woman, rosy and silver-haired, well bundled up against the chill, and very willing to chat. "I saw some troopers this morning going in the old firehouse. The firefighters just moved out. They got a brand-new building out on the road between Burgoyne and Kirkbridge. Nothing wrong with the old building, but they've got a lot of new equipment. Cost a fortune, they say. At least the troopers are getting some use out of the firehouse. Great balls of fire," she said, and laughed. "Happy New Year," she added as she walked away.

It was easy to find the firehouse. Mary walked in. There were two desks and some chairs scattered in a space meant for firetrucks and there was only one man visible. It was very different from the First Precinct, or the Ninth, where she had gone to complain of street noise during Quent's illness: she might have been back in the firehouse where her father had painfully hung on to his job, but there was no bustle of old buddies to greet young Mary. Whitewashed, cold, and almost bare, it was forbidding. The sergeant, however, gave her a seat politely, and was attentive once she said her name.

He was fresh-faced with red cheeks, brown eyes, and a shock of brown hair. Except for his gray uniform he might have been a farm boy. Like farm people he was practical, explaining carefully, without fuss, what had been done and what was going on.

The state troopers from Merivale were conducting and directing the search, but other troops were cooperating. This building had been taken over as the local center of the search. A helicopter was flying over the area. The house had been ransacked, the attic, the cellar, the garage, the space under the garage, every inch, since early morning. They had also made a sweep of the immediate area and were now fanning out in wider and wider circles. He didn't tell her about the bloodhounds.

"All the houses that are closed up for the winter. Everywhere they could possibly be. But you could give us some help, Mrs. Christopher. We have photographs, but you can tell us what the children were wearing. And you can give us a list of people up here that the children knew, their favorite places, somewhere they might have slipped off to."

Already there were men over at Maplewood Lake, looking for cracks and holes in the ice. Unless they found something, there was no point bringing that up either. The sergeant was a local man. He remembered the Beecham woman, three years before. She'd fainted from the shock when they'd found young Artie's body, although the kid had been going out on the ice all winter, nearly every morning. Just blotted the idea from her mind, the doctor said. Anyway, these kids had disappeared at night in the dark and icy rain.

Mary gave him all the information she had. Both children were wearing blue jeans and long-sleeved cotton shirts, Tom's blue and Linda's white. They had brought with them Tom's green loden coat and Linda's new red one. "She would have it red. For Christmas . . ." The children did have friends in Spenser and the sergeant took all the names. More uniformed men came down from upstairs. Somebody brought her coffee while the men made the telephone calls. She could see, by their manner, that none of the people who answered had the children. A man was sent to check on the houses where there had been no reply. Mary remembered that she had drunk coffee that morning—it seemed such a long time ago, as

though weeks had passed. She had no hunger but she was thirsty
and she drank the coffee down in gulps. They were noisy gulps and
one of the men looked at her, startled.

A cold gust struck as a man came in from the street, a tall, well-
built, older man. He threw his car coat over a chair and came and
stood next to the officer behind the desk. He was very neat in a
navy blue cardigan over a blue shirt and gray slacks with a knife-
edge crease. He was leaning over, reading the sheet the officer had
completed.

"Sergeant?" He spoke quietly, but the sergeant sat up, his manner
more formal.

"Mrs. Christopher, Captain Bassett, Bureau of Criminal Investigation," he said. Bassett nodded but continued reading. His skin was
pink from the cold and well shaven; his silver hair glistened under
the light. When he looked up at last Mary saw that his eyes were
small, clear, and sharp.

A Bassett. The area was full of Bassetts and Baileys.

"Inbred, really," Quent had said. "Outpost of Empire. Just as well
we're getting a splash of your Irish blood."

"Just one more question, Mrs. Christopher." Bassett's voice was
crisp. "Since you arrived in New York last night, did you receive any
calls or messages about the children, other than the ones from your
mother-in-law?

"No," Mary answered blankly. "And my mother-in-law didn't mention the children."

He nodded and walked away. His black shoes were highly polished, even the heels, Mary noticed. Her gaze followed until he
disappeared up the staircase.

"You drove from New York this morning?" the sergeant in charge,
whose name she had never caught, asked her and she said she had.
"Perhaps you should start back now, Mrs. Christopher, if you want
to get home before dark."

"Start back?" She looked at him stupidly, not comprehending.

"There's nothing you can do here now. Everything possible is
being done. Everything. The mounted patrol has been called in."

Everything, he thought, except the FBI. But there was no reason
to bring them in. The woman had received no calls, no ransom note.
The idea of the Christopher kids being taken for ransom seemed far-
fetched to him. The Christophers weren't short of money, but they

weren't rich, real rich, like some of the city people who'd come up to Burgoyne.

Mrs. Christopher was still sitting, staring at him with big blue eyes that looked dark with those thick black eyelashes. Her face was white; the hand that held the coffee cup—she had drunk three cups—was shaking. She hadn't answered her phone all night. A widow for four years: Fiona Derwent had given the information. A good-looking young widow.

"What would I do at home?" she asked, still staring.

"You'd be comfortable. And the Christopher house is closed."

It wasn't officially sealed, but Ernest Burgoyne, who was Alice Christopher's lawyer, had made the arrangements. Sensible, while the house was unoccupied. And that suited the troopers. Make it easier when and if the case developed. The children had been missing now for twenty-one hours. It was almost certain that the case would develop. Captain Bassett was the big cheese from the Bureau of Criminal Investigation. He rarely left his office in Merivale—his investigators did that—but he was a Burgoyne man and when the call went out he had been first at the scene. And he wasn't here to look for kids at a secret pajama party.

Of course, Mary thought, the police wouldn't understand. But she couldn't go back without the children. They were lost *here*; she had to find them. She could go to a hotel or stay with one of the Baileys. They were so kind, so helpful; she felt a throb of warmth at the thought of the Baileys and the Bailey children and grandchildren. There was a warm family up here; she was not alone. They had been so good when Quentin—but first she must go to Slade Memorial. If she couldn't see Alice, she wanted to ask about her.

"We'd like to know where you are—to get in touch with you."

"I'll let you know," she said as she rose. As if she wouldn't be on the phone to them, constantly.

She must try to see Alice. Nothing had been said about the children in the phone messages; the police hadn't known that. The whole thing could be a mistake. Alice, not feeling well, had *sent* the children somewhere. Or called someone to pick them up. Someone that Mary hadn't thought of, perhaps didn't know. In the crisis of her attack, people had misunderstood—the children were safe and sound. Turning back, she blurted it all out, excitedly, to the troopers, but they didn't respond as they should.

"I don't think you'll be able to talk to your mother-in-law yet, Mrs. Christopher. But we'll follow up on that. People around here know each other pretty well. Everyone she knows will be checked. When we got the message from the city this morning that the children weren't with you, announcements were given to the local radio stations. They have begun broadcasting, so someone might call in at any time."

Alice Christopher had called the police before she was stricken— to get in touch with her daughter-in-law. And Alice Christopher wasn't crazy; she was a sharp woman. But everyone would be checked out; nothing would be left undone.

Mary thanked the sergeant, picked her jacket up, and walked away. That morning she had pulled on the nearest clothes to hand: dark wool pants and a white sweater, a bright red down jacket. Although she wore flat shoes, her well-rounded body looked seductive as she moved. She had done nothing with her hair; shining and improbably black, it fell over her shoulders.

A new recruit, just out of the academy, came from upstairs where he had been telephoning. He had a stack of memos in his hand, but he stood and watched Mary as she left.

"The kids' mother," the sergeant remarked.

"That's *her*? Some dish," the rookie said.

The sergeant didn't answer. He was just staring at the door, although Mary was already gone.

The street was full of people, walking in and out of the post office and coffee shops. A lot of women scurried into stores carrying bright Christmas boxes—it was gift-returning time. Mary stopped suddenly and a woman bumped into her, apologized, and dashed ahead. Getting into her car, Mary sat motionless behind the wheel, staring at a row of hooded parking meters, in the gathering dusk.

I can't just sit here, she thought, but she couldn't think where she should go first. She wasn't all that far from Susan's. Susan lived about twenty-five miles from Burgoyne. She was a sensible girl, though she was younger than Mary; she would have some ideas. Driving along the north road to Susan's, Mary longed to see Alice, Alice so practical, so full of love. But Alice was struggling for life. And it was Mary's fault. She had left the children for an appointment with an editor. Not just because of Quent. Gene Meyer had been flattering, and Mary had begun to think of a writing career.

A wave of terror swept over her, while the guilt was still bitter in her mouth. Susan. She would think of Susan. The children called her aunt, but she was Quent's cousin, a Bailey, though she was Mrs. Taylor now. It had amused Quent that despite the considerable difference in their ages, he and his cousin had had their young families at about the same time.

"I was a late starter," he had said to Mary. "A good thing you rescued me or I would have been a grandfather to my first child."

Susan would be upset at disappointing the children. Their parents would understand why the party had to be canceled, but certainly the children wouldn't— Or would she tell them that Tom and Linda— Tom and Linda. Her mind froze and she drove mechanically until she saw the familiar white house with the green shutters.

It was easy to see from a distance, all lit up with Christmas lights; as she approached she heard voices ringing out: ". . . and a partridge in a pear tree." Children's voices—Tom and Linda were there. They *had* gone there, after all. Not waited—or Susan had called for them last night. Just as Mary had thought, someone had taken them.

At the noise of the car some of the children looked out. Mary was at the wreath-bedecked door just as Susan, flushed and breathless, opened the door. She pushed a lock of hair back from her cheek, leaving a trail of white confectioners' sugar: it made pretty Susan look like a child herself.

"Mary!" She stood, embarrassed, on the step. "Jimmy, don't touch the candles," she called back into the room.

Turning to Mary she said, "Such a mischief, Jimmy, and Frances couldn't stay—"

She broke off, then continued apologetically. "We decided to go on with the party after all, not to spoil the children's holidays." She dropped her voice. "We haven't told them yet about Alice and—"

The tip of her pink tongue popped out and ran around her lips as if it were trying to escape. "I'm so sorry—I do hope it turns out to be all right—Linda and Tom. Mary, would you like to come in and have a cup of coffee—it's so cold. I'm afraid the house is noisy, but—"

"The Twelve Days of Christmas" was over. A familiar booming, crashing noise took its place; the stereo was on, the Brimstones' new album—Tom had wanted it but Mary had refused. It sounded like a hundred wailing banshees accompanied by a chorus of pneumatic drills.

"No, thank you," Mary said desperately. "I have a lot to do. A lot—"

"I'm so sorry," Susan repeated. "So—"

There was a crash of china from the room behind her and Susan started off, leaving the door ajar.

Mary lingered on the step, but the sound of children's voices rose in argument behind the door. She walked away slowly. Chagrin struck her belly into a lurch as if she'd dropped a thousand feet. Not there. Tom and Linda weren't there. And they'd had the party without them. She started to cry. Of course, Susan had had to— But the children weren't there.

Standing on the narrow country road, with the wind whistling around her ears, she felt very cold. This cold—were Tom and Linda indoors? Tom? Linda? The noise of the Brimstones was cut off, and the children began "The First Noel." Mary, taking shelter in her car, put her head down on the steering wheel and wept. The sky was dark. What should she do? Where should she go? She couldn't seem to think.

Her hands and feet took over and she was moving toward the highway as if the car were a horse, trotting back through the night to its stable. When she reached the city, there was no trouble getting into her parking lot and she was soon at her own front door, slipping her key into the lock. Then suddenly she woke up, outside the empty apartment. *What am I doing here?* she thought. And then she screamed.

3

Mary's cry did not go unheard. Someone called Carmel Attard, the janitor, who helped Mary into her apartment. His wife, Rita, was the first to give her comfort. The Attards were fairly recent Maltese immigrants and Rita wasn't fluent in English, but she soon understood Mary's trouble. She sat with the distraught mother and at last gave her a glass of warm milk into which she had stirred two sleeping pills. Her doctor had prescribed the medicine to make Rita rest during a bout of flu but she had never taken any of it. She had a young child and could not lie drugged in the night.

"God help her," she said to her husband when she rejoined him in their basement apartment, and she went to the room of her own three-year-old son and sat there until she fell asleep.

The next morning Rita was summoned to the apartment of Regina Valenti, an elderly woman, a longtime tenant of the building. To the small-boned Rita she seemed tall and grand. Rita had learned quickly that Miss Valenti was a person of some importance. She expected special services and she paid well for them. That morning she had been to early Mass and she wore a dark dress of thin wool with long sleeves and a high neck, set off by a heavy rope of pearls, white and gleaming like the crown of thick hair piled high on her head. Her eyes were dark and very sharp.

Miss Valenti wanted to know what had happened last night. It was she who had heard the cry from the poor mother, but Miss Valenti never opened her door after dark so she had called Carmel. Rita explained about the missing children and Miss Valenti shook her head slowly and then asked about the mother, a "new person," though Mrs. Christopher had lived in the building for four years.

Leaving, Rita opened the door for Mrs. Ferraro, another elderly neighbor, as short and plump as Rita herself, a friendly woman who liked to stop and chat. Both Mrs. Ferraro and Miss Valenti were ladies who did much charitable work. They would help poor Mrs. Christopher. Rita left with a lighter heart.

Outside, the day was bright, but Regina Valenti made sure that in her *salotto* the light was shaded by heavy draperies at the window. The floors were dark and highly polished; the tapestry rugs yielded soft color and the antique furniture had been shipped from Italy. The two women sat on gilded armchairs by a small, low marble table and drank espresso while they talked of the terrible happening.

"I heard from the super there was trouble," Connie Ferraro said excitedly. "He saw two police officers leaving yesterday and they asked him when he had last seen the Christopher children. He told them the last time he saw the children was a week ago; they had been with Mrs. Christopher when she had taken down his Christmas present. The children were excited—they were going to the grandmother's house for Christmas."

"The children were with their grandmother and they are lost?" Regina's brow wrinkled. "How can that be?"

"One of the officers, a woman, told the super that the grandmother had been taken ill."

"The boy, Tom, he is a big child. He would have telephoned for help. How could they be lost?"

The two women gazed at each other. They had lived long lives. They often deplored the world they lived in, but they understood it.

"Poor Mrs. Christopher," Mrs. Ferraro said sadly. "Always so pleasant, always with the children. Not like so many of the young mothers today."

"We will go to the seven o'clock Mass tonight," Miss Valenti said. "We must pray for those children."

Captain Bassett, back in his office in Merivale, was talking to the First Precinct in New York City. He learned that detectives from the First had gone to question the mother after they got the reports from

Billops and Nunez, but they had failed to reach her. Missing Persons had been informed and duplicate reports had been transmitted.

"Mary Christopher was in Burgoyne yesterday," he told them. "She went to the temporary HQ on Oak Avenue. I saw her there. She had nothing to offer; states she left the children at the family house in Spenser when Mrs. Alice Christopher returned from a visit. Mrs. Alice Christopher was in the garage, the mother says, when she left."

Detective Pidusky, who had caught the case, was anxious to question Mary, and Bassett told him that she had been advised to go home. When he put the receiver down he turned to the pile of reports on his desk. The search was being conducted intensively all over Dutchess County and in neighboring counties. Police were cooperating in New Jersey and Connecticut. Even the new Cessnas from the highway safety program had been coopted for the emergency. Three mounted patrolmen were searching the woods and all Troop T men were on alert the length of the thruway. But apart from a few mistaken identifications, there had been no leads. The dogs had failed to find a scent.

The case was officially a New York City matter, for the children were city residents. Meticulously, Bassett sent the precinct copies of his reports. But the children had disappeared from Spenser, near the town of Burgoyne, not only in his NYSP region but on his home territory. No one knew the place and its people as he did. And from his experience, he was almost certain that this would not remain a Missing Persons case, to be transferred to One Police Plaza in the city. It was *his* case, not the NYPD's, not the sheriff's in Poughkeepsie, and not the FBI's. And he was going to stay right on it.

Mary's drugged sleep was shot through with spasms of pure terror and patches of recollections that turned to nightmares. Quentin's face hovered before her, stark and cold as she had seen it last, yet his eyes were open with an expression of deep reproach, forbidding, with eternal condemnation. Then the image changed and the emaciated Quent was sweating and moaning with pain on his sickbed, while four-year-old Tom, still smooth with baby fat, confused and sulky, gazed at his father. Tom, telling her neighbor that his father was not sick, it was just the baby coming; Tom, after the memorial service, trying to push Linda from her cot—"Daddy, I want Daddy."

Then Tom, gasping and wheezing, thin and pale, the battle with asthma begun. And Tom, nine years old, under the Christmas tree at Spenser. Grabbing Linda, he had her out in the dark and cold and— Mary woke, moaning and weeping.

When she arose, it was still dark. She moved, jerky with panic, fumbling for some clothes. Could it have happened? Could Alice have been stricken earlier, a small stroke, falling perhaps, unable to speak, apparently as helpless as Quent in his last days? Had it brought back Tom's old fears, his old resentment? Had he run away from sickness dragging his sister and then— Only God could know what then.

Still in her nightmare she grabbed a jacket and hurried out of her apartment, not stopping to get the car, almost running to the precinct house. The skies were lighter now. Already there were a few people about in the bleak, forbidding area near the West Side Highway.

As she grasped the double door, she remembered her last visit there, with her neighbors, to talk to the community relations officer about protection for the neighborhood. Slowly the nightmare faded, but its fading brought little relief. The fear remained.

Entering, the first thing she saw was a Christmas tree, stripped of its decorations, the evergreen somber by the bright blue wall. Soon someone would cart it away. Christmas was over.

She turned to the uniformed man at the desk. He looked young, young as the trooper in Burgoyne, but without his fresh complexion, and he looked tired. A city look. "I'm Mary Christopher," she said. She gave her address. "Two of your officers came to see me yesterday—" She stopped. Was it just yesterday? Of course, she realized. How could the children be missing more than one night? She was losing her mind. "I would like to see the detectives."

The desk man had heard Daisy Billops talking about the Christopher kids the previous day. "It don't sound good," she had said. "Two kids just vanishing that way. And way up in the country. I've got a bad feeling about it. A bad feeling."

Billops's hunches were pretty reliable.

"Detective Pidusky's on the case," the desk man said. "I'll go and see if he's upstairs."

The case. Tom and Linda weren't a case . . . As the officer ran up the steps, she wondered why she had come. The dream, she had felt she must tell someone her dream. But it was a foolish dream. Tom had recovered from all that years ago. Tom . . .

The switchboard was busy. Officers came and went briskly, the doors banging, their voices loud and clear: "Helluva Christmas. A jumper on King Street." . . . "And my wife's cousin came and brought some guy we'd never met. That made thirteen." A man was brought in handcuffed, seedy and downcast. This place was full of life that had nothing to do with her or hers. What could she learn here? They knew nothing of Tom and Linda. The children were in Spenser, not here. She must go back.

She had turned to leave when the sergeant spoke from halfway down the stairs. "Mrs. Christopher, Detective Pidusky is up there. He'll see you now."

Mary hesitated, wondering if she should linger. For a moment she stared at the far wall. High up, someone had placed a seven-branched electric candlestick. She recognized the menorah, shining for the Hanukkah holiday. A time of hope. It should have been turned off. She followed the officer up the stairs and into the detective's tiny, crowded office.

When she left the precinct house about half an hour later and walked out into the morning, bright now but with a sharp, cold wind, she felt deflated, bewildered. Detective Pidusky had shared his office with two other detectives. One of them had kindly given her his chair. They were all busy. Pidusky, a big man who looked about fifty, had a broad face with an open look and gray eyes that seemed warm and sympathetic, but he had little to offer.

He had asked her some questions about her visit to Spenser and her leaving the children with Alice—the same questions she had been asked by the officers who had come to the apartment and by the police in Burgoyne. Then he had doodled on a piece of paper and explained police procedure. Or tried to.

"You see, Mrs. Christopher, this is our case because the children live here in this precinct. But of course the search started up in the Burgoyne area because that is where they were last known to be, and they are really on the job up there. Doing everything possible, you can be sure of that. Here, this precinct is very busy and the squad doesn't have the manpower or resources to handle a Missing Persons case like this. The Missing Persons squad down at One Police Plaza are fully equipped for this kind of work and their investigation is nationwide. So we've already sent them copies of what we've got from upstate. They're probably trying to reach you at your home and they will want to talk to you right away, the sooner the better."

The telephones had been ringing, and the other men answered, talking constantly: ". . . reported to Homicide." . . . "He just went out." . . . "The keys were thrown in the yard of the building next door." . . . "Murphy went over—a shooting on West Street." This place was a department store of crime, she thought distractedly.

Detective Pidusky had given her a slip of paper. "You go down there and show them this at the desk. Ask for Detective Keegan. They'll take care of you. They'll want recent photographs of the children, better than what we got from upstate, so you go home first and pick out the clearest you can find."

He'd watched her as she rose. "Would you like to have one of the officers drive you? He can wait while you find the photographs and take you downtown."

"I'm okay," she'd said, but she'd wobbled a bit as she was walking away.

"Sit down," he'd told her, and gone out. Another detective arrived and then Pidusky returned with a mug of hot coffee. She hadn't wanted it but he had made her drink it down and when she stood up again she was steady on her feet. He had left the office with the telephones ringing and walked with her downstairs.

"Sure you don't want a ride?"

"I live close by," she'd told him, but of course he knew that.

He had seemed to hesitate as he held the door open for her.

"They'll take care of you downtown. Try not to worry yourself until you get sick. It won't help the kids."

A kind man. Probably a father. But when she left and faced the stream of people going to their jobs in the office buildings scattered through the district, she had again the feeling of being in the wrong place, wasting time, going through prescribed motions—*yet where were the children?*

She went back to the apartment and took two large photographs from their frames, the silver frames on top of Quent's piano. She had had the photographs taken for Alice, on her last birthday, and had kept copies herself. They were good likenesses, head and shoulders, Linda pretty and prim, and Tom with a smile that resembled Quent's so much. That was easy, but the detectives might want full-length photographs. She hadn't been keeping up with her album since Quent had died; all the snapshots were in a huge envelope and she would just have to sort through. Sitting on the sofa, she hurriedly dumped the contents of the envelope onto the cushion beside her, a jigsaw of rainbow colors to her fogging eyes, Linda and Tom, Linda and Tom, over a hundred Lindas and Toms, laughing and playing in the orchard at Spenser, jumping about in Washington Square, sitting at the table with birthday cakes . . . She couldn't. She couldn't choose. She pushed all the pictures back into the envelope, along with the two portraits and left the house again.

It seemed quicker to take the subway than to drive and park, but when she got down to Brooklyn Bridge station she found herself wandering in a maze of tunnels. She saw a transit officer who could have directed her, but he was moving swiftly. Breaking into a run, she tried to catch up; she stumbled and dropped her envelope. The thin paper burst and the snapshots were all over the cement floor, already littered with paper wrappings, cups, soft-drink cans, take-out food containers, and black flattened wads of dried chewing gum, and permeated with the smell of urine.

In spite of herself, Mary began to cry. Most of the passengers went scurrying by and some of the pictures were trampled, but a woman and a young man stopped to help her. They worked quickly and the young man, who had long straggly hair and looked like a bum, packed the photographs neatly and efficiently back into the envelope, folding it so that the torn section was on the inside. He then produced a bit of string from the pocket of his duffel coat and tied the package swiftly. That accomplished, he disappeared into the throng, but the woman directed Mary to the right exit. She was a social worker and watched Mary as she ran off. One Police Plaza. All those pictures of two kids. She felt a surge of pity for the weeping mother. She had *trouble*.

Mary was eased by the kindness but she came up to unfamiliar territory, walking east into a large square that she didn't remember seeing before, with people streaming across, hemmed in by construction work in progress and a large metal sculpture that took up much of the space. Inside the headquarters building she had to take her place at the end of a long snake of people, working their way toward a desk to be given a pass to the upper floors. Everyone stood silent in this bureaucrats' purgatory, each intent on his own affairs, and Mary was alone again. The building was modern but the lobby was grim and gloomy, dark stone reaching up and up: she was at the bottom of a well. Although she had felt cold, now she was sweating and dizzy.

Then a man walked by with a swift, confident stride, snapping up her gaze and her attention. He was tall, broad in the shoulders, with a homely Irish face. Bypassing the line, he went through a private entrance without seeing her, but there was something familiar about this man; he was a calm spot in a whirling world. She was still trying to place him when her turn came at the desk and she was sent on her way.

On the upper floors there were no more imposing effects. When she left the elevator she faced what could have been factory offices, each with rows of desks under harsh fluorescents, metal cabinets, and a partitioned cubicle. She blundered into one that had nothing to do with Missing Persons and was directed a few feet along to the correct space. An officer near the door took her name and went over to the cubicle. He returned quickly.

"The detectives are out, Mrs. Christopher, but Sergeant Purcell can see you now."

She walked into the little office, her hands shaking. Sergeant Purcell greeted her kindly. He was an upright, gray-haired man, with a fatherly look and manner, and he tried to make her comfortable and at ease. But the first thing she had seen were two posters on the wall to her left; one was an old black and white photograph of a dignified elderly man whom she didn't recognize, but the other, in bright colors, was Etan Patz, the small boy who had vanished from Prince Street, a few blocks from her home. How many years ago? She remembered the knock on her door when the police had come around, asking if she'd seen him. The sergeant saw where she was looking and took her hand.

"Now, don't let that worry you. The poster is there because it's most unusual for that to happen. You must remember this: nearly all missing persons are found, most within seventy-two hours. And two children of four and nine are very special. Everything, really everything, is being done and will be done. And remember this, too: when children are missing it is very, very rare that the worst has happened."

He had a list of the children's clothes that were left in Spenser—a lot of their things were up there. Not the coats the children had worn to the country—she had already told the other officers about them—Tom's old green loden coat that he loved though it was getting too short and Linda's new scarlet coat with the brass buttons.

The sergeant, in a quiet, soothing voice, explained in some detail how Missing Persons went to work. Posters—he was glad she had brought the photographs. They would be sent down to the special photographic unit and posters would go out all over the country. Right now, the state was sponsoring poster displays at tollbooths. And there were fliers. A whole nationwide alert. And up in the Spenser–Burgoyne area a massive search was going on. Detective Keegan was handling it here in the city and the First Precinct was still on the case and cooperating.

After he took the photographs, Sergeant Purcell got her some coffee and explained more of the procedures. Her mind was fuzzy. The sergeant was speaking clearly but she found it hard to follow. It seemed to have nothing to do with Linda and Tom . . . except the coats. The two missing coats. Of course, the children had put their coats on before they went out in the cold. Linda loved her new coat. Bright red for Christmas, she had wanted that, not the light blue that Mary had picked out. And the buttons. She had begun pulling the buttons at once—Mary remembered, suddenly, that one was lost. She had noticed when they had arrived in Spenser. But she couldn't scold, not at Christmastime.

She began to cry and couldn't stop. Sergeant Purcell made a call and an officer arrived to drive her home. "Stay in touch with Detective Keegan," he advised her. "He'll keep you up to date."

In the next few days she was to call many times, as she called Merivale and Burgoyne. But there was no news. No news from Spenser or anywhere in the Burgoyne area. Sergeant Purcell, Detective Keegan, Captain Bassett—they had all said that everything was being done. Yet it seemed that nothing was being done: there was no word, no hint, no idea of where Tom and Linda might possibly be. Where *could* they be?

Her neighbors, when they met her in the lobby or the elevator, would look at her with compassion and some of them tried to give her words of comfort. Friends—some that she had hardly seen since Quent's death—called with an embarrassed sympathy. But no one in the family called. The Christophers and Baileys were reserved peo-ple; they had no good news and, she thought, probably hesitated to intrude, not knowing what to say.

Only Alice could know what to say: Alice, who must know where the children were. Mary telephoned the hospital several times a day, but Alice was still in Intensive Care. Alice could speak to no one.

Mary argued with Captain Bassett. The children must be with some friend, neighbor, or acquaintance of Alice's; his men should inquire. Bassett responded that everything along that line had been tried. And he reiterated that Alice had called the police through the telephone operator *before* her stroke, stating her belief that the chil-dren were with Mary.

"But surely," Mary expostulated, "she was ill before the actual stroke. Something must have happened, a precursor; she was mud-dle-headed, forgetful perhaps . . . She will remember; we must *know*."

"I'm not a physician," Bassett said. "And her physician will not allow questioning at this time. But I will tell you that we've had a man there, in case she spoke. From the few words she has said, she still appears to believe that the children left with you."

Mary put the receiver down, sick at heart. Alice must know, but her illness had wiped out her memory. She would remember, but— Mary had to know *now*. She pressed her knuckles against her throb-bing temples. There had been broadcasts. Why had no one come forward? Who was it who listened to no radio, watched no televi-sion, read no newspapers?

Her mind raced with horror stories, but she pushed them away. Even the sergeant at Missing Persons had said it was very, very rare that— No. There was a perfectly simple explanation. There must be. If only Alice—

Yet the next time Mary called the hospital she had a shock. The telephone operator told her that Mrs. Alice Christopher had been discharged. Eagerly, Mary called the house in Spenser. It seemed an age since she had called there, the ring of the telephone strange in its familiarity. But no one picked up at the other end. During the day she called again and again, but there was no reply. Puzzled, Mary called Susan. Susan answered, a little breathless as usual. Mary could hear the children's voices, clamoring.

"They want to go to the pond," Susan said apologetically. "You

know how they are in this weather— Oh, Mary, I'm so sorry. Have
you heard anything?"

"No," Mary said, "I need to talk to Alice. I found she's left the
hospital, but she's not at home."

"She's gone to Boy Burgoyne's," Susan told her. "In that house,
there are people to take care of her, you see. It was a bad stroke,
Mary, but she's a little better. My Beth has to go into the hospital
next week, an operation on the membrane of her tongue. But it's
nothing, really, the doctor says . . ."

Mary made a polite response, but inside of one minute she was
dialing the number of the Burgoyne house. Once again, it was Fiona
who answered. After greeting her, Mary asked to speak to Alice.

"I'm afraid you don't quite understand the situation here, Mary."
Fiona's voice was cool as usual. "Alice is still very, very ill. But she
wanted so much to leave the hospital that Boy discussed with the
doctors what could be done. She needs twenty-four-hour care. And
so we have the nurses and Mrs. Denby is coping and I am here to
help as much as I can. But Alice is allowed no visitors yet and she is
far too weak to talk on the telephone. I must go now. My time is
hardly my own."

She rang off. Fiona hadn't mentioned the children. It was Mary
who should have been with Alice—but Boy Burgoyne hadn't consulted her. She would rather have been up in Burgoyne than in the
city, for all that the police called it "a city case." The children had
been upstate and that was where they still were. Surely no one
doubted that.

Detective Keegan, at Missing Persons, had suggested that Mary
take something to relax, something to make her sleep. But she didn't
want to sleep. There were things, she knew, that she must do. No
one else was doing anything. Or not enough. Posters. Milk cartons
. . . but that was a private effort on the part of the milk companies,
Keegan said.

Time after time, she put her coat on and went out, determined to
do *something*, but once on the street she would stop, frustrated, not
knowing where to go, what to do. Sometimes she would flick on the
radio or the television set; perhaps there would be an announce-
ment, the children had been found . . . But there was just the usual
babble, no mention of the children, or if there had been she had
missed it. They were lost far away, in the country; they weren't city

news. Late at night, she turned on a cable station and it was rerunning an old series on the FBI.

Why not the FBI? Suddenly, she was seized with new energy. The police kept saying "Missing Persons, nationwide." The FBI were nationwide. First thing the next morning, she rushed to the FBI offices on Federal Plaza. They were nothing like the background of the television series set in the twenties; now the FBI was housed in a tall, squared-off glass building like many others. Pedestrians maneuvered around another big metal sculpture—Quent had called such works "the rust belt," to the indignation of his colleagues.

Inside, Mary had to wait at a desk, explain her business. But she was lucky; although she had made no appointment, a special agent agreed to see her. She was surprised to find that the special agent was a very attractive young woman, tall and as well formed as a model, with stylishly cut blond hair. But she could tell Mary no more than the police.

"We have not been called in, you see. Missing Persons is handling the case, and they are very good. When it's children who are missing, the greatest efforts are made."

She went on talking to comfort the mother. But the children had been missing for eight days. No ransom note. No estranged husband who might have spirited them away safely, though surreptitiously. While she spoke, Mary's eyes were raking her, trying to read her expression, desperate for reassurance. The special agent of the Federal Bureau squeezed Mary's hand as if they were old friends, before she was escorted to the crowded emptiness of the street below.

Mary returned to her apartment, drained and exhausted, and lay down on her bed. No help from the FBI. No hope there. Unless—unless the police asked for their help, that young, pretty agent had said. Then . . . It was Detective Pidusky's case. Mary ran to the telephone and called the precinct. She must persuade him. She could not wait until Alice recovered. It would take too long. But she found that Detective Pidusky was out. She left her name and number.

It was late at night when Pidusky returned her call. He apologized for the delay but explained, in a weary voice, that it had been one hell of a day in the precinct. She told him of her visit to the FBI offices and what the special agent had told her. Pidusky sounded very patient. He repeated his assurance about the great efficiency of the Missing Persons squad. He knew Detective Keegan personally and he was a fine officer. The matter was officially a Missing Persons case now, transferred from the First Precinct. There was no evidence of any crime having taken place and—

"No," Mary said, "no, of course not. There's no *crime*. But we must *find* them." He was tired, of course, not stupid. No one had suggested a crime. But no one seemed to understand that they must be found *at once*. Or perhaps something might— Her mind turned away from the thought.

Still fully dressed, she returned to her bed, but she had no wish for sleep. Red numerals flashed relentlessly on the electronic bedside clock. 11:15 . . . 11:16 . . . 11:30 . . . 11:55. Quent had bought that clock, but she had always disliked it. "Far more efficient," he had said when Mary regretted the plain white face and elegant hands of the old one. "You can't be a prisoner of the past." She was a prisoner of the present, she thought. 12:58 . . . 12:59 . . .

She jumped up, taking her jacket from the living room sofa where she had dropped it that morning. The night was cold but dry and there was no wind. To the north, the great column of the Empire State Building glittered; to the south, the sparkling twin towers sliced into the sky. Above, the stars were shining.

Her car was over on the side of the crowded parking lot and she had to maneuver carefully, but she emerged without damage, without sweat, almost as though her way was being cleared. There were no cars or trucks between her and the West Side Highway and there was little traffic on the roads. It seemed but a moment until she passed the George Washington Bridge, brilliant between the sleeping shores.

After she reached the Saw Mill River Parkway, the car seemed to fly; she took the curves easily and all the lights were green. On the Taconic, the rolling road the children loved, nothing was in her way; the trees stretched protectively on either side and when she passed the sheer rock she had no fear of falling stones; the middle of the road was hers. She branched off to the east and she was in Spenser when the clock in the dashboard gleamed 2:31.

Her headlights faintly touched the farmhouse on the Johnson land, dark among dark trees, and then she reached the lane. Slowing down, she gazed at the Christopher house, the warm red clapboards black under a night sky. The old lantern on the porch was not lit; no night light glowed from the children's rooms. The house was barren;

she went on. At the end of the lane she took the road leading into Oak Avenue that passed through Burgoyne.

The road was empty, silent. On either side now was the Burgoyne family land. The handsome three-story house was dark behind its screen of shrubs and trees; if Alice slept here it was like the sleep of death. Mary's car moved, silent as a hearse, through the town, the white-painted church rising like a ghostly backdrop by the road.

The car turned; she drove on, away from the town, climbing through hills and descending, passing through orchards, gliding by streams, not knowing where or why she was going, and found herself twenty miles away on the shore of Maplewood Lake. On she drove until she came to the high ground; looking down, she saw the surface of the lake like frozen milk. 3:09. She stopped, got out of the car, and looked about her.

The sky was bright with stars. Below there were no headlights; nothing moved. The windows of the houses were all dark. She saw no living soul. Mary returned to the car and drove on slowly. The road sloped down and soon the lake was hidden by the houses and the trees. She stopped and her head sank onto the wheel. She was nowhere. The children were nowhere. They were gone.

The next morning she hardly remembered her drive home, but the late-morning sun awakened her as she lay on her bed, and she cried. But, as always, light gave her strength. She had had a waking nightmare, that was all. She took aspirins and drank coffee and soon hope rose again. It buoyed her up and kept her busy, running to One Police Plaza, calling Merivale and Burgoyne, furiously active by day, restless at night—until the detectives came.

4

The children's bodies had been found not by the county police or the state troopers but by an inquisitive dog rooting around the bushes not far from Tony's Tavern. Because of the hard frost that had held since New Year's, the bodies were in a good state of preservation, except for the damage done by the dog. The owner of the tavern had seen the dog dragging something and strolled over to see what it was. When he saw, he lost his breakfast. Then he went and called the police.

The state troopers had their instructions. They called Bassett's office at once and he was there in thirty minutes, accompanied by one of his investigators, Lieutenant Hayes, a big, slow-moving man, grim-faced as he stepped from the car. The wind blew unchecked across the flat acres of grass, slapping against the patrol car where the troopers were hunkered down. The body of the useful dog was sprawled beside some scraggly bushes; one of the troopers had shot him.

Bassett didn't need to disturb the site to identify the bodies. The grave in the bushes was shallow; the killer had been in a hurry. A shoulder was sticking up in a green loden coat, dusted with snow. The little girl now lay face downward in a red coat and blue jeans—the Christopher children, for sure. More men were arriving; he left Lieutenant Hayes in charge and went inside the tavern to find the owner.

As the photographers began their work, and the forensic men

took samples of earth, snow, and ripped cloth, they were gripped by the cold and spoke enviously of Bassett's comfort in the warm tavern.

"Though, God knows, he doesn't care," one of the photographers remarked, stamping his numb feet. "About as much idea of comfort as those guys who go in for ice fishing. I've known him for fifteen years. He wouldn't take any notice if his piss froze."

Lieutenant Hayes was a few yards away. He had made a careful inspection of the site. As he finished, he saw little strings of something flapping from a ragged bush. He went closer, peering down: thin strips of plastic, attached to a torn, large piece, ridged—it was one of those folding hoods that women kept in their bags, ready for a sudden shower. It could have been there for a month or more, but— He called a photographer and then had it collected with the samples. Best to be sure. A man of about Bassett's age, he was chilled to the marrow. Getting too old for this, he thought.

The owner of Tony's, not a Tony but Jerry Crump, was unshaven and red-faced under his silver stubble—too fond, Bassett guessed, of his own merchandise. His yellow leather coat was soiled and he had a seedy look, but he was a talker. He had previously identified a photograph of Mary for the troopers, but stated that he had seen no children. Repeating his story to Bassett, he told him he had no trouble with the identification.

"I sure remember her. A great looker. She caused quite a rumpus." When he finished, he supplied Bassett with the names and addresses of other witnesses. "Mostly local folk stop in here. We don't get many off the road."

The place did not look prosperous. It wasn't far from the highway, Bassett had noticed, but it was tricky to find. And isolated. But Mary Christopher had found it.

He arranged with Crump to come to Merivale and make a formal statement. Then he returned to the scattered bushes beyond the macadam where the team was finishing up. The meat wagon had arrived and Dodgson from the county ME's office was kneeling over the bodies, his plump rear bulky in his overcoat. Both bodies were now lying face down under a dusting of dirt and snow. The dog's teeth had torn the boy's pants and scraped his leg. The little girl's right ear had been ripped from her head.

"No way of telling when until we see the contents of the stomachs," Dodgson said. "The frost preserved them well. But they'll decompose quickly."

Doctors loved to state the obvious, Bassett thought, but Dodgson was better than most: he was a forensic pathologist. And he soon redeemed himself.

"Look here." His fingers touched the back of the children's necks. Both were swollen, with purplish-red bruises. "Could be a break in the cervical spine. Might be your cause of death. Clothing undisturbed," he said reflectively.

Bassett hadn't expected to find sexual molestation, but the tests would have to be made. The doctor's face was red with cold when he stood, glancing at the van, ready for the removal of the bodies. But Bassett lingered, the doctor thought, as if it were a day in May, crouching down in the brittle grass, staring at something grasped in the girl's right hand.

"Didn't dare touch it," Hayes remarked. "Could be glass. Have to wait till the rigor passes off."

Bassett peered more closely at the brightly painted little ball.

"Metal, I think. But we'll wait. A Christmas tree ornament," he said thoughtfully.

Dodgson, who had been eager to leave, waited while the bodies were placed in the van. They'd been nice-looking kids. A Christmas tree ornament. Just a few days since he'd taken his own decorations down; the grandchildren had loved them.

A car drew up: a reporter and a photographer from a local paper. "Get going," Bassett told the driver of the van. "I'll talk to them," he said quietly to Hayes. "We're not going to mention anything that might have been found on the bodies."

The place where the children had lain was now just a shallow pit of dirty snow. The doctor felt a familiar melancholy. Captain Bassett, he saw, was frowning in concentration. A shiny ball, Bassett thought. He had seen the ornaments on the tree in the house at Spenser. Old, like the ones he had had as a boy. His daughter had them now. He was sure this ball came from that tree. The children had come here directly from the house with their mother on the way to the city. It was just as he had thought it would be. And to the doctor's surprise, he smiled.

*   *   *

The homicides had taken place within his region; they were now officially Captain Bassett's case. Missing Persons was notified and Detective Keegan relieved of his duty. Captain Bassett called Lieutenant Pidusky at the First Precinct. "I'd have liked to come down to inform Mary Christopher myself," Bassett said. "See how she jumps. But the newspapers are on to it."

"I'll go over," Pidusky replied. "Before she catches it on the radio. But it might not make the papers today. Murder's not hot news these days. We had a young kid's corpse, or the remains of it, in a *garbage compactor* at a supermarket this week—no radio or television report, just a line or two in one of the dailies. Fun City."

He asked a few questions and Bassett told him the preliminary findings from Dr. Dodgson. No evidence of sexual molestation of either child. In both cases, the cause of death appeared to be fracture of the cervical spine. The contents of both stomachs matched the supper given to the children in Spenser as reported by the mother—turkey soup, ham, bread and butter, milk. The time of death wasn't established yet but it looked like not much more than an hour or two after the ingestion of the meal.

"We've had someone make the ID," Bassett said. "The grandmother is still in precarious health, so Bartholomew Burgoyne, an old friend of the family, came in. But of course we need the mother. Dodgson will be finished tomorrow. I'll come down tomorrow morning and pick Mrs. Christopher up myself, but I'll stop in to see you first, if you can arrange your schedule. There was an item you sent us I'd like to discuss."

"I'll talk to Captain O'Rourke, chief of the squad," Pidusky told him. "He'll want to be in on it. I'll get back to you."

Captain Bassett's meeting at the First Precinct was satisfactory. The city men, though hard pressed, were cooperative. Earlier, they had checked out Mary Christopher's route through the city on the night the children had disappeared and transmitted copies of all the reports. Now they discussed the homicides, and Mary Christopher's response on being informed of the discovery of the children's bodies: "Quiet," Pidusky said. "Dazed, maybe. Didn't seem to be taking it in." And he showed Bassett the original report on the item that had interested him. It was from Narcotics and it was instructive reading.

Before he left the precinct house, someone brought in an early edition of an afternoon newspaper. On the third page were two short columns on the case under the large headline THE BATHSHEBA MURDERS.

"Bathsheba?" Pidusky had asked. "Is that the town?"

"A village," Bassett told him. "Not much of anything. Supermarket. Gas station. A few scattered houses. And the tavern, up near the highway. So they're running the story."

"They like the name," Pidusky said.

There were pictures of the children, the ones Missing Persons had run, already stamped on Bassett's mind. The boy, dark-haired like his mother, hardly a child, not yet adolescent; the girl, a pretty little thing, fair, with a look of Alice Christopher. Or she had had a look of Alice Christopher. He remembered the mutilated, frozen corpse and anger struck him with more force than he had felt at the crime scene. These murders were an abomination. He could, at least, see that the killer was brought to justice. His anger was hot inside him, but his demeanor was cool though courteous.

"Father Frost," Pidusky commented when he left.

"It's a type," O'Rourke said. "Old English stock. Lean, mean, and snotty."

O'Rourke liked his food and patted his expanding waistline with regret. "But he has a big rep up there. A good man. Bloodhound Bassett, they call him, since the Pemberthy case—oh, a few years back. A front-page case. Murder by poison. It was the wife who did it."

On the way up to Poughkeepsie, Bassett asked Mary few questions. Pidusky had telephoned to notify her that the upstate investigators were coming. When Bassett and Hayes had arrived at the apartment door, Mary let them in. She was still in her bathrobe, although it was noon. Her hair was tousled. There was a smell of liquor on her breath. The apartment was dusty and untidy. The windows were wide open, letting in all the frigid air.

When he asked if she was ready to go to identify the children, she disappeared into her bedroom and dressed quietly. She went to the car without fuss and she sat beside him on the back seat.

Inside the car it was warm, but she began to shiver, her teeth chattering.

Was she acting? Or was it some form of hysteria, Bassett wondered. When the shivering stopped, she became curiously rigid. In the closed car, she smelt of soap and fear. Her dark, shaggy wool coat muffled her body and its upturned collar partly hid her face. When he spoke, she answered him in monosyllables or not at all. The drive was long, but he was a patient man. There would be plenty of time for questions in the weeks ahead.

Lieutenant Hayes was driving. He said little. Normally, this should have been his case and he would have been asking questions. But Bassett had made it clear that he was handling this personally. Hayes would merely assist. It was natural enough—Bassett knew the family and he was a Burgoyne man. Hayes lived in Poughkeepsie, but he and his wife had bought a house in Virginia and now, just a few months from putting his retirement papers in, most of his thoughts were on his new home.

He was a tired man and it showed, he knew, in the slouch of his shoulders and the folds of skin around his eyes. He had never been ambitious like Bassett and he had not fretted when he knew there would be no more promotion. The work had become more grinding, more plain rotten over the years. Drugs, murder, rape, and child abuse—everywhere now, a reflection of the carnage in the big cities. Lieutenant Hayes wanted out.

And now this. Two kids. It hadn't been a sex molester. It didn't look like a kidnap. He knew which way Bassett's nose was pointing, the obvious place. But something about the woman bothered Hayes. He couldn't think why, but he was uncomfortable. He glanced back and it came to him. She was alone, except for Bloodhound Bassett, shrinking into her clothes. It seemed unnatural that no one had come with her, family, friend. Not even a lawyer. She probably hadn't thought of a lawyer. Or she had, and was just acting dumb. But still it didn't seem right, somehow.

The two detectives shepherded Mary into the hospital. Hayes felt a certain relief that it was this bright, modern, cheerful place, with flowers in the lobby and glimpses of the Hudson through wide windows. In the waiting area children were playing quite happily—but that wouldn't help. He saw Mary's eyes fixed on a sign: PLEASE DO NOT LEAVE CHILDREN UNATTENDED. Christ!

Hayes had made arrangements with the morgue, and they took Mary there directly. Or as directly as possible; these modern hospital rooms were built on a century-old base and were labyrinthine. Here there was less light, the walls were dull gray cinder block, and there were obstacles on the path, crates, boxes, and bags; he had to hold the arm of the stumbling woman. They came to the metal door, gray-painted, black-streaked, and scarred from rough use like a warehouse door, and he saw the mother stare, as if she wondered why they were pausing here.

Then there was a hitch. The door was locked and no one answered Bassett's knock. A passing workman went in search of the morgue attendant, who came in a few moments, smiling, with the key. He asked them to wait. In not much more than a minute or two, he opened the door and the three of them walked into a small corridor.

Here the light was dim. Of the two fluorescents on the ceiling, one was out. At the end of the corridor a printed curtain had been drawn to hide the mortuary table and all the equipment of this place. Perhaps there was work in progress. Like all morgues, it smelled of formaldehyde, but not too strongly. Hayes looked with concern at the mother; she might faint, become nauseous, hysterical. But she just stood there, as if she were waiting to be moved on through another corridor, following Bassett's lead.

The attendant disappeared into the room on the left. Soon the door was opened wide: a long metal cart nosed out into the narrow space, twisting as the attendant pushed it up toward the curtain while he dragged another cart behind him. The bodies were covered with white sheets, and Hayes, so close to the woman, felt her draw back in some last effort not to see, not to admit . . .

Hayes knew that the bodies had been cut up for the autopsy and watched as the attendant carefully pulled the sheet down to uncover the faces only. It was awkward, viewing the two bodies in the small space, but it was done. The faces had been cleaned and someone had drawn the girl's hair forward in an attempt to hide the torn flesh where the ear should have been. But the mother saw it anyway. Her hand went forward as if to touch the injured place and then stopped abruptly. For a moment she stood, her hand raised, still as the corpses. An odd little sound escaped from her, like the mewing of a cat.

In a matter-of-fact voice, Bassett asked her formally for the identification; she answered as she had in the car. When they left the morgue, he suggested that she might like to go to the reception room and sit down, or perhaps get some coffee or a soft drink. They were due at the district attorney's office, but the decencies, he thought, should be preserved. Mary asked if there was a water fountain.

Sergeant Sweet from Merivale was waiting in the lobby: he had been detailed to meet them and later drive Mary home. He would also be useful, Bassett had considered, to testify, along with Hayes, about Mary's appearance and manner. Defense counsel would challenge any statement she made now. "This distraught mother . . ." It was best to be prepared. He found Mary a seat in an empty row and left her with Hayes while Sweet went to get the water, and he made a call to the district attorney to say they were on their way.

Morton Kramer was on the line at once. His voice was raspy and his feet, Bassett thought, had turned cold. "Forget it for today. I've got too much on my desk, and I have to be in Albany tomorrow before the Probyn Commission. Besides, any statement she gives now would be thrown out. No sense going through a ritual dance. Did she break down?"

From where he stood at the reception desk, Bassett had an unobstructed view of Mary Christopher, sitting in the empty row with Hayes like an old nurse standing beside her. She was sipping the water. Apart from a slight tremor in her hand, she showed no agitation. She handed the cup back to Sweet and, as if aware of his own gaze, she looked up. The overhead light shone full on her face. She had put lipstick on when she dressed, red lipstick. He noticed it was crooked on the right side of her mouth and she had left a smudge on her chalk-white skin. For a moment her face seemed like a cheap, badly made mask, and he felt nonplused. Then she asked for more water in a steady voice and he recovered.

"No," he replied to Kramer. "No change."

"Hmm. No reports of child abuse in the city?"

"We've checked it out. Nothing."

"Lizzie Borden," Kramer said gloomily. "No conviction. But stay with it. Remember Françoise Pemberthy."

"Yes," Bassett said. He could hardly forget. It was his biggest case as an investigator and had brought him where he was. Twelve years ago. No one had believed that the Belgian woman could be convicted. But she was still in jail.

"I won't trouble you with a lot of questions today, Mrs. Christopher," he told Mary, before he took his leave. "But there is one thing I would like to ask, if it is all right with you."

"Ask anything necessary," she replied.

"You've been asked this many times before. But now, when we have a clear case of murder, I must ask you to think again. Is there any person, or group of persons, who might have any real or imagined reason to hold a grudge against the children, the family, you personally? Anyone who might want to hurt the children?"

"No one." Her voice now sounded tired. "No one at all. It could only be a stranger. A maniac."

People still said "maniac" at times like this, Bassett thought. Otherwise it was "mentally deranged." Or even "mentally handicapped." Or "pervert." As a matter of routine, when the children were reported missing, he had assigned men to check on known sexual degenerates over a wide area, but they had come up with nothing useful. As he had expected.

Sergeant Sweet had felt curious and a little apprehensive when he'd received his orders to escort the mother home. But when they met, she had seemed composed enough. An earnest, ambitious young man, he had taken a three-week course on the effect of crime on the family; the aftermath of shock had been discussed—sometimes an inability to express grief, the need for communication. But he soon found that Mrs. Christopher had no wish to talk. She sat in the back seat and the only words she said were "thank you," when he offered her a peppermint. After that she didn't seem to hear his remarks. If her eyes had not been open, he would have thought she was asleep. He was left to contemplate the roll of fat that had appeared under his chin. With his pink complexion and light eyelashes, he thought it gave him a piggy look. He must cut down on the deli sandwiches and get back to working out. Starting tonight.

By the time he reached the city, it was five-thirty. The southbound traffic was slow and he could see it backing up in the northbound lanes; it could only get worse. Impatient, he swung off the highway at Seventy-ninth Street and soon found himself in the thick of traffic. Jammed. He had made a mistake and he had to inch his way almost to the tip of the island. If he got home by nine that night he would be lucky.

When he finally reached her apartment house, there was nowhere to park but the bus stop. Politely, he escorted Mrs. Christopher to the door of her building. There was no doorman and he waited until she got inside. Then he ran back to pull his car out; a city bus and a large vegetable truck were jockeying for the space.

Mary walked four feet, reached the inner stairs, and collapsed.

5

Regina Valenti stepped out of a long black car, which was double-parked. Her brother Paul had driven her home, after her visit to his apartment in Little Italy. She told him not to bother to escort her inside, "for the Brownies and the police are quick to give out tickets here. These days, if you want to see a police officer, double-park your car. Otherwise . . ."

She shrugged and turned to the house, as she considered the irritating ways of the police. Where were they when Connie Ferraro had her purse snatched on Varick Street? Nowhere in sight. As she pushed the outer door—it was really too heavy, she should have let Paul come in—to her annoyance she saw a figure huddled on the steps. A street person. The super would have to be called. But a direct look convinced her that this was no street person: the figure was clean and tidily dressed. The woman's face was against the marble beneath the handrail, but the fall of dark hair was enough. It was her neighbor, the *irlandesa*. The mother of the lost children.

Without a word, she leaned down and took Mary's hand in a firm grasp. Gently, she eased her up. Mary gave her a blind stare, but she must have recognized her neighbor, for she allowed herself to be guided, docile as a good child. Inside her own apartment, Regina sat Mary in an armchair while she brewed a pot of strong espresso. She was wrong, she thought, looking at the stunned, broken creature: there was nothing childlike in her passivity. The red-slashed white face could have been a clown's.

Regina laced the coffee with anisette and held Mary's trembling hand while she drank it. Some dark drops ran down her chin and Regina wiped her face with a white linen napkin. She fed her a morsel of light sweet biscuit, but Mary choked on it. She didn't speak until she said, quite suddenly, as if to someone in the middle of the room, "Her ear."

There was no doubt in Regina's mind about the cause of Mary's collapse. It could only be one thing. The children had been found dead. She had been sure it would be so. Such children were not "lost." There had been that long hunt for the little girl in Queens, but it was her dead body that was found in a park. Yesterday the super's wife said Mrs. Christopher looked very bad. The poor woman.

Although she was not as strong as she had been, Regina put her arms around Mary and got her up on her feet and then, still holding tight, helped her walk to her apartment door. Taking the key from Mary's purse, she guided her inside and it was a shock to see, while she was supporting the mother, the two empty silver photograph frames, facing each other across the piano. Somehow she got Mary's clothes off, found a nightgown, and put her to bed. She was tired when she finished the task, but her duty was not yet done. Mary was lying flat on her back, staring at the ceiling, like a corpse herself, her neighbor thought.

"Shall I call your doctor?"

Almost soundlessly, Mary refused.

"Can I call someone in your family?"

Mary stared, as if she failed to understand. Her forehead wrinkled and at length she murmured, "Alice." Then she gave an uneasy start and said, "No, not Alice."

Tears sprang from those dead eyes. Her body shook in convulsions. Beads of sweat formed on her skin and soon her nightgown was soaked. Harsh cries and low mumbling sounds came from her distorted mouth.

Perhaps it was better, Regina thought, than that dreadful stillness. But this woman needed care. She sent for Mrs. Attard and asked if she knew Mrs. Christopher's doctor.

"I have the number," Rita Attard told her. "She left it with me when I sat with the children."

While Regina telephoned, Mrs. Attard, the young mother,

watched the figure writhing on the bed and shook her head. "They were killed?"

"Murdered," Regina answered, and Rita sat down and held Mary's hand.

The doctor came and gave Mary an injection. The women had expected him to call an ambulance, but he was reluctant to do so. Dr. Linley was a young man who had taken over the practice of the Christophers' family doctor just eighteen months before. The children had been in for one annual checkup: both had been in excellent health, Tom having lost all traces of asthma. Dr. Linley had been busy the last few weeks and he had not heard of the tragedy. Miss Valenti explained, with admirable brevity.

"It's delayed shock," he told them, "but there is nothing else wrong. What Mrs. Christopher needs is just someone to tend her for a while until she recovers. One of the family. She doesn't need a trained nurse. I'll phone the druggist and have some pills sent up."

He paused for a moment on the way out, although he was in a hurry. He had been called away from his dinner guests. "Those two fine children," he said. "And up in Burgoyne. Not the city. Who could have imagined . . . ?"

He was gone. The three of them had left the drugged Mary to talk in the living room. The two women looked at each other in the sudden quiet. Regina motioned Mrs. Attard to sit down and they consulted in low tones. The super's wife knew all about everyone in the building; she was an unofficial concierge. But Mary Christopher seemed to have no family.

"She never spoke of brothers or sisters. I take her mail when she goes upstate and a card always comes at Christmas from Ireland, from a Kathleen. Mrs. Christopher told me that her mother had returned to Ireland after her father died, and she died herself, not long after. I think this Kathleen is the mother's sister."

After some prodding, Mrs. Attard remembered that the children had talked of cousins upstate, but she didn't know much about them. Cards and packages had come from the children's grandmother. Mrs. Christopher had talked a lot about her mother-in-law, but now, it seemed, she was ill. "Bad luck brings bad luck," she added, but Regina had gone on to her own thoughts.

No brothers, no sisters to come and help. Regina had always thought that a family limited to one child was a selfish family, if not sinful. A solitary child. "The poor creatures are defenseless in the world," she told Mrs. Attard, who agreed.

Regina gathered up some help. She knew all the older residents of the building; many of them were related and almost all of them were friends. Mary, a "newcomer," had never been part of the group. Although she was said to be a Catholic, no one had ever seen her in either of the two Catholic churches nearby.

"Do you think the children were baptized?" they asked each other fearfully. But Mary was a neighbor and needed help and Regina Valenti had suggested they give it. They took turns sitting with her for a few days. They brought her soups and other easy-to-eat foods. Regina saw to it that the children's belongings, scattered about the apartment, were put away neatly in drawers and closets. Mary wished at first that they would go away and leave her in peace, but eventually such continued kindness touched her. She made efforts to regain her independence for their sake, and soon she found, without pleasure, that she was growing stronger.

When she first went into the living room, she saw immediately that someone had taken the empty photograph frames from the piano. She had given the photographs to the police. Had they returned them to her? She looked at the piles of unopened mail. The police had no need of the photos now. She wept, and the weary desolation flooded her. Turning back, she decided to return to bed. A pill would send her to sleep, a blank, dead sleep if she was lucky. But at the windowsill she paused.

The streets were still covered in snow. It must have been very cold, for the piled-up hillocks along the curb were covered in glistening ice. People were slipping and sliding and on the corner she saw the plump figure of Connie Ferraro, wrapped in a heavy fur coat and hat with a scarf blowing in front of her face, unsteady on her feet, carrying a grocery bag. Mary's supply of bread and milk was low, Connie had remarked earlier.

Mary felt a pang of shame which for a moment pierced the despair and grief that had possessed her entirely. This could not go on. She bathed and dressed and when Connie Ferraro came up, triumphant, with her purchases, Mary had fresh coffee waiting for her.

She resumed her household tasks. Her neighbors still visited and they persuaded her to go to Mass with them. They had had Masses said for the children. She agreed to go, although she couldn't take communion. It was peaceful to stand in the congregation in the big, old, rather ugly church—it had amused Quent to see it decorated for Christmas, its bulk heavily draped with bands of lights, "like a fat old whore smothered with sparklers," he had said, but the interior had dignity. At first she missed the sonorous Latin of her childhood; then she just stood quietly. She couldn't pray, but for a moment she felt eased from the frantic despair that was only masked by the strong drugs she had been given. Then she thought of the children's funeral. Sometime soon the police would return the children's bodies to her, but where and how could it be?

The recollection of her wedding at City Hall was with her, sharp and clear. She and Quent had giggled at the earnest official who had married them, a plump and solemn man who tried, as he told them, to "give the occasion some dignity." Mary had amused Quent by arriving in a white dress and hat, after all. They were both agnostics. The children hadn't been baptized. Alice hadn't minded; she was relieved, perhaps, that the children were not to be brought up as Catholics. She and her husband, Joe, had been agnostic themselves, though in the way of country people they belonged to the church in Spenser, which was the social meeting place for the scattered households. She had suggested baptism there, as each child was born, just for the sake of form, "and the minister would like it—Mr. Gaylord is such a nice man." But Quent would have none of it.

"Hypocrisy," he had said, and the discussion was over. For both Quent and Mary, hypocrisy had been the one unforgivable sin. She had agreed and never mentioned her sudden longing, when Tom was born, for the christening ceremony, with the child in an heirloom robe and all the family present. And now— She had managed not to think about the autopsies, with the help of strong drugs, but the funeral *must* take place. She would have to get in touch with the police.

As she left the church, she saw children playing in the new fall of snow that lay over the ice. A little girl, with a cap on her head and a bright coat like Linda's, ran and slid with a shout of laughter. Mary's sudden flood of tears troubled Connie Ferraro, who got her to take another pill and helped her into bed, though Regina was disapproving.

"She must make an end of that," she said.

But Regina, Connie thought, was a woman of iron.

Mary was asked to go to Poughkeepsie to give what information she could to the district attorney. She had no car—the police had taken it. "Routine," they had told her. So an officer drove her there and back. She answered the same questions she had been asked so many times before, getting through the day with an extra dose of tranquilizers, and that night she took four sleeping pills.

The next afternoon, the telephone rang and Mary heard the voice of Fiona. It seemed like months since they had spoken. Mary's head was still heavy from the drug she had taken the night before and she wondered if she had missed a call that morning, because Fiona was telling her that the police were releasing the children's bodies. Certainly, they must have tried to reach her first.

Fiona was talking briskly, though Mary's mind was still caught in her first words. What did it mean, "released"? They were ready, like a parcel, to be picked up? By an undertaker, she supposed.

"What did you say?" She felt stupid. "The line . . ."

"I was saying that Alice has had to be told that the children are dead. We didn't want to tell her, of course. In her condition there is always a risk. Yet she had to be consulted. We found that she had expected the news."

Fiona sounded curiously unpleasant; it was almost as though she was blaming Mary. Well, she blamed her for Alice's stroke, no doubt.

"But, of course, she had a relapse," Fiona continued. "Nevertheless, she has made it clear what she wants done about the funeral arrangements. The children should be buried next to Quentin. Quentin had bought one additional plot; Ernest is arranging about the other. I don't suppose you object to that."

It wasn't a question. Quentin had bought the plot for Mary; she had liked the idea of their lying side by side. But there was no better place for the children; the graveyard at Spenser was well kept; Joe was buried there with a place for Alice beside him. Baileys and Christophers visited regularly and brought flowers, and on the Fourth of July the Stars and Stripes flew over Joe's grave—he had been a proud veteran. The children would be with the family, beside their father. It was difficult to speak, but she agreed.

Yet Fiona wasn't finished. She continued with hardly a pause for Mary's reply. "Alice, as you must know, has never liked the idea of the family being present at the interment. Far too morbid. So arrangements have been made to bury the children quietly without ceremony and for a memorial service to be held a week from this Tuesday at two o'clock, unless you prefer another date."

Dr. Bristow got on the line. He was Boy Burgoyne's doctor—all the Burgoynes went to him and he had looked after Alice since her first stroke.

"Allow me to add my thoughts, Mrs. Christopher. It would be impossible for your mother-in-law to attend a graveside ceremony. I could not think of allowing it if it were during the spring, let alone in this weather. She might—I only say she might—be able to get through a quiet service in the church here. And it would give her over a week to gain strength after the shock of the bad news."

Mary had no reason to refuse. The doctor rang off. Fiona apparently had no more to say. As Mary put the receiver down, she found herself wishing once more that she and Quent had been religious. Her mother had talked of the old funerals, with black coaches, black-plumed horses, black-clad mourners honoring their dead.

The images haunted her and followed her into sleep, but she woke, startled, before dawn, with another thought. Her conversation with Fiona—it had been strange. Fiona had spoken as if Alice had been the children's mother, not herself. Mary lay in bed in the dark, wondering. But as the first gray light came through the windows, common sense returned. Naturally Fiona, with Alice in the house, was thinking first of her welfare. Yet that thought brought little consolation.

Then it came to her that Alice would be with her. Alice would be at her side. They would mourn together as they had not been able to do before, kept apart by the barrier of Alice's condition. She felt a sudden easing of her pain, for she would no longer be alone.

6

"So there's nothing else. We're releasing the car to her today," Lieutenant Pidusky said. "Any luck with the button?"

"Mm," Captain Bassett said. The Merivale man kept a close mouth, Pidusky thought, a Yankee type. But that morning the man on the other end of the line continued. After all, Pidusky had cooperated well with him. "It matches the other buttons on the girl's coat. The bit of thread matches the loose ones where it broke off."

"Could have broken off before that night, though," Pidusky said, reflectively.

"*Could* have," Bassett answered. "We're not releasing the information yet, by the way."

As soon as Mary knew her car was being returned she called Carol Grafton. When Carol had read about the death of the children, she called Mary with warm sympathy and an offer to help in any way she could. Mary had been too numb to talk, but after her conversation with Fiona, she had roused herself to ask Carol if she would drive her up for the funeral. Carol had agreed at once, but mentioned she would have to pick up her car on Staten Island, where she had left it until she got settled.

"And so you needn't trouble to collect your car, Carol. Just meet me here on Tuesday morning—"

"Oh, Mary, I'm so sorry," Carol's voice cut in. "I was going to call you, but I've been in a sweat. I got word from the top brass—they're in Chicago, believe it or not—I have to be ready to start on Monday; the woman who was there decided to quit early. It had to be now when I'm having all sorts of trouble with Steve. Well, most likely it's his bitchy mother, though my lawyer thinks he's got another woman. The lawyer wants me to go back and live in the house and throw Steve out to protect my claim, but my God, imagine the commute— I'm awfully sorry, Mary. Everything piling up at once . . ."

"Don't worry, Carol," Mary replied calmly. "I hope everything works out. It has to take time, I suppose. And really, though I would have liked it if you could have come, it makes no difference. I can manage."

"Well, thanks, Mary." Carol sounded relieved. "I suppose nothing makes much difference really. Hell is hell. But when things calm down, let's get together. Maybe at Fanelli's . . ."

Mary had been sincere, but after she hung up she found she had been wrong. It did make a difference. But why?

She paced about the apartment. It was already tidied and dusted. There was little to do anymore. The children had filled her life . . . She could turn out the china closet, but she had done that a few days before. Sitting down at her desk in her bedroom, she looked at the pile of manuscript. The work had been going well; she should try to get back to it. Gene Meyer—she had never kept that appointment. He had sent her a kind note of condolence. She knew he had liked her work on the early part of the book. She picked up the folder with the completed chapters and glanced at them. Early Hellenic myths, almost forgotten goddesses . . . Sometime. But not now.

Her hands were shaking. Her belly was quivering. She paced the apartment, consumed by the sick anxiety she had felt while Linda and Tom were missing, blundering through every room except the children's. There she could not go. But why should she suddenly feel worse? Once again, her heart was banging against her ribs. Why should she feel apprehensive about going up alone? The worst had happened. There was nothing left to fear.

It was the place, she knew suddenly. The place: the house, Spenser, Burgoyne. Christmas country, Christopher country. The place that had meant home. Now it seemed drenched with evil and the very thought of it brought on nausea like the stench of death.

Stumbling to her desk, she clutched the corners and very deliber-

she said. "You have to try to stop torturing yourself, as time goes on. Jake always felt for me as much as he did for Bobby. You know, I was driving the car. I hardly got a scratch. Jake was going to come with us that day, but he had papers to grade. If he had been driv- ing—I don't know. It happened so fast. If only—"

If only. Guilt lasted longer than anything, Mary supposed. Miriam was still looking at the ifs all these years later. As Mary was now. Why the devil had it seemed so important to get that train? Why didn't I wait for Alice to come into the house? What could have possessed me?

The question that no other friend or acquaintance would ask, the bereaved mother asked. "What do you think happened, Mary?"

Reporters had come to her door but she would not speak to them. The newspapers had called the death of her children "the Bathsheba murders," after the name of the place where Tony's Tavern stood. She had not known it had a name. Just a lot of waste ground . . .

"I was afraid, from the beginning," she said slowly, "when they disappeared." It was difficult, still, to get the words out. She had had to talk to the police. Probably she had made little sense. From the young trooper in Burgoyne to that Captain Bassett, they had all looked at her as though she wasn't making much sense. And so had the district attorney.

Now she could only answer Miriam's question with another, the question that haunted her own days and nights: "What *could* have happened?"

Under Miriam's steady gaze, she went on. "Tom is always inclined to be restless." She heard the *is* and her stomach lurched. "I left the house in a hurry to get the train. My mother-in-law was there, but she was busy in the garage. I expect that Tom ran out and of course Linda followed, because she always did. But she wouldn't have liked the dark and the rain. Someone driving by must have seen them there, two beautiful children, alone. I don't know what he could have said—"

"He?" Miriam asked. "Do you know . . . ?"

Mary stared. "No. I just thought it must be . . . The police said they were not molested—sexually. But that had to be the purpose. Tom was a big boy; he fought and got his neck broken. Linda—too noisy, and she would have been a witness, and so— It must have been quick."

Her voice trembled. She could talk no more. The thought of her children and their lost lives overwhelmed her. Miriam was kind and understood. Really understood. Mary, with a new clarity, saw that Miriam and her husband had been only half living since their son had died.

"At least you know they're gone," Miriam said. It was the best comfort she could offer. "Not like the parents of children who are missing and *never found*. That's the worst of torments."

Mary supposed that must be true. But in the night she wished she had died with Linda and Tom.

In his office in the large, light modern building in Merivale, Captain Bassett was reviewing the progress of the case with Lieutenant Hayes. The chief had put in a lot of time on it, Hayes knew, and it looked as though he had been right from the beginning. Like the Pemberthy case, all over again.

"Circumstantial," Bassett said shortly, in answer to Hayes's congratulations. "We haven't pinned anything down. No one saw the children in the car. Or *admits* to seeing the children in the car."

"They could have been in the trunk," Hayes said reflectively. "She could have done it at any time. Right by the house if she liked. Kids wouldn't have had time to holler."

"She's not a professional killer," Bassett replied. "She wouldn't be certain of that. No, she was looking for a lonely spot, off the highway. Like Bathsheba. Not much off her route."

"Then she went into the tavern and said she was lost. Advertising herself. Now, why the hell—" Hayes stretched his legs and stared in front of him, a habitual attitude when he was perplexed.

"Useless speculation," Bassett said witheringly. "A passing car— she could have been afraid she was spotted. She might really have been lost and was arrogant enough to think that we'd swallow any story from Mary Christopher. You can't gauge the balance of fear and arrogance in that kind of killer."

"Well, we've got the button—"

"Defending counsel will be quick to point out that it could have come off at any time. Alice Christopher isn't the sort of woman to leave a child's coat with a button off and the threads hanging, but that's not evidence."

"And there's the plastic hood. We know Mary was wearing it when she left Spenser."

"No use to us. We could never prove that it was hers. And she might not bother to deny it. She has already admitted to being in the area. The wind could have blown it around."

Bassett regarded the pile of statements on his desk with only limited satisfaction. There were plenty of witnesses to testify that Mary was in Tony's Tavern, but not one could say that the children were with her. Alice Christopher, in the garage, was aware that her daughter-in-law had driven off, but had not actually seen her go.

Alice Christopher, he thought for a moment. He had taken her statement himself, in her bedroom. Alice, looking like a very old woman. But she had tried to sit erect and she kept her dignity through it all.

"And the handyman, the one that drove Alice Christopher home, he didn't remember seeing her go either," Hayes remarked. "He's one of the most tight-lipped guys I've ever come across, but I got that out of him. He was in a hurry to get back to his boss, that Burgoyne. Thought he was needed again that night."

Captain Bassett was rereading Lesska's statement. "He said that when he was turning the Cadillac around, young Mrs. Christopher's car was still under the tree and she was getting into it. He hadn't seen the children. But their mother says she left them on the porch—a brightly lit, glassed-in porch. If they were there, he *must* have seen them."

"Yes, well, if he'd stopped there we would have had something. But you'll notice later on he says he didn't pass the porch and he hadn't been looking at the house; he was looking at the road. It was bad driving weather that night and the guy is a careful driver."

Hayes had checked the records: Lesska had never received a ticket for a moving violation. "And he's not a nosy guy. People in Burgoyne say he's a loner. It's likely he didn't look."

Captain Bassett, deeply vexed, regarded the offending statement. One witness who could have proved the woman was lying. But he wasn't nosy. He hadn't looked. Just bad luck he wasn't like Jerry Crump from Tony's Tavern or his customer, Jack Curlew. A couple of useful blabbermouths. But it was a good distance from Spenser to

Bathsheba. Someone must have seen those children. It was just a matter of time before he found the witness.

The beautiful three-story house at the western limit of Burgoyne saw more activity on the day before the memorial service than it had for some time. At ten o'clock Boy Burgoyne returned from a trip and greeted his sister, Fiona, who was still staying there. Alice was resting, in preparation for Dr. Bristow's visit. Ernest arrived at one o'clock, hurrying from his office on Oak Avenue, and the three of them conferred in the library on the west side of the house. They could not disturb Alice there; she had a big, sunny bedroom on the third floor facing east.

Bristow arrived at one-thirty and was taken up to the family. Marcus Bristow was in his fifties, an energetic, busy man with a good practice. He made few house calls and he was due at the hospital at two, but the Burgoynes had always been special patients, not only for him but for his father, who had been a general practitioner also. The Burgoyne connection had been the making of his practice, his father had said, and he had remembered that a lot of Burgoyne money had gone into Slade Memorial. So Bristow attended their guest, Alice Christopher, and he was ready to listen to what the family had to say.

When he had been shown to the library instead of Mrs. Christopher's room, he had expected a conference. His patient had not been recovering as well as he had hoped and he knew that there was the children's funeral to be faced. But that was not the only subject of the discussion.

Boy was majestic as always, and greeted the doctor with a handshake that conveyed a special distinction, a distinction that amused yet pleased him.

"We are glad you've come to help us, Marcus. We have to make a decision and your advice is necessary. Vital."

"We know that you've done all you can, doctor." Fiona was brisk. With Fiona, even at her best, a compliment was inclined to contain a sting, and he waited for it. "But Alice simply isn't gaining enough strength. She talks to me, as another woman, and it is very clear that she is obsessed by guilt. We had to let her know that the children's bodies had been found—the suspense, we thought, was hurting her the most. But now her guilt is more intense. She feels that it was her failure to go straight into the house that caused the children to be restless and run out."

Bristow had guessed as much; it was natural that she would feel that way. The better the woman, the greater the guilt.

Fiona went on. "So it seems essential that she learn the truth. Then, at least, she can cease this self-reproach. She will know that nothing she could have done would have made any difference and the guilt rests firmly—elsewhere. Then she might gain sufficient strength to get through this memorial and perhaps, after a while, regain some measure of independence, which would mean so much to her."

"The truth?" Bristow asked. "Have the police found the killer?"

There had been nothing in the newspapers, but of course the family would be notified first. And the Burgoynes were unofficial family.

"The police have always been certain about the identity of the killer," Boy told him. "There was really only one possibility. But they had no proof; nobody had seen the children in the car. But now *we* know."

Bristow did not have to ask whom the police *suspected*. It had been all over Burgoyne from the beginning.

Ernest gave a lawyerlike cough. "There is a witness, Dr. Bristow, a witness who places the children in the car, a reliable witness. But he refuses to go to the police. He told his story to Boy and then to me, but he cannot be persuaded to go further. There is no point, of course, in our going to the authorities with this story without his corroboration."

"No point in pretending we're not relieved to let sleeping dogs lie." Boy's rich voice filled the library. Discretion was not part of Boy's nature, Bristow reflected. It was a quality that he had never needed. "A trial would certainly kill Alice."

"But we had to consult you, Doctor." Fiona's high, cool tone was astringent. It matched her lean body and her face, handsome with its good bones, yet with no erotic appeal. He wondered about old Derwent. Had he married her for the Burgoyne money? Or had she been softer, more appealing, then? "Only you can help us decide what is best to do for Alice now. To learn the truth, however shocking, and stop her anguish? Or let her remain as she is? The dosage of tranquilizers and sleeping pills that she's taking is rather high, isn't it?"

Bristow was hampered by the thought that the police should have had a crack at the reluctant witness. By the deep wrinkle on Ernest's forehead, he knew that the lawyer had the same idea. But if the witness refused to come forward, he supposed the family were not obliged to report his remarks. In any event, that wasn't his business. Fiona was right about the medication. Alice could not continue at that level of barbiturates and tranquilizers without a harmful interaction with the essential blood thinners and pressure pills. He thought of his patient receiving that news.

"Well—it won't be much of a consolation to her, will it?"

"All nonsense." Boy Burgoyne, standing by the chimney piece, looked down on them as though they were pygmies. A log was burning in the grate and its warmth brought his usually florid complexion to a high flush, exaggerated by his thick white hair, and he seemed to glow. A giant of a man, but well proportioned, and his custom-made tweeds disguised the belly that was becoming more pronounced.

"I know Alice. She can face the truth. Always could. Knew Joe was dying long before his doctor told *him,* and she kept a smiling face. Get the nonsense out of her head, eh, Marcus?"

Bristow had to agree. Perhaps nothing could be worse than that self-reproach. Ernest was a steady, sensible man and he seemed to think so. And he had always respected Boy, for all his tendency to bombast. Generous to the town in time as well as money, always approachable. And his devotion to Alice Christopher was of long standing. The Burgoynes had obviously made up their minds on the matter; this consultation was, he believed, a matter of form. And so he did agree.

As he walked down the fine staircase after looking in on his patient, he wondered who the reluctant witness was. And then he thought about the children's mother until he reached the hospital, when his mind filled with other problems and the Christopher case was forgotten for a time.

Before the doctor's car had left the driveway, Boy, Ernest, and Fiona were crossing the floor into the east wing. A nurse was sitting beside Alice's bed; Fiona gave her an expressive glance and she left. Alice was lying down but she was awake. A hairdresser had been coming to the house, and her hair was arranged in its usual style, in deep waves from a center part and curling lightly on the nape of her neck. She had worn it that way since she was a young girl, and when the blond hair turned to silver it hardly seemed to change. But her face, Fiona noticed, had aged in the last weeks. Pale and drawn, Alice was showing her years.

Alice smiled at her visitors. "I'm only lying here," she told them, "to save my strength for tomorrow. I've gotten terribly lazy. Sit down, all of you. You look very *serious*, Boy."

Ernest saw the fear behind the attempt at lightness and felt a stab of pain for Alice, pain mingled with some fear of his own. He had expected Bristow to stay until it was over—Alice might need something. Of course, she was well supplied with tranquilizers, but she might need an injection. She might have another stroke—they couldn't just go ahead— And so, as always, it was Boy who went ahead.

"It's because of tomorrow that we're here," he said. "There is something you have to know. You're well enough now; Bristow thinks so."

"Doesn't matter what Bristow thinks," Alice answered tartly. "If there's something I should know, tell me. I'm not in my dotage yet."

Boy nodded in satisfaction, but Ernest could see the fear in the pallor of her cheeks and the tightening of the muscles around her mouth that made deep furrows he had never seen before.

"There is no longer any doubt that Mary committed the crime," he said. "We've told you the suspicions of the police from the beginning."

She closed her eyes. "But I still don't believe it. Won't believe it."

"They have always believed she did it. But they can't arrest her because no one has come forward to say that the children were in her car. You didn't see them and Lesska said that he didn't. I wondered about that and I've questioned him, privately, more than once. Alice, you know that he is loyal, not only to me, but to all of us. He thought he was protecting the family. But he confessed to me that he knew the children were in the car."

Alice made a small sound and turned her head into the pillow. Boy went on. He never hesitates, Ernest thought. I agonize and do nothing. Just let myself be towed along in his wake. Ernest longed for the comfort of his office, where he could handle other people's problems within the guidelines of the law and leave the turbulence of trials to his partner. How could a family like theirs have become involved with something like this? It was Quentin Christopher, he thought. Quent, whom he had liked as a boy, but who had become a city man, an intellectual with contempt for the values of a place like Burgoyne. It was he who had brought that woman into all their lives.

Boy was still talking. "Lesska has not lied to the police. He hadn't *seen* them in the car in the strict sense of the word. But he told me something else. I had a long talk with him recently, first just the two of us, then with Ernest present for the information of the family. Alice, I think you should hear what he has to say."

Alice lifted herself from the pillow. She didn't speak, but she looked at Boy and after a moment bowed her head.

Boy opened the door and ushered Lesska in. He looked as he did every day, dressed in neat chinos, a checked khaki shirt, a zippered leather jacket. His light hair was neatly combed. A slight reddening along the nose and cheekbones from the bitter wind was the only mark of something different on his pale face, and his eyes held no particular expression.

"Tell Mrs. Christopher what you told me about *everything* you saw in Mrs. Mary's car, Lesska."

Lesska looked at him. "It was dark inside. I told the police. Couldn't say I saw the children."

"But what did you see?"

"When I drove up with Mrs. Christopher, the white Toyota was under the branches of the big tree near the house. Mrs. Mary came over to the Caddy, talking. I wondered why, if she was in such a hurry, she was just standing there, and why she hadn't taken the car around to the front and got it going instead of putting it on soaking grass. City woman. After I took Mrs. Christopher to the garage and turned the Caddy, she was still standing there, fumbling with her keys and fussing with her hair. The car was still dark, but as I swung round there was a little light dancing about inside, like a bit of mirror reflecting the headlights. I didn't know what it was. I went on my way."

It was a very long speech for Lesska. Alice was quite still. Remembering, Ernest thought. For the thousandth time, no doubt. She said nothing.

"Thank you, Lesska," Boy said and Lesska trudged out, leaving Alice to stare up at Boy, her eyes fearful.

"*City woman.*" Boy was amused. "You'd think Lesska was born and bred in Burgoyne. Hates the city. But the important thing is that dancing light. It would have meant nothing to me, either. Then. But the police had some information that they didn't give to the press, but Bassett, of course, told me. A very decent fellow. We're lucky we got a Burgoyne man. We might have had some young investigator who would want to make a splash in the newspapers. Poughkeepsie is getting more like New York every day."

Alice's body was shaking.

"Get on with it, Boy," Fiona said. She was the only person who spoke to Boy like that, Ernest reflected. The only one, ever. Alice had teased him, but with Alice it was pleasant.

"Well, Bassett had told me that when Linda's body was found, she was clutching one of those metal balls from the Christmas tree in her hand." He paused.

"Lesska couldn't have known that," Boy added reflectively. "So that clinches it."

Alice was still. Her arms were folded across her chest and her eyes were closed. Since the children's disappearance, she had refused to consider the possibility of Mary's guilt. Such an idea was unthinkable. But as time passed, she had been forced to think of it, though steadfastly holding that Mary was innocent. After a few moments, which seemed very long to Ernest, Alice opened her eyes and faced them all. Her face was livid, but she seemed calm and her voice was clear.

"Lesska was right. The police must not be informed. Mary was Quentin's *wife*. The children's mother."

Her fingers dug into her arms, her nails scraping her flesh. She must be hurting herself, Ernest thought uneasily, we should stop her. But he didn't move.

"There must be no trial," Alice said. "Let it rest. But I don't want to set eyes on her, ever again."

The brothers and sister looked at each other. Tomorrow, Mary would be at the church. But Alice had closed her eyes again and wished to speak no more.

"Sufficient unto the day . . ." Fiona said quietly as they left the silent room.

7

The small white church in Spenser was creditably filled with mourners. Boy had suggested the larger, more imposing gray stone Episcopal church in Burgoyne, but Alice had wanted the memorial to take place at the church she had attended with her husband and the children at Christmas, Easter, and Thanksgiving. And the Reverend Peter Gaylord should not be slighted.

Alice's Bailey cousins, their children and grandchildren, were there in the front rows of seats, greeting each other quietly. They had come in from all the villages around Burgoyne. There were no Christophers; old Joe's brother had moved from Poughkeepsie to Santa Fe for his health and died there. His daughter, Mildred, was an archeologist and she was on a dig somewhere in southern Mexico.

The rest were Alice's friends and neighbors, come to give her comfort in her sickness and distress. Mrs. Pritchard, the organist, played softly, and the voices of the congregation were muted as they waited for the minister to take the pulpit, but there were some whisperings. Already it was past eleven, the time set for the service, but no one had seen the mother of the children.

Mary had left early. The day before she had been eager for the next morning to come; she would see Alice, share her burden. Yet the night had brought troubled dreams. She tried to shake her depression and anxiety—no reason to be anxious, she told herself. The worst had happened. There could only be comfort in being once again with the family, with Alice. Alice would be weaker than she remembered, but she, Mary, must be stronger. She must comfort Alice, an old woman, bereft of her gift to the future. You've been drowning in self-pity, she told herself. It is time you thought of someone else.

She took little time dressing. She had got her mourning clothes out the night before. For Quent, she had worn no real mourning; he had asked her not to and she had respected his wishes. But she had had to wear full mourning when she went to Ireland for her mother's funeral; anything less would have hurt her Aunt Kathy and offended the neighbors in the small country village. It seemed appropriate now.

As soon as she got in the car, it began giving trouble. It had seemed all right when she got it back from the police, but now the engine was running rough and it felt as if it had lost a lot of power. She pulled in at a garage and she was lucky; the mechanic wasn't busy and he found the problem right away. It was just a wire that had come loose from a spark plug. The repair was simple, but the detour had taken twenty minutes and now trucks were unloading in front of her. Another ten minutes passed before she got through the traffic to the highway and then it was a slow ride up to the Henry Hudson. After that, the roads were fairly clear. She traveled through the bleak winter landscape, keeping her mind on her driving, pushing away the thoughts of her other drives on these same roads when she was still tormented by uncertainty. Now there was no uncertainty. She took a curve in the road too fast and for a moment had the sense of losing control. Reducing speed, she drove carefully the rest of the way. At last she arrived the church set in the dun-colored lawn and entered to the sound of the organ. The hymn was "Abide with Me"—she had heard it last at Quent's memorial.

She went through the door beyond the small porch into the nave. The minister was already in the pulpit. The organ music died away and the heads of the congregation turned to see the latecomer. Some of them had never seen her before: a tall woman, with thick black hair surrounding a startlingly white face. Of course, the mother.

To Mary they were a blur of faces. An usher tried to lead her to the front pew, but she felt dizzy and hesitated. The organist went on to finish the hymn; the minister was waiting to begin the service.

Quickly she slipped into a seat in the back of the church, blinked, and found herself among strangers.

The congregation recovered its manners and lifted its gaze to the pulpit. Mary found she was conspicuous in her mourning; everyone she could see was wearing ordinary clothes. The fashion of informality had reached Spenser. No wonder people had stared.

Mr. Gaylord based his sermon on "Suffer the little children to come unto me." For a time she was caught up in his words. The sermon was moving and she had to struggle to keep from breaking down. The service ended with the congregation singing a hymn, but Mary couldn't make a sound. She saw people turning discreetly to glance at her and then quickly looking away. They seemed embarrassed to have met her gaze.

Miriam had described the nightmare quality of her son's funeral. "I was the mother who had driven the car. 'She didn't get a scratch.'" Now Mary was the mother who had left her children with a sick old woman. These people—she didn't recognize them. The Baileys must be in the front. Did Alice manage to come? It was a hard, cold day for an invalid.

She peered forward, trying to make out the front row, but she could only see Boy's head and shoulders, towering over the rest.

The hymn drew to a close. Mr. Gaylord climbed down from the pulpit and walked slowly to the side of the nave and down the aisle to the door. The organist continued playing. The congregation remained still, waiting for something. Of course, they were waiting for her to move first.

She prepared to rise, placing her hand on the back of the pew as she felt oddly weak. And clumsy. Suddenly she was stifling in her heavy black coat, so right for Ireland, so wrong for this place. Half standing, she thought she saw Susan near the front—Susan, closest to her of all the Bailey girls. And there was Marjorie, from Pleasant Valley . . . Her gaze searched for Uncle William, Alice's cousin and always Mary's favorite, but his tall figure was not to be seen.

Then she saw a stirring in the front row and hesitated: Boy Burgoyne had risen and Fiona, dressed in pale gray, with hat and gloves. Boy was splendid in a dark suit; brother and sister always had the look of the lord and lady of the manor. Then the rest of the congregation rose deferentially. Soon Boy was in the center aisle. His brother Ernest was close by, sober-looking, anxious. Fiona came last, but now Mary could see that Boy had a woman on his arm, between him and Ernest, small among the Burgoynes. They advanced slowly.

The woman was not small, Mary perceived; she was stooped and using a cane. Old . . . Then the woman, who had kept her eyes to the ground, looked up. It was Alice.

"Alice!" she called. "Alice!"

Alice looked so very old. Mary had hardly recognized— Her face, so pale and drawn, her movements, so slow. There was nothing of her bright look, her vigor. As she moved, with several pauses, down the aisle, the organist started to play again. Mary's heart was beating fast; she could not think why. Down the little party came, in some strange travesty of a wedding march, Alice and Boy, Ernest as best man, Fiona the matron of honor. But the stumbling Alice wore dark clothes; there were no nuptials here, only death as consummation.

Alice did not look up again; she had not seen her.

"Alice," she said again as the little party drew level. Alice paused. She stood, hunched over her stick. The congregation was quite still.

"Alice!" It was a cry.

Alice moved, stumbled, and, recovering, caught Mary's gaze. Mary wasn't quite certain if she had recognized her. The expression on her face was strange: obviously she was still weak, still very sick; the look could have been that of fear, or horror.

Mary's words died in her throat. She followed them out, with the rest of the congregation. It was cold and raw; sleet was pelting down. The Cadillac was waiting in front of the church with Lesska at the wheel. Boy and Ernest were helping Alice into the back seat. Fiona put a hand on Mary's shoulder and drew her back onto the porch.

Mourners Mary didn't know were rushing to the car to say a word to Alice. Burgoyne people, probably. Some of them paused to murmur a condolence to Mary as they went.

"I hope you liked the service, Mary," Fiona said. "I thought Mr. Gaylord did very well, under the circumstances. A lot of people came, considering the weather." A middle-aged man, dressed in a duffel coat and jeans, stopped and murmured something to Fiona; then he paused for a moment and shook Mary's hand.

"Sorry," he said. "Sorry about the kids. Good kids. Always liked them."

Mary recalled who he was as he moved off swiftly. The man from the gas station. Tom had liked to talk to him about cars. Quent had always denied any knowledge of the "beast under the hood." "I leave the entrails to the car doctors," he had told Tom. "Or the car butchers, as they sometimes turn out to be." So Tom had chatted to Billy Robinson. They had been friends.

"A lot of people," Fiona went on. "I can't think who some of them are." She saw Mary's eyes searching the mourners as they streamed out. "Oh, you won't see William and Isobel, I'm afraid. Isobel came down with one of these new influenzas, a very bad case, and William is at the hospital with her today. They weren't certain she was going to pull through; there were complications, but I heard this morning that she seems to be taking a turn for the better. So fortunate—William was really quite distracted. I think all the Bailey girls came, except Anne, who's about to give birth. Jack and his wife are still at his post near Frankfurt—rather worrying these days."

People were rushing to get to their cars, out of the sleet.

"Mary, you see how Alice is," Fiona went on, smoothing her gloves. "We must get her back to bed immediately. She should have absolute quiet. We couldn't arrange anything for the mourners, obviously. You know Alice. She would have wanted to greet them, and the effort . . ."

Mary could only nod and Fiona disappeared into the Cadillac, which rolled away at once. There was nothing, Mary thought, that she could have said. Alice had not known her. Was Alice's mind gone and the Burgoynes reluctant to talk about it? But surely the doctor would have told her that when he spoke of the problems Alice would face at a lengthy funeral. Mary had been hot in the church, but now she was shivering uncontrollably. She had been like a child, she adjured herself, wanting to run to her mother to be comforted. But Alice was the one needing comfort now. And, it was clear, she wasn't looking to her daughter-in-law for that comfort. It wasn't just Fiona keeping them apart. Alice's eyes had shown no recognition, but she had stopped and bent her head because she had heard Mary's voice. She must have heard it; she must have recognized it.

The thumping of Mary's heart got worse and she felt a wave of nausea. She tried to push it away as a few more people came to offer condolences. The freckle-faced Marjorie, usually a laughing young woman, fond of practical jokes, stood, frowning, under the hood of her quilted coat, her arm clutching her solid young husband.

"I hope you find peace, Mary," she said, before her husband took her away. The words, doubtless, were well meant, but somehow they struck Mary as . . . She didn't know. They were—unsatisfying. She couldn't think why.

Several of the other Baileys who passed by said the same thing. But then, she remembered, no one could think of what to say at such a time. Not she herself, in Rome, writing to Miriam. Easier to run through the sleet back to a warm house. The crowd was thinning; she was about to leave, but then Susan came, clutching the hand of Jimmy, her eldest. Susan was crying, the tears running down her cheeks. "Oh, Mary," she said. "Oh, Mary." She stood, dabbing her eyes like a little girl, unable to stop the flow. A pretty little girl.

Jimmy began to cough, a deep racking cough.

Susan looked at him; her sobs stopped at once.

"I was afraid of that," she said. "Penny's been coughing. That sounds *bad*. I must get him in the car, Mary. I *told* you to wear your parka, Jimmy."

"None of the kids are wearing them," Jimmy said.

"Now speak to Aunty Mary and I'll take you to the car."

"I'm sorry about Tom and Linda, Aunty. Tom was going to teach me his backhand next summer."

"Beth and Jane have colds," Susan said, distractedly. Jimmy began to cough again. "Mary . . . I hope you find peace." Susan, holding Jimmy's hand, ran away home.

Perhaps it was a phrase the family used. But Mary had not heard it after Quentin's death. Susan had come over to Alice's and the two young women had cried together in the bright living room.

The church was emptying fast. People Mary did not know saw her on the porch, murmured a few words, and headed promptly for the line of cars parked on the grass verge. She felt conspicuous and gazed around for her own car—she had left it in a space somewhere, but could not remember now just where it was. Several people glanced back curiously but for some reason she couldn't move, and for a moment she closed her eyes and stood, her rigidity broken only by her shivers.

Captain Bassett, who had been sitting with some town officials from Burgoyne, had not left with them. He had watched Mary since she entered and he had passed her on the porch, but she had not noticed him. Despite her silent passivity, to his sharp gaze she looked disoriented. He had an urgent wish to take her in, now, for questioning. This was the time to break her down.

Yet he couldn't do it. His colonel had told him a decision had been made, on the highest level, to proceed very carefully, discreetly. The new DA, Kramer, wasn't like his predecessor, John Blessing, who had let BCI tend to its own business. Kramer was always looking at the political angle. Interested in higher office, that was for sure. The county wasn't big enough; he had his eyes on Albany. "A great help to the Probyn Commission," the newspapers said. Yet another commission on police forces in the state. A carpetbagger, the men called him, because he had come to Poughkeepsie from Hartford.

And Kramer remembered the Peter Reilly case and he was not going to let anybody forget it. He talked to the commissioner in Albany and he had him running scared. "We'll have a horde of lawyers and God knows who from the city on this one. A lot of eggheads jumping all over us. 'Persecuting the bereaved mother.' *And* the newspapers. She's a looker, too, prime meat for TV." And so the only person who could have killed the children, the one person who stood to gain by their deaths, was walking around scot-free.

From the shelter of his car, with the sleet crackling against the glass, Bassett watched the woman on the porch. It was almost clear of departing mourners now, but she was still standing there, as if she was waiting for someone. Who? he wondered. Not the family. They believed Mary Christopher was guilty, he knew that. Boy Burgoyne had made it clear, in his own way. He had also let him know, obliquely, that they didn't want a trial and a conviction. Bassett understood. It was typical of the kind of people they were. He admired them for it, but he was a police officer.

"The scandal," Boy had said. "We have to think of Alice."

Alice Christopher. Bassett had seen that long, agonized walk down the aisle, the bent, shuffling old woman who looked as if she had been shattered in one great blow. And on that cold gray day he remembered the young Alice Bailey, a bright-eyed, fair-haired, lively girl, full of fun, and yet the most respected girl for miles around. He had just come from the Academy then, a hard-working young trooper, with little money and a lot of dreams. Some about Alice Bailey. But Alice, a few years older, had married Joe Christopher, an established, prosperous man.

By the time he made sergeant he had recovered enough to marry Dolly Westcott. They had got along together well enough and their two daughters were married and had children of their own. When Dolly died three years ago, he had mourned her sincerely, but he had settled, happily enough, into his widower's existence. He liked the quiet of his old house in Burgoyne after the hustle of BCI. But Alice Bailey Christopher had remained in his mind as someone very special, and even here by the church and God's blessing, he felt a deep anger for that city woman who had brought her to this.

He lingered, hoping to see whom Mary was expecting. Talking with Lieutenant Hayes, he had gone over the possibility of an accomplice—the likelihood of a lover—but they had found no leads. The First Precinct had nothing to offer on that score—but they were a busy precinct. Something could have been missed.

The woman still stood, a spectacle in the ostentatious mourning, dressed for a grief she couldn't feel. Like Françoise Pemberthy, he thought. She had been all grief at her husband's funeral, in dark colors—brand-new expensive clothes. Pemberthy. He had been a good man, at a loss after his first wife's death. He had gone on a European tour, met the young Belgian woman, and been drawn into a quick marriage. Pemberthy was a man of property with a good income and he had no children. Within two years of his marriage he died of a heart attack, though he had no history of heart disease. He was approaching seventy and his doctor signed the death certificate.

Bassett was already an investigator. If the doctor was satisfied, he wasn't. And he had gone out on a limb and asked for an autopsy. He got the court order, to the widow's fury, but he had understood that if nothing harmful was found, his budding career in BCI would be over.

The medical examiner found that Pemberthy had died of a heart attack, but he gave serum samples to the toxicologist. And in a routine check for controlled substances, it was discovered that Pemberthy had taken a potent narcotic analgesic, dextromoramide. Pemberthy's doctor was certain that he had never prescribed it.

Bassett's first excitement was quieted when he learned that the dextromoramide could not be pinpointed as the cause of the heart attack. The lab had no standard for the compound; the dose could be lethal or not. The federal Drug Enforcement Administration had no knowledge of it and referred the inquiry to a pharmaceutical company. The company could only tell them that the drug had not been available in the United States since the 1960s. It was, however, still produced in Belgium.

While the lab waited for a sample to quantify, Bassett had flown to Belgium for consultation with the Brussels police on his own time and at his own expense. Checking on Françoise's background, he discovered her cousin and lover, one Jacques Perigord. The Brussels police were very cooperative, for, though they had no interest in Françoise, they had copious files on Perigord, who had an unsavory history of parting widows from their money: a common, sometimes vicious, swindler. His affections had been centered on the young Françoise; but after interrogation by the Brussels police he had soon broken down and implicated her. He confessed to sending her supplies of the drug, claiming that he was told she needed it to quiet her husband, who importuned her with his surprising virility.

By the time Bassett returned from Europe, it had been discovered that the drug found in Pemberthy was enough to kill a young man in good health. Françoise was arrested and tried, though Perigord escaped prosecution by testifying.

Mary Christopher, Bassett felt in his heart, had needed no accomplice. Instinct told him that she had worked alone. It made it that much harder for him, but he would not concede defeat. That greedy young woman from the city who had married foolish Quentin Christopher and wrought all this havoc would pay the price. If only that damned fool of a mechanic had looked into the car when he changed the wipers! But all he had noticed was that the woman was good-looking. "Real tasty," he'd said, "but in a hurry. The good-looking ones are usually in a hurry. Well, most of them." And he grinned. Pleased with himself. So both children must have been in the back, where Linda's coat button had been found. Someone, somewhere along the route from Spenser to Tony's Tavern, must have seen those children in the car. In the white car he could see now that the others had moved off, the small white car alone outside the church.

*   *   *

When Mary got into her car, she found that her hands were shaking. Her whole body was still shivering, and the shivering and shaking didn't stop after she started the engine and the heater was warming the car. Her eyes weren't focusing clearly and she was surprised to hear herself speak aloud.

"I can't drive," she said.

She hadn't thought about going home. All her thoughts had been about getting to the church—seeing Alice. The house in Spenser was still closed up and somehow she hadn't thought of staying with Alice at the Burgoynes', but if she had thought, she would have expected one of the girls, probably Susan, to ask her to stay for the night. But Jimmy had a cough and Penny was sick; naturally she would think of them first. Perhaps each of the others thought that someone else was taking her home.

The sermon had been comforting. The minister in his black robe had the air of a priest and his words held the promise of eternity. She was really a believer after all.

"When it suits you." She could hear Quent mocking her a little in his dry way.

Yet now she couldn't move. Her heart had started to pound again and her belly was queasy, worse than it had been on the way up. Much worse. Part of her mind was clear and wondered why she should feel so much worse; it made no sense. Nothing could be more final than the scene in Poughkeepsie, when she had stood in the morgue and seen the corpses, her Tom, her Linda, yet no longer Tom and Linda. It was only then that she had known they were gone, and she remembered the bitter, cold despair, the taste of death on her tongue.

So why was she agitated now, when everything was already lost and nothing really mattered?

Mr. Gaylord had said goodbye to the mourners inside the church; he had not yet succumbed to a winter cold and he was wary of the drafty porch. A few long-winded parishioners had caused him problems out there on more than one occasion. Particularly funerals and memorials, he thought. But when he emerged he saw young Mrs. Christopher sitting alone in her car, when everyone else had departed. It didn't seem quite right.

He went over to the car and looked down. Mrs. Christopher tried to open the window, but she seemed to be having trouble. When she finally lowered it a few inches, he saw that she was shaking and looked ill.

"You aren't well enough to drive," he said. "I think you need someone to drive you home. The sleet seems to be getting worse. Why don't you come back inside the church, while we make some arrangement?"

His face was perplexed. She saw that he didn't know what to do, but as a minister—and perhaps as a kind man—he felt he should do something. He was embarrassed. She was being a nuisance.

"I can manage," she said mechanically, and thanked him for his thoughtfulness. The short exchange steadied her hands and she drove off, leaving him free to go about his business. Without his robe, he looked like an ordinary man.

Once more, she made the journey that she had taken so often, with pleasure, with joy, through Christopher country, along its roads through all the seasons: white with snow, pink with spring blossom, blue with summer lakes, green and gold with woodland. Now it was bleak, grim, black-yellow, nauseating, poisonous, deadly, and stinking.

You are going mad, she told herself soberly, but the evil stench was not merely a thought; it possessed her mind and it did not lessen. No hope left. No hope left. Yet as she saw the George Washington Bridge in the distance she felt a slight, indefinable relief. She had passed through the storm, hardly noticing that the sky had cleared, but here the sun was out. She rolled the window down; the air was milder. As she drove along the West Side Highway, the Hudson below sparkled blue, looking, from that distance, clear and fresh, happily deceiving the eye, disguising the filth in its depths. Going by the Twenty-third Street exit, she noticed the traffic piling up and she abruptly turned off at Fourteenth Street.

A passing truck hooted; a mass of cars and trucks were trundling down the street, all coming in her direction. "Oh, hell," she muttered. How in the world—this stretch, lined with loading platforms, was one-way. The wrong way. Then the light ahead changed to green; the traffic stopped and she barreled through to the two-way lanes and went straight into a pothole with such a shuddering thrust and bounce she was afraid the car would get stuck. But it pulled free and after that she watched the road carefully. The roads, like the pavement, were full of people—men, no women. Men nodding in doorways and on the sidewalk, while others strolled in the street carrying goods of all kinds, pots, pans, carpets, television sets—and drugs: she noticed the pushers were out already.

The entrepreneurs weren't brisk and cheerful; many of them had glazed eyes and surly looks. They had no look of North America; she could not guess their origins; they wore short, colorful, dirty blankets against the cold and ignored the traffic—they had made this place their own.

"Calcutta," Quent had remarked, when they first saw the people sleeping in the streets, "the armpit of civilization."

And there hadn't been as many street people then. But it wasn't Calcutta, it was New York. A home for all kinds. She stopped at a light and a man rushed up to wipe her windshield with a filthy rag. He was a giant of a man and his look was menacing. She felt no fear and handed him a dollar as the tribute he demanded. The place was a cesspool. Yet this city was her place. Not Christopher country. She had no hope left, but it was a relief to be back.

8

"You should go back to work," Carol said briskly. "Or get another job. Look how I've been run off my feet since last month. I've been trying to get to see you since the memorial, but it's one thing after another. What you need is to be so busy you don't have time to brood. Everything that could go wrong did, right? So that's the end of it and you have to make something else."

The two women were sitting in Fanelli's. Mary hadn't wanted to go there; it reminded her of Quent, of— But Carol only had time for a drink; she had a business dinner to go to at a restaurant nearby, so it was convenient for her. And Mary had wanted to see Carol. Lately Mary had taken to walking around the streets aimlessly, wishing she could burst through her skin, be someone else for a day, go back to the time before it all happened. She was still seized by the fear that had come when the children were lost: the cause was gone but the terror remained, existing on its own behalf. She was like a laboratory animal, she thought, fixed up to circuits that prodded the brain. Now fear, now horror, now despair. And now the suicide circuit. The idea would come, always the idea of jumping from a tall building, the Empire State, the World Trade, or any handy roof. Just an idea . . .

"The children were my job," she said.

She saw "the look" on Carol's face. She had come to know that look. After the memorial, she had longed to see her old friends, to talk of her anguish and her despair, of the limbo in which she lived, to draw some comfort from her own world, the world that she had shared with Quent.

And it was some relief to be in the company of city people, with the talk of politics and art and theater, spiced with the latest municipal scandals. There was no reproach in their gaze; here she wasn't "the mother who left her children." They were considerate and attentive, but—

Her first visit had been to an art gallery on Prince Street where Erik Lindstrom, an artist friend, was having a show. Blond and baby-faced, always a sunny man, he was glowing that day with his modest, but marked, success. Afterward a few of the guests went up to his studio for a late supper. She knew most of them well; they had been acquainted for years. They offered their condolences; they asked about the progress of the case. There had been none; there wasn't much to say about it. In that warm setting, after she had drunk a large brandy she began to talk of her mystification, her horror—and she first saw "the look" on her listener's face. She was speaking to Peter Tilney, a tall, thin, bearded young man with heavy-rimmed glasses. Like most of her New York friends, he was interested in psychology, from Freud through Werner Erhardt, alpha waves and cosmic consciousness. He was an astrologer and had made up a chart for her three years ago.

"Pluto has been transiting your Mars," he said. "That's heavy. Very heavy. But in a few weeks' time, this will change. Jupiter will transit your north node. A benign influence—"

"Let me give you some more brandy," her host interjected. "And you must try this quiche. And don't tell me that quiche is too boring, because I spent as much time on it as I did on that small figure study you liked and if I say so myself it's magnificent."

She saw "the look" again as his eyes met Tilney's, and she had understood. She was being tactless, showing bad taste. Her misery was too heavy to dole out at a social gathering. But she only saw her friends at social gatherings . . . And today was a social gathering too, a small one—Carol's pause between a full day at the bookstore and the challenge of a business dinner.

"A lot depends on how I strike Blakey and the rest of the Chicago contingent," Carol was saying. "The way I read it, it's move up or move out. And I'm going up, I can tell you. You wouldn't believe it from your old library pal, but I tell you that marketing is really my bag. I actually took courses in college, but I got nervous and went the library route. Am I glad I rerouted myself. Old Abe Schulte, who's in charge of the New York sector of the operation, is almost ready to retire and not before his time. A real dodderer, hates to make a decision. Upper management needs fresh blood and I'm it . . ."

She talked more about it over a vodka and tonic. "This is good," she said with a happy sigh. "At the dinner I'll just have white wine. Or perhaps just Perrier. People look at that sort of thing now."

But then she went on with her suggestions for Mary. "You need people," she pronounced doggedly. She had decided to be bracing. "You're letting yourself go, Mary. We're old friends, so you won't mind my telling you. Those clothes—well, they might have been okay upstate, but here they're so out of date, they're gross. It doesn't matter in the Village, I guess, but get yourself a good haircut, some sharp new outfits. Look like a smart New York woman; it'll do you a world of good. I've got to run," she added, rising. She reached for her coat, a cloth coat, Mary noticed, but very stylish. It slipped easily over the equally well-cut suit and the bright striped scarf at her throat. Carol walked out with a brisk step, much more brisk than that of the leisurely, gossipy Carol of her library days. Steve and Staten Island seemed to be quite forgotten. Carol had found her métier.

Mary left the bar. There was a chill wind blowing down from the north, piercing the seams of the down jacket that Carol had despised. She saw other people wearing padded coats and almost any kind of garment one could think of—old, new, practical, weird. Carol was getting very uptown.

The thought of returning to the apartment was grim. Mary knew she should eat dinner, but her appetite had not returned. The drink she had had with Carol had not dulled her senses; it had left her feeling more depressed. She walked up to the private park at University Village and let herself in at the gate. No one challenged her. The park was empty and the security guards were not to be seen. The branches of the trees were black against the sky, the gray of the day deepening into twilight. In the center, the square basin was empty, dry. The blue-painted concrete, strewn with implements, was garish, ugly.

She and Quent had sat here in their courtship days. Later Tom, and then Linda and Tom, had played here. She could not think why she had come. She rose abruptly and walked and then ran back to the apartment, letting herself in with clumsy haste as though she were fleeing from a mugger, but when she got inside the panic was still there. Now she understood how people could take to drink or drugs. Anything to stop the sick, whirling fear.

Instead of taking a pill she stood by the window and did deep-breathing exercises; she remembered the method from Quent's yoga days. Calmed a little, she reflected that Carol was right. She should go back to work, though she could feel no interest in her old duties. Libraries were changing before she had left. The Minetta branch, under the direction of her senior, remained better than most but it could not escape computerization, new cataloging methods, new sections for cassettes—a moving away from the old quiet world of books.

There was Quent's book . . . Gene Meyer had been patient, but he had called last week to ask how she was getting on, if she had returned to writing. He had not said so, but he had his schedule to consider.

Her desk, in her bedroom, still looked neglected. She had dusted it perfunctorily, but when she lit the lamp there was more dust and the pages she had left on top were stacked untidily. Clearing every-thing off, she dusted and polished, and arranged the draft pages in a neat pile. The desk had always been a refuge. From the time Linda had been old enough to leave her crib and share a room with Tom, this had been her own private space and she had enjoyed it. She had been apprehensive about the necessity of taking Linda back as Tom grew older— How absurd that seemed now! Almost wicked. She turned her mind away resolutely.

The book. Since the horror time had started, the only mental exercise that sometimes gave a little relief had been the book. Think-ing hard, concentrating on Zeus, Hera. And Pallas Athene, the vir-gin goddess, without natural parents, sprung from her father's head. Goddess of intellect, she was cool to contemplate. Lying in bed at night, Mary had forced her mind to tune in to that channel, Pallas Athene and her deeds, trying to lock herself there, on occasion suc-ceeding for a little while.

She recalled an idea that had come, which she had never got down. Before she knew it she was writing, with a blunt pencil on scrap paper; her typewriter was put away. She wrote and filled the sheets. It was laborious, too laborious, writing by hand, and she went to the closet and pulled out the portable machine, setting it on the desk. Then she went back for the half-empty box of typing paper. She could go on, she realized. That she could do.

As her hands moved on the keys, it came to her that though everything else seemed to be gone, her confidence in the work was not. At first when she began after Quent's death, she had been unsure. She had shown Gene Meyer two chapters she had written from Quent's notes, trying to follow what he had begun. It had not seemed right; it didn't match, try as she would.

After he had read them, Gene Meyer had asked her to come to his office. "This is good," he told her.

"But—it's not like Quent's," she had said. "I tried, but—"

Gene had smiled and taken her to lunch. She had thought of him as a gray man—gray suit, gray hair, a rather gray complexion, and kind gray eyes. But a drink, some wine, and a good lunch warmed him and brought some color to his cheeks.

"Quent was a professor, a classical scholar. His prose style was on a level we don't see much in this country anymore and his wit gave it a pleasing edge. With that, and the results of his new research, we knew we would have a creditable book. A book for other scholars, for libraries—not a book for the general public. He wasn't proceeding too fast, you must have noticed. I think the research interested him more than the writing itself—as you know, there were only two complete chapters."

"But he had all the notes," Mary had said. "He was thorough—"

"Of course," Gene said. "That's what makes it simple for us. For you."

The coffee was very good. The two of them had been relaxed and easy. Mary was a fairly new widow then and she had been surprised at her own enjoyment.

"Just go on," Gene advised, "as you are doing. Write naturally, in your own style. When you are finished, you will probably rewrite the first two chapters—slightly," he added, observing her distress. It was *Quent's* work.

"I can't write prose on the level of Quent's," Mary had said. "And I'm not witty, either."

"You have a fine flow," Gene said thoughtfully. "Rhythmic. Natural. Pleasing. It puts me in mind of Frank O'Connor. And you bring those characters to life, Mary. I was caught up, as if I'd never heard of them before."

"Not a celestial soap opera," Mary had said, still gloomy. "Quent *despised* that sort of thing."

Gene laughed. "Those old boys and girls were supersoaps. But Quent's notes will keep you straight. You can't help it, Mary. You have the Celtic gift. And that might propel this book into a popular success for all its good academic underpinnings. You have to accept this gift from your ancestors gracefully."

Gene had seemed very amused. She had thanked him, got on with the job as best she could until—shifting her thoughts violently, she typed on. And only when she noticed it was past midnight did she stop typing so that she wouldn't disturb her neighbors. In the morning she woke to the relief of knowing there was work that she must do.

Every morning she went out and got a newspaper, a tabloid—it had become a habit. She would glance over it, quickly, to see if there was anything in it about the Bathsheba murders, as the papers were still calling the case. It was silly, she told herself as her eyes scanned the pages. If there was an arrest, she would certainly be informed.

But she was never informed of anything. Her calls to Merivale were always answered in the same words: "No new developments." As there weren't any old developments it seemed that nothing was being done.

Erik Lindstrom stopped by to see her after a talk with a new, prestigious gallery owner who showed interest in taking him on. He was in a buoyant mood, but he was a good friend and he listened.

"There probably aren't any developments," he said, sounding reasonable. "The police don't have anything to go on, do they? A passing child molester who took a chance and panicked, as you say yourself. How could they find him—or her, if you want to stretch your imagination? Where could they begin? Think of the Etan Patz case—very similar. And those parents still don't know what happened. At least you do know, Mary, about the children, anyway. That's over now. And if the police do find the killer—then it won't be over. A big trial, reporters at your door, and it could go on for years. Perhaps it's better this way."

"So that the killer can go out and do the same to other children?" Mary said bitterly.

"You don't know that." Eric had come to say goodbye. He was going to visit his family in Sweden, arrange a showing of his work, lecture at Uppsala—he was full of plans and projects. "In any event, you have no control over it. And I still believe if there's no arrest and no trial it will be easier for you and it's you we should be thinking about. Remember what happened to the Lindberghs. And now people are saying that Hauptmann didn't do it after all."

Mary understood what he said and knew that he meant well. It was true; yet she couldn't wish that the murderer of her children would go unpunished. She did not, she realized, wish to turn the other cheek. She felt as vengeful as the Furies and knew that she would feel suspended in time and place until she heard *something*. Anything.

Erik was pleased that she was working on her book and suggested that she set herself a deadline. He was going away for three months. She was sorry he was leaving, though it would be a good trip for him. But that was the city; people were always coming and going. She and Quent had been a stable point for their friends. They would call with news of arrivals and departures, bringing tales of their successes and sometimes their sorrows.

"Old reliables. Mom and Pop," Quent had said, grinning, and the coffee pot was always ready and drinks on hand in the evening.

City people—not like Burgoyne and Spenser with their close-knit families who stayed in one place for generations. The thought jogged her memory; she had not heard from her close-knit family. She had expected that some of the girls, at least, might have written a word after the memorial, but not a word had come. Nothing . . . For a few days she had gone down and waited for the mail and looked through it while the mailman was still distributing the envelopes, side by side with the super's wife, who collected the mail for absent tenants. Mary had been conscious of Rita Attard's eyes upon her as she waited and received no personal mail, nothing except a condolence card from Aunt Katherine. Mary had written to her, telling her as simply as possible about the children's death. Aunt Kathy had disapproved of Mary's marriage, of her giving up her religion, of her bearing two children outside the sanctity of the church and leaving those children unbaptized. Her remarks, like Mr.

Gaylord's, were based on "Suffer the little children to come unto me," but, unlike Mr. Gaylord's, they didn't sound too hopeful. The message was not consoling.

A brief note came from Uncle William, expressing his grief and offering sympathy. He mentioned that Isobel was recovering from her illness and its complications, but was still very weak. He planned to bring her home and help nurse her himself. Poor William, he must be distracted. His intense love for his wife had been a matter of affectionate humor in the family, rather rueful humor on the part of wives who were loved more sedately. Isobel—certainly something of a trial for women of her own generation, Mary reflected. No one ever said of Isobel, "Still a handsome woman" or "You should see her photographs; she was such a lovely girl." Isobel was pretty and elegant now. Nutty Nell, a Burgoyne character, had been heard to remark, "It's the devil's work." Isobel, who had a keen sense of humor, had been delighted. It was usually Isobel who wrote, friendly, chatty notes. Would she have written if she could, Mary wondered, if even Susan . . .

And a card had come from Mexico, bearing a cheerful message from Mildred Christopher, with a joke about her colleagues at the dig—she had not heard, obviously, about the children. There was no mention of her return.

Mary stopped waiting for a letter. A mother judged guilty of neglect, she would not hear from Spenser, or Burgoyne, or any of the villages where the family were living. Not from young Marjorie or old Uncle Burt or— She had to stop thinking about it. But she was wrong. She did hear from upstate, but it wasn't from the family. The postmark was Spenser and the name printed on the envelope was CROSSROADS SERVICE STATION. She looked at it blankly, then took it up to the apartment and opened it.

It was a note from Billy Robinson at the gas station. She had never known it had a name; it was just Robinson's. Billy was Quent's age; they had known each other as boys and she always got her gas there. He had been at the memorial, she remembered. He was one of the people who had come up to her while she stood on the porch with Fiona.

The note was written by hand.

"Dear Mrs. Christopher"—Billy always called her Mary, but this was a business letter—"We have the antenna you ordered on December 14. I have been holding it until you came up, but didn't wish to bother you at the Memorial Service. I expect you will be up soon now that Mrs. Alice is home, so I thought I would let you know."

Mary had completely forgotten ordering the antenna. The old one had broken in the car wash. She hadn't bothered with the radio—she hadn't used the car since the memorial— But those thoughts just flickered through her head, while she took in the fact that Alice was home.

Home. She was well enough to be in her own home. Recovered. And away from Fiona and Boy and . . . Mary's mind was racing. She was excited. Perhaps after all there was some shift, some change. Alice, restored to even part of her normal vigor and acuteness, would not blame her, hate her for the children's loss. They had both made terrible mistakes: Mary, in going off before Alice was in the house; Alice herself, to some degree, in lingering in the barn. But neither of them could have thought, dreamed of— Alice, always full of understanding, would know that. If Alice was well, then—

She rushed to the telephone, her forefinger dialing the number of the Spenser house, while her mind was picturing Alice, back in her home. Mary's heart was racing again, but this time it wasn't panic, it was hope.

The ringing tone stopped. Alice had picked up. "Hello?" It was Fiona's voice.

"It's Mary. I'd like to speak to Alice."

There was a pause.

"Mary, she's only been home a few days. She is still very, very weak. She should really be back in the hospital but she had a great longing to come home. Dr. Bristow would only give permission if we have nurses here at all times. She is in bed now. She comes down very little; the strain of going back up the stairs is physically too much for her. Her heart is enlarged and very weak."

"But she can just pick up the extension; it's still by her bed, isn't it?"

"We removed the bell from upstairs, of course," Fiona said.

"Well, please go up and tell her that I am calling," Mary said, with a decisiveness that had been foreign to her for so long.

"Very well." To her relief, Fiona consented and put the receiver aside. Mary's mind followed her as she mounted the stairs and went into Alice's sparely furnished, cool white bedroom, which in Mary's mind was always full of bright sunlight.

She thought of Alice's hand on the receiver, of her familiar voice— But there was silence. After what seemed like a long time, Fiona's voice returned. "I'm sorry, Mary, but you have to know. Alice isn't well enough to talk on the telephone and there is no use your calling again. I'm afraid she doesn't want to talk to you. I thought you would have realized that after the memorial. She refuses and I am certain she won't change her mind. It could only do harm if you badger her. When I told her you were calling she was so upset I had to give her a sedative, and Dr. Bristow won't be pleased."

"But why?" Mary asked desperately. "Why?"

"You know why, Mary. The children. You must understand. But as long as you *have* called, I should remind you to get in touch with Ernest. I think he expected a call from you."

She rang off. Mary listened to the angry-sounding buzz and replaced the receiver. She stood for a moment, just staring at the telephone. She couldn't understand the reference to Ernest, but it didn't matter. Alice had recovered enough to want to go home, but she still didn't want to see her. Mary thought herself a fool to have believed that she would. Alice did still blame her for the children's deaths. In truth, Mary knew, she was at fault. She was the principal guardian of the children, the one who should have put their welfare before any other consideration, and she had not. It had seemed more important to catch a train. Vanity, carelessness. She could never forgive herself, so why should Alice? The gray winter day seemed dull and endless.

On Sunday the sun was shining. Carol stopped by in the afternoon; she had been shopping on West Broadway.

"Well, I don't go for the downtown look, but these shoes are marvelous—do pay attention, Mary. And they're so comfortable as running shoes, which I can't wear with my business clothes no matter what everyone else does.

"You know," she remarked, looking around, "this place could use some livening up. A fresh paint job and you could do something else with the windows. More plants and take down those old drapes."

Mary brought the coffee in on a tray and didn't try to defend her possessions. She had been meaning to paint before . . .

"But what you *should* do," Carol went on, "really, is offload this apartment. You can get a great price for a two-bedroom right now, but the market is softening. I really know, because I've been looking around myself. I only have my place for six months and I think I'll buy. My share of the house will help. Why don't you get a smaller place in a different neighborhood, maybe on the Upper East Side? It will take you out of yourself; you won't just hang around in the old familiar places."

Mary supposed she was right. But it seemed an impossible undertaking. She could hardly bring herself to go into the children's room, much less dispose of it. And she couldn't imagine herself away from the Village. Besides, "I don't know if I can," she said doubtfully. "It was family money that went into it." Some of the money, anyway, she remembered. It had come from the Christopher Trust. Looking back, she recalled signing papers; she really didn't know how those matters stood.

"Then find out." Carol was full of energy. She certainly looked well; her new life suited her. "But I have to tell you, Mary"—she giggled and looked more like her old self—"I did meet a guy. Quite a hunk. And, would you believe it, one of the Chicago crowd. It was at that dinner I went to after we met at Fanelli's. I thought they were all coming in with knives drawn. Well, they were, in a way, but I got a quick look at him and— I'm not going to get too involved, though. Chicago! Staten Island was bad enough. But he's being a real help with the Abe Schulte business and I tell you when I'm with him I think about getting back to the apartment, even when he took me to the Four Seasons—"

"Then watch it," Mary said, reverting for a moment to the professor's wife, and Carol laughed.

"Seeing him tonight, to tell you the truth. So I'll watch it."

She left in a happy glow, pressing Mary's hand. Carol's grip was warm and swift. For Carol, life was still going on. Mary's hand felt weak and clinging; for her, life was over.

But some of Carol's talk lingered in her mind. About the apartment. Mary had no problem there. The income from the trust still arrived; it was sufficient for herself alone, even with the stiff maintenance charges. Regina and Connie had been kind and the super's wife was friendly. No, she couldn't leave. Yet Fiona had said she should call Ernest. It was Ernest who handled the trust. Mary had no inclination to call him, nor anyone upstate. The mere thought was painful. If Ernest had wanted to get in touch about the trust, he would have written. He was a conscientious man. No, it must have something to do with Alice. Perhaps Ernest had some legal paper, barring her from attempting to talk to Alice. They would not need it. She would not try again.

Ernest had wanted to get in touch with Mary, but on that same day he met his brother in church and walked back with him to the Burgoyne house, where they lunched together in the dining room under the portrait of their grandfather, another Bartholomew Burgoyne. After the housekeeper had cleared away, Ernest brought up the matter that was on his mind.

"Boy, as trustee I should be winding up the Christopher Trust. Mary is the last heir and—"

Boy snorted. "You can't give it to that woman. We have absolute proof of her guilt."

"Well, some proof. But—a flash in the dark, a shiny metal ball in a child's hand—enough for a jury, perhaps—"

"Don't niggle, Ernest," his brother said. "Along with everything else, it's incontrovertible."

"But she has not been charged," Ernest pointed out, screwing up his forehead in a caricature of worry. "It's our fault, Boy. Put it any way you want, but we are withholding information from the police. And as matters now stand, I don't see—"

"Fiona told me last night that she'd asked Mary to call you. Been talking it over, you two?"

It was Boy and Fiona who usually foregathered. Ernest could see that Boy was annoyed. It had been that way when they were children.

"I don't see that you need to do anything unless Mary asks you to," Boy continued. "Probably happy to keep on getting the income, no questions asked. Let sleeping dogs lie. She won't want to stir anything up. The case is still open and she's the only suspect. Bassett might move any day." He nodded his leonine head portentously and spread himself back in his chair until it creaked. Boy always had the air of knowing more than anyone else, Ernest reflected, and often it proved that he did. Boy was a great clubman, and his friends and acquaintances were inclined to drop a word in his ear. Bassett kept him informed, Ernest knew, and he wondered what was in store. Boy would tell, when he was ready.

"But there are other concerns, Ernest, more important," Boy went on. "Alice's concerns. She's spoken to you, I know, and she's anxious to get them handled."

"Oh, that's no problem." Ernest relaxed. "I gave that to Franklin Lacey and he's been working on it. He only has to take the papers over for her signature. This is the time I always want a cigarette," he said, with a sigh. "It seems to have a soothing effect on a full stomach."

"Have one, then. I think there's a box in the library—I keep them for old John Strethem."

Ernest shook his head.

"The reluctant Puritan." Boy mocked him, lighting up his own cigar with relish.

"So we leave it that the winding up of the trust will wait, pending—events. I don't suppose the court could object to that."

"It's settled, then." Boy blew a puff of dense smoke up toward the pure white plaster of the ceiling. "You'll be at the dinner on Thursday?"

It was the annual Burgoyne dinner, held in the old Burgoyne place, a mile out of town: a monstrous turreted stone edifice that embarrassed Ernest and amused Boy. A nineteenth-century Burgoyne had built it, after acquiring great additional wealth by speculating in railroads and gold. Most of that wealth was lost in the crash of 1869 and he had left "the Castle" to his reluctant heirs. It was an uncomfortable place to live in and required a huge staff of servants. The speculator's grandson had been happy to donate it to the town as a cultural center and move back thankfully to the lovely wooden house built by the first Burgoyne, who had married a patroon's daughter. The complex was now run on town, county, and state funds, with private contributions, a large part of which came from the annual dinner. Renamed the Burgoyne Center for History and the Arts, it was still "the Castle" to the people of Burgoyne.

Ernest shook his head. Boy, in happy contemplation, hardly noticed. Ernest's stomach could not deal with a banquet and he found the long drawn-out convivialities tiring. He would send a handsome contribution and his regrets. Boy would enjoy it all and represent the family. Bassett, it occurred to Ernest, would be there, and doubtless would tell Boy the latest developments. If only things would not develop, Ernest thought dismally; if only they could remain as they were. But he was certain in his heart that they would not. Bassett was determined to bring the killer to justice and Bassett wouldn't fail.

9

Regina Valenti left the church after evening Mass, walking the short distance home, when a woman came blindly around the corner and slammed against her. Regina drew back sharply and regarded her assailant. It was her neighbor, Mary Christopher. Mary looked startled, like a roused sleepwalker. Tears were running down her face.

Mary had been on one of her aimless walks. She had gone to a supermarket but found herself unable to enter. A girl and boy, playing by the curb, had suddenly reminded her— She tried to apologize to Miss Valenti, who stood looking at her, but the words confused her tongue.

Regina had been growing more concerned about Mary. She had seemed to be making an effort to recover, but lately . . . She was disheveled. Her pants were hanging loose from the waist; she had lost weight, doubtless. The red down jacket looked shabby and should have gone to the cleaners if it wasn't thrown away. Her hair was too long and bushy, badly in need of a hairdresser's attention. She was too much alone, Regina thought, as they returned to the house together.

The super's wife had told her that none of Mrs. Christopher's family had come to stay, or even to visit. Something was very wrong there. Steps must be taken. As soon as she was in her apartment she telephoned Connie Ferraro to come and join her. Connie came in with a concerned look and no time for her usual warm and lengthy greeting. And Regina soon learned that there was more trouble in store for Mary.

Connie had been at a meeting of the Community Board, which she attended regularly. "There were police officers talking about the same old things, more lights, more locks." Each of the women already had three locks and they muttered over their coffee. "A waste of time. But my cousin Marco was there and he said he'd met some of his old friends from the precinct at a Knights of Columbus dinner last Tuesday and they told Marco something *dreadful.*"

Marco, who owned a restaurant, was a police buff. He wasted his time and money, Regina thought privately, encouraging active officers to stop by, eat, and chat. They repaid him with lurid tales, which he passed on, doubtless exaggerated.

"They drank a lot of good wine, I expect," she said. "What was it, the prison barge on the pier? That matter is still in the courts."

"They told Marco"—Connie was breathless—"that a woman in the precinct was a suspect in the murder of two children up in Dutchess County."

Regina's coffee cups were porcelain, very fine, and decorated with gold. They had been in her family for generations, but now she clattered the cup down on the saucer almost hard enough to shatter it and she didn't notice what she had done.

"That couldn't be," she said, without believing it.

"Two little children, that *ubriacone* said."

The two women talked, coming to no satisfactory conclusion. After Connie had gone, Regina wondered who Connie had meant when she said "that *ubriacone.*" Was she calling her cousin Marco a drunkard or the police officer? It didn't matter. The story must be true. It began to explain many things.

That night Regina couldn't sleep. Her heavy curtains were drawn over the windows, keeping out the distant sparkle of light from the World Trade Center and the pale glow from the dome of the Municipal Building. She lay in the big carved bed that had belonged to her parents and had been sent from Italy, but its comfort and its family associations failed to settle her mind. She remembered Mary Christopher as a mother, happy, content with her children. She thought of the woman bolting, distraught, through the streets. The wound was not healing. Regina had known that something was wrong, strange. And now this. *What was going on?*

She rose, wrapped herself in a brocade dressing gown, and poured herself a glass of anisette. Then she sat in her *salotto*, in a high-backed chair, to sip and think. What could be done for that woman, alone? And it came to her. This was an affair where a man was needed. There were such times. Carefully she reviewed and considered the men in her family for their brains, helpfulness, and special abilities, and decided on the one who could be useful. By then it was one in the morning. She picked up the telephone and called her nephew Danny Valenti. Never before had she called upon him for a serious matter; he was in her mind a half-nephew. But for this business he was her choice—Danny, the policeman, the Italian with the Irish face.

Staring at his broad, freckled face in the bathroom mirror while he shaved, Danny found he was amused by his aunt's call, though it had broken his night's sleep. It was like Aunt Regina to call at one o'clock because that was when she had wanted to speak to him. He was used to her imperious ways. The elderly woman had the family trait, but in her it was softened by her lingering beauty and her tart, dry charm.

One of her neighbors, she believed, was in trouble. Aunt Regina had simply ordered him to take care of the matter and had rung off, assured and content that he would do so. "You must help her," Regina had said. "She is being murdered by her own family."

Though Aunt Regina had always liked him, he knew it was somewhat against her will. His Irish mother. And then his joining the police—only a fool would do that, she had told him severely. A *cafone*.

But now she needed a detective. And though he was in the Special Frauds squad in Manhattan, and the case she was interested in was a double murder in Dutchess County, that made no difference to Aunt Regina. It would have been a waste of breath to argue.

It was a strange thing, he reflected; the building she was living in was full of women, but he remembered that one. Christopher. Irish, obviously. Quiet. Good-looking. Regina had said she was a widow.

He scraped his chin and gazed more carefully into the glass. Swiftly, he felt an unaccustomed gloom. The sun was pouring in from the high window and he saw clearly that his sandy hair was light with gray. He was as wrinkled as a spaniel. He had never been a beauty and now he was looking like an old man. Well, he was forty-five. His two boys grown and independent. Fifty was just around the corner.

Mary Christopher. A pleasant woman. He had always seen her busy with her children. To a girl like that he would be an old man. Aunt Regina said she couldn't have done it. Danny had always had considerable respect for Aunt Regina's judgment. She was a very shrewd woman and though she'd never married, she had a sharp eye on the doings of men and women—as bad as a priest. There really wasn't anything he could do, but he would stop by the First Precinct. They would have been in touch with the state police. Maybe Mary wasn't a suspect after all. What Regina had told him sounded more like a family feud.

The First Precinct, always busy, was busier than usual. All of the detectives were out.

"Helluva week," the desk man told him. "On top of the usual grief we've got this girl-chopper. Just great."

The plastic-bag murders, the papers were calling it. Young girls' bodies, three so far, turning up in Dumpsters and garbage cans tied up in plastic bags. All in the West Village.

Detective Keegan, an old acquaintance of Danny's, now with Missing Persons, came through the door and greeted him as he stamped his feet and pulled off his muffler.

"Another one," he told Danny. "We thought it might be one of ours, so I went to see the body. It wasn't. Guess nobody's missed her yet. Can you believe it?" It wasn't a question. Keegan had spent years at the First Precinct, working with Pidusky, before he'd made the Missing Persons squad. And he could be a cynical bastard, Danny thought, but he looked shaken.

"I'm going up for a cup of coffee," he said. "Come on." And he went to the detectives' room upstairs. "Looked about thirteen," he told Danny, after he'd swallowed two cups of black coffee. "We'll probably get a call soon. Have the thrill of getting the parents to the morgue."

He was a decent guy. He had called Danny recently when an elderly widow that he knew had been swindled out of her savings, about thirty grand, by a new acquaintance. It had been no sweat for Danny. The widow had identified a photograph down at One Police Plaza. The man was well known to Special Frauds and not very bright. Danny had picked him up fast and recovered most of the money before he'd spent it—the cash had been all over his apartment.

Keegan listened to Danny's story. "Pidusky went over with the body to the morgue. I can reach him. Don't suppose he'd mind you looking at the file."

He made the call and soon left Danny in the room with the Christopher file. "Leave it on Pidusky's desk when you're through. We turned everything back to him, but actually it's a guy called Bassett's case, up in Merivale. Not Pidusky's. He's going to sweat some suspects on the girl killings, but his guess is that this is new talent around here. No familiar features . . ."

It wasn't a very thick file. Of course, the Christopher case was in the hands of the state police and the precinct was merely cooperating with this Bassett. The early records were there. A telephone call from Spenser, upstate. A worried old lady who had thought her daughter-in-law was going to leave her children behind, but who seemed to have taken them down to the city. And the daughter-in-law who could not be reached by phone.

Two uniformed officers had gone to the Christopher apartment to check on the whereabouts of the children. Their reports were in the file, almost identical. They had arrived about 9:20 A.M. Mrs. Christopher had been reluctant to open the door. She had been wearing a bathrobe, drinking black coffee. There was a second coffee cup with dregs in it, but they did not see any other person. Mrs. Christopher said she had not played back her messages the night before. The officer who checked her telephone line said that it was in order. Officer Billops added that Mrs. Christopher's hands were shaking and she appeared anxious for them to go. Captain Bassett, Danny thought, could make a meal of that. Mrs. Christopher said she was going to Spenser, where she had left the children.

Precinct detectives had checked her movements in the city the night before. She had driven into the city after dark and instead of going to her usual parking lot, she had parked her car on the street outside the Corner Bar on West Broadway. The bartender there had not remembered her, but it had been a busy night. Mary Christopher claimed to have gone directly to a supermarket across the street at about ten-thirty. One of the help who had been stacking crates recognized her in the photograph the detectives showed, though he said she looked different. The photograph was of Mary with her two children. She had been wild like, the stock boy said. And all splashed with mud. He couldn't remember the time, except that it was late. That night Mrs. Christopher had met a Mrs. Carol Grafton, unemployed, who had just separated from her husband, and the two women had gone to another local bar for a few drinks. The waitresses in the bar remembered her being there. Mrs. Christopher said she had arrived home alone at about twelve, had taken a bath, and gone to bed.

The next precinct report was on the car, but Danny left that for a moment and went on to material sent down from Merivale. Mary's statements. Alice Christopher's statement. Statements collected from witnesses along her route to the city.

Mary had left the family house in Spenser in time to catch the 7:15 from Brewster, but she had missed the train and driven to the city. She had stopped at a bar near Bathsheba on a desolate dark road. It was about a hundred yards away from where the children's bodies were later found. Danny was frowning as he read.

Mrs. Christopher had told the bartender and the patrons that she had taken a wrong turn and couldn't find the road to the highway. Several people remembered her—she was a striking woman. They all said at that time there was no trace of mud on her. "You would have noticed," a Mrs. Jarvis had reported. "She had on some fancy white raincoat, like it was never going to rain."

A male witness said he had offered to help her find her way. It *was* tough to find the turnoff. He hadn't used his own car to get to Tony's, but he had offered to drive her car and show her the way if she would then turn back and drop him off at the tavern, but she had become excited, refused abruptly, "bit my head off," and rushed away. He hadn't gone with her to the car and he didn't know if the children were in it.

Danny turned back to the precinct's report on the car. After the bodies had been found, at the request of Captain Bassett detectives had made a search. They had found a button from the little girl's coat. There were some cookie crumbs behind the seat in the back left-hand corner. No blood—but the way the children had died there wouldn't have been any unless it was the murderer's.

He looked through the autopsy report. No blood or tissue under the fingernails. These children had been taken by surprise. No marks of any struggle. They had gone into a car to their deaths, it seemed, with someone they knew and trusted.

There was one more set of papers: financial information, most of it from Burgoyne and Thrale, a law office in Burgoyne, some from statements of witnesses and some from the personal ferreting of Captain Bassett. Details of the Joseph Christopher Trust, about $270,000, left to Quentin Christopher, now deceased, and his family. With the children dead, Mary was the last heir and the capital would go to her. Mary Christopher, six months before, had written to the trustees complaining that the income from the trust, very conservatively invested, brought in a low return. She had not been employed. Her husband had been dead for four years. Because of the language of the trust, if she had remarried she would not personally have any more rights in the trust, which would have devolved in its entirety on the children. And Mary Christopher was up to her ears in debt. She had been paying it off, but it must have been a hard row to hoe with two growing children.

Slipped in with the Merivale copies, he came across one more report that should have been with the precinct's original file. In fact, he noticed, it was dated more than four years earlier. Nothing to do with this case. It puzzled Danny. Mary Christopher had been spotted by an undercover narc making a buy from a known heroin dealer in Washington Square Park. Heroin. That fresh-faced woman? Maybe a little pot. The husband had been a professor. A lot of that crowd thought nothing of it. But heroin? The undercover man had got it all balled up, he thought. It happened. The pusher was pushing. Mary Christopher, known in the neighborhood and easily identifiable, had been in the vicinity. He looked back at the statement of Mrs. Jarvis, one of the patrons of Tony's Tavern.

"She was high and flirting with the guys. Got one lover-boy so excited he tried to go with her to her car. But then she brushed him off real quick."

Some crusty old bitch, maybe. But it didn't look good. A lot of this stuff didn't look good. Aunt Regina's neighbor was in a lot of trouble. Arrests had been made on evidence no stronger than this, Danny thought, and he wondered why Merivale was holding back, but only for a second. Of course. No one had actually seen the children in the car. He went back with renewed interest to the statement of the mechanic at Highland Falls who had changed the windshield wipers. No help to either side. He hadn't noticed whether the children were there or not. A hot young stud in the rain.

He sat, pensively tapping his finger on the sheaf of documents. From time to time the phone rang, three or four rings, and then there was silence. To him it seemed crazy. If the woman had murdered her children, why would she make herself conspicuous in a tavern and then bury the bodies about a hundred yards away? True, it was dark and there were bushes nearby, but— Perhaps she'd been afraid of being remembered, in her white car, going off the New York route when she left Brewster, looking for some dark and solitary place. Her appearance in the tavern could have been a bold move. He was thinking like a detective on the case. A stranger. But this was Mary Christopher.

Mary. She seemed like the all-time reliable good mother. But then, so had Sally Mandrell, mousy-haired, sweet-faced, not *too* pretty. Sally had hit on a new blackmail racket. Posing as a young widow, she had moved around a lot in the affluent suburbs, in Long Island and Westchester, mostly. She would strike up an acquaintance with a nearby household, one without children. On various pretexts, contrived emergencies, she would persuade the couple to mind her children. Afterward she moved quietly and discreetly. The wife would be informed that the children had complained of sex abuse. Her confederate, posing as a doctor, made up medical reports confirming the allegations. Once the first shock and outrage were over, Sally would suggest, with apparent decency, that she had no desire to go to the police, for her children's sake, but it would be better if she moved away. Of course, that would be expensive . . .

The couples all knew it was a scam. But they were professionals or business people who could be badly damaged by allegations even if they were proved false. One retired couple had nothing to lose that way, but they paid the most, dreading the scandal and upheaval in their quiet lives. She might still have been in business, but she made the mistake of choosing a bright young movie director who had gone straight to the police. He was delighted with the publicity and was raising money to produce a film around the story. Sally was in Bedford Hills Correctional and the children were in a foster home. The director, a generous man, had put up money for their psychological treatment.

Appearances . . . No, they didn't mean much. Yet Aunt Regina was convinced of Mary's innocence. What was it she had said? "She is being murdered by her own family." Mary was getting the cold shoulder. Obviously, they thought she was guilty. And they knew her. They had known her for fourteen years, much longer than Aunt Regina. He got up and left the small office, away from the phones that were still ringing. To please Aunt Regina he would talk to the woman. But if those guys upstate found someone who could place the children in the car, there wouldn't be much anyone could do for Mary Christopher.

For the next few days Danny was busy, chasing an old acquaintance, Handsome Harry, a big, jovial, good-looking guy, over forty now but still charming the pants off the women. A little love, a lot of attention, and he would convince them that investing in one of his nonexistent businesses was the safest and most profitable thing to do with their money. Considering his life work, he hadn't done much time. Usually the women, after hysterically complaining to the police when he disappeared, were moved when they saw him again, and after his arrest they often withdrew their complaints, saying the money was a gift.

But this victim, a paralegal in her late fifties, looked as though she would stick with the case. Danny made a special effort, searching through all the best hotels in New York and the casinos in Atlantic City where Harry usually went to get parted from his loot. Finally he ran into him in the arcade of Trump Plaza, where Harry was buying a few trifles in an English specialty store.

Aunt Regina became impatient. Danny was at his desk in the squad room at One Police Plaza when he heard his name and looked up to see Mary coming toward him. She was very pale and much thinner than he remembered and there was a tremor in the hand she held out to him.

"Regina says I should talk to you, if it's all right. She says there is fraud . . ."

Aunt Regina had original ideas. He asked Mary to sit down, wondering how she had managed to reach this floor. The people in the lobby were not supposed to let anyone up without a pass or a memo from the precinct of their domicile.

"I mentioned your name." She was still an eyeful. They must have thought . . .

He had to explain to the distraught woman that his work was

based in New York City and, though the Special Frauds squad did at times assist other jurisdictions, that was by their request. Also, Special Frauds handled certain clearly defined offenses and he had no connection with and no right to interfere in any homicide investigation. She listened quietly but she looked as though she were drowning. He could almost see the wash of despair that overtook her. It was worse than watching tears. And she was nothing like Sally Mandrell.

"But I'll do what I can, privately," he found himself saying, wondering what he *could* do. Or if he would have said that, if she hadn't been young and so poignantly lovely. A blue-eyed Irish beauty. His father, old Rocco Valenti, had taken as a second wife an Irishwoman from Hell's Kitchen, to the surprise and less-than-delight of the Valenti family. "At least she's Catholic," had been their attitude, but they had accepted her and Danny had loved his Irish mother, who had died young, killed in a car crash with his father while they were touring Italy.

He asked Mary to write out for him everything that had happened on the day she left Spenser after Christmas up until the time she had arrived back at her apartment in the city and gone to bed. Then he would visit her, in a day or two, and they would talk some more.

Mary agreed and promised to call him. She felt a certain confidence in Danny. He was the man she had noticed on her first visit here, downstairs, while she was waiting. She had felt a familiar warmth, without remembering that he was Regina Valenti's nephew. As she left the elevator on the ground floor, the lobby looked less grim. A statue stood near the exit, a bronze of a police officer, with a look of an earlier era. His hand was on a small boy's shoulder, and his face was kind. Mary stood before it in quiet reflection. The officer resembled her father, but his features were stronger. She was thoughtful with memory as she walked away.

Danny was caught up with another case and it was two days later when he called her, but there was no reply. Aunt Regina didn't know where she was, but promised to arrange the meeting. "Here, in my apartment," she said. "Mary must preserve her good name."

Danny was amused. "Things are a lot different now," he said.

"Not so different," his aunt remarked tartly as he hung up.

Danny remembered the reports in the file. Mary in her bathrobe at nine A.M. Two coffee cups. Reluctance to admit the officers. Aunt

Regina was right, as usual. And Mary's troubles had started in Burgoyne: a picture-postcard little place. Prosperous. Not run-down like some of the towns in the Hudson Valley. He and Joan had passed through it years back, when they had vacationed upstate, long before her illness. "Old General Burgoyne would have been proud of it," she had remarked. "But he lost," Danny had replied. "Not here." Joan had had the last word. Yes, Mary, the city girl, would be an outsider in that place. In time of trouble, not a good thing to be.

Mary had heard from the cemetery that the children's names and dates had been carved into the headstones. She was filled with longing to see their graves, however painful it might be. And she knew also that while she was in Spenser she must go to see Alice. She could not simply accept Fiona's message. On reflection, she could not understand why Fiona had been at the house. Alice had always disliked her, though she had managed not to show it. But to Mary she had said, "Silly woman. More snobbish and showy than Boy, and she doesn't have his talent and distinction to justify it. Only the name. If she wasn't so thin," she had added with a mischievous smile, "you could say she's too big for her britches."

No, Alice would not choose Fiona as a spokeswoman. Why Fiona wished to interfere, Mary could not fathom. But she and Alice were fully adult and they should speak to each other plainly.

The sick apprehension that always struck her now when she thought of Spenser and Burgoyne, the family—it mustn't get in the way. Alice was reasonable, she told herself. There was nothing cruel about her. She had said no word of reproach to the old doctor who had been treating Joe over two years for "indigestion," which was discovered at last to be stomach cancer, but not until it was terminal.

"He feels it enough," she had said. "He is retiring. We were all at fault. Joe had always been so healthy."

Next morning Mary was at the flower shop as the doors were opening. She stood, hesitating over the fresh-cut blooms. Yellow for Tom, strong, bright, cheerful—they were only pompoms, but she took a large bunch—and some pink blossoms for Linda, pretty, fragile things; she didn't know what they were. She was about to ask the owner, who was wrapping them up in paper and plastic, but she found she couldn't speak. Flowers. Linda was not a flower girl; Tom was not a page; they were dead. Mary stood stock-still as if she had never known it before.

The owner of the shop, watching her, didn't speak. She had owned the shop for thirty years and she had seen that look before. A parent perhaps? A husband? The blue-eyed woman was still young. She looked stunned. The owner felt pity for her, though that morning she had much to occupy her mind. The lease on the premises was up; soon she would be gone, retired. The business of shopkeeping would be forgotten. But some moments, like this, she would remember.

The cemetery was on the outskirts of Spenser; there was no house in view. Only the spreading lawn, set back from the road and screened by the surrounding trees and shrubs. Mary had taken early violets for Quent, as she did every year. The children were on either side. Thomas Christopher. Linda Christopher. And the dates. She would have preferred to have a verse as well, but Alice thought that nonsense. Still, Mary thought, she should have had it done. But she had been too . . . Sighing, she let the thought go. Just now, she felt a certain calm. The fresh-cut turf had been neatly placed; a passerby would not notice . . . Tears chilled on her cheeks, but she did not break down. The new headstones sparkled in the sunlight. Mary had loved the high, blue skies of winter in Spenser, the feeling of openness, of freedom . . . She sat there for a time, though it was bitter cold. A flock of snow buntings wheeled above her, a swirl of large snowflakes to the earthbound. In the silence of the cemetery, their plaintive little calls were sweet and clear, a familiar part of Christopher country. Yet they were seasonal visitors, Canadian birds, strangers like herself.

She followed them out of the cemetery down to the road and started the car, still in the calm of the company of her dead. But as she approached the house her heart was pounding again.

The back door was unlocked, and she walked right into the kitchen. Then Fiona appeared, standing in the doorway of the kitchen that led to the rest of the house. Of course, she must have heard the car on the quiet lane. She raised her hands, barring the way.

"Mary, you must not try to see Alice. I've told you that she's not to be disturbed."

Fiona was well dressed, as usual, in a gray coat and skirt of an excellent cut and a beautifully laundered and ironed white silk blouse, edged with lace. She had been out—the tip of her nose was red from the sharp cold. If only I had come a few minutes before, Mary thought, but she pushed past the startled Fiona and went into the living room. It was as she had imagined—Alice, dressed, sitting in her familiar chair, though her feet were on a footstool. She looked stronger than she had at the memorial and Mary ran toward her.

Alice looked up, startled, and cringed. Her face was screwed into a look of revulsion, mixed with fear, and her trembling hands went up, as if warding off a blow.

Fiona, close behind, put a hand on Mary's shoulder.

"Why must you come here?" Alice said. Her voice was thin and tired. "Go away, please. I can't see you again. Ever."

Mary stood like a stone, unable to move or speak. Fiona took her arm and steered her to the door. "You had better go back to the city and stay there. It will be easier for all of us."

In the bright, serene, midday sun in icy Christopher country, Mary drove away, she supposed for the last time. Alice, weak and distraught, still blamed her for the children's deaths; perhaps she always would. Mary remembered her father's last days. The drink had affected his mind as well as his liver; delirious, he had accused her mother of fornicating with strange men in the streets—her mother, that Catholic puritan whom, in better times, he had named "All the Virtues." His rages and vile words had been distressing, a grief among all the other griefs to be endured, but that was all. Not a hammerblow. Not like this.

As the cars moved along, the familiar scenes struck her gaze and she saw again all the beauty that glimmered in the ice on the ponds and on a frozen waterfall, set among the black branches of the maples holding up the bright blue sky. It was there, but it no longer spoke to her; it was alien country. She was sore, she was desolate, she was afraid.

At the Three Corners, she was stopped by a long red light. Coming out of the Three Corners Superette was a familiar figure, Nutty Nell, awkwardly clutching a big bag of groceries. Her short white hair stuck out around her coarse red face under the battered gray broad-brimmed hat—a man's hat. Mary had often stopped for a word with the strange old woman, as Alice had. "Eleanor was a lovely girl," she'd told Mary, "always outspoken. It took a lot to bring her to this."

Nell would blurt out anything, things no one else would ever say. She had a partial paralysis down the right side of her body, including her face, and it gave her a strange, twisted look. Small children were afraid of her and the older ones, especially in the absence of their parents, would giggle.

She caught sight of Mary and came over to the car. Mary rolled the window down and greeted her. Nell's face looked stranger than ever as she peered over the cola bottle poking at her chin. Her head gave a familiar little jerk before she spoke. "You're the woman who murdered her children," she said. She made a sound between a bark and a laugh and turned away.

PART II

10

Before Mary left for Spenser, she had given Regina an account of her journey and arrival in town on the day of the children's disappearance. Regina called Danny downtown and left a message that he should come over. By the time he had finished with Handsome Harry and had made a long court appearance on another case, a few days had passed before he arrived at his aunt's apartment.

She settled him in an armchair and handed him the sheaf of papers.

"Mary is home," she told him, bringing him coffee. "She is very bad. Not eating. I took her some panettone. Even if she cannot eat, she might take some sweet thing with her coffee. Connie Ferraro took her yesterday to her own doctor. A good man. Mary has palpitations of the heart. From anxiety, the doctor says, but why should she be anxious now? Poor child. For her, the worst is over, or should be. And her insides are like water, Connie says, like a baby's."

Danny thought that if she were guilty, she had reason enough for anxiety. Bassett was hot on her track. Remembering the trust fund, he asked: "Does she have a boyfriend? Boyfriends?"

Regina, though spending the evening at home, was wearing a dress of maroon velvet, the same color as the silk on her chairs. Her shoes were of finely worked leather, hand-made in the neighborhood, and her white hair, piled high, was perfectly arranged. She looked like an old aristocrat, but she spoke like all the neighborhood

Italian women he had known since his boyhood, upholders of the moral order.

"No one," she answered firmly. "Not ever. Not like these other young women, no husband, no children, always different men."

This apartment building had had an influx of yuppies in the last few years and the old ladies disapproved strongly. "We saw her always with the children. She took the boy to school and brought him home and she went with the little girl to kindergarten and *she stayed there with her.*"

Before Danny could wonder at the efficiency of the intelligence network in the house, Regina ended with a flourish. "Mary is a good mother, a good woman. Like your Joan."

Danny was taken aback by this reference to his wife, dead now for thirteen years. He hadn't heard anything like that in Joan's lifetime. The family had been somewhat distant to the Protestant girl from Utah, and Joan had never been easy with the very Catholic Italian clan of family, friends, and neighbors. Nor did she care for his other clan, the NYPD. But for all that she had been a good wife and a very good mother, bringing the boys up to be strong and independent. And they were: Mark was finishing graduate work at Stanford; Henry, already married and living with his wife in Salt Lake City. Joan. A fond memory, but a memory.

He began to read Mary Christopher's recollections. She had handwritten the few pages, a clear hand that suggested a parochial school, though it seemed to waver at times, as though she were suffering from a nervous affliction. He hadn't read very far when he put it down, puzzled. Something Mary had mentioned didn't appear in the file he had read in the First Precinct. Certainly, that wasn't complete. Merivale wasn't obliged to send them duplicates of everything, only what was necessary for the jobs they were asked to do. And yet—

He finished the strange, sad little story. It had the ring of truth. Of course, a lot of con artists managed a ring of truth that could deafen you. He looked back over the description at the beginning.

"Can I talk to her now?" he asked.

His aunt left, and came back with her arm about the sick young woman. She put her in what passed as a comfortable chair in that room, and brought her coffee and cookies—pasticcino from a neighborhood baker. Mary looked tired and more worn than when he had seen her downtown, and even then she had been very different from the fresh young woman he had seen promenading with her children in the little park by the house.

Aunt Regina left them together, saying she had letters to write. She kept up a regular correspondence with the relations in the old country.

"I've read your recollections of what happened that night," he said. "You don't mind if I ask you some questions now?"

Mary shook her head. Her hands were on her knees; her shoulders were slumped. She had no objection, it seemed, but she showed little interest in their talk.

"You said there was someone else there, at the house, when you left the children."

She stared at him blankly. "No. There was no one in the house. Just Tom and Linda."

"But here, on the first page, you mention a man named Lesska. He was there when you talked to your mother-in-law."

"Oh, Lesska. He wasn't in the house. He just drove Alice—he works for Boy Burgoyne. Sort of all-purpose help. Caretaker. Looks after the cars. Drives for him."

"Did he leave before you or after you?"

She answered indifferently, as if she was unaware that she was building the case against herself. "Before."

"Are you sure? Think carefully," he urged.

She didn't have to think. "I'm sure," she said. "You see I was late for the train. I had brought the car out, but I didn't put it in the driveway because Alice had to get in. I parked it just on the side under the tree and I was going to drive right off when she arrived. But Alice talked for a minute . . . There was something she wanted from the garage."

She was staring ahead blankly, not seeing him or the room, he thought; she was watching a moving picture, back in time, that she had run before, over and over. Yet she was still caught up in it, to the exclusion of anything in the present.

"She gave me a plastic bonnet to put on, because of the rain. I was fiddling with the strings when I went to get in the car, and I had my keys in my hand—I dropped them in the grass. I was bending over, picking them up, and I guess Lesska had already turned and he just shot right past."

That was that. "Which way did he go?"

"I don't know. I wasn't looking at the car—it was the Cadillac, I remember. He might have gone down the lane and turned into the road at the bottom. It's a longer route, but often it's a quicker way to Burgoyne. Anyway, I didn't look."

Danny was frowning. "Didn't your mother-in-law ask the driver to wait until she came out of the garage to drive her back to the house as it was raining so hard?"

"No. He probably had to get back to Burgoyne. I was thinking, then, that Alice would be okay when she came out because she has a whole collection of old umbrellas and raincoats in there. Boots. Everything. She's always prepared. She—"

Suddenly, Mary broke down in tears. Her sobs were violent and shook her whole body. Aunt Regina reappeared and shooed Danny away. As he walked back to his own apartment, a bitter-cold wind was blowing. He noted it absently; his mind was occupied with Mary Christopher. Strange. It was the mention of her mother-in-law that had caused her to break down. Not a sudden recall of the death of the children. Was she refusing to accept the fact that they were dead? Could she simply not face it at all? Or was something strong and healthy in her beginning to handle it, slowly, obscurely? Certainly, it was the break with her late husband's mother, the sick old lady, that had finished her. Ruth and Naomi. Poor Ruth, amid the alien corn. That alien corn could give you a pretty sick belly.

In the morning, however, while Danny was showing the much-thumbed photographs of the usual con men to a couple from Iowa— they had been taken right in a bank for two thousand dollars' worth of traveler's checks—his mind went back to the undeniable fact that there had been someone else at the scene of the abduction. No one could really know how long the old lady had been in the garage, poking about. She might not have noticed the time herself and, with her stroke coming so soon after, her recollection might not be the clearest.

While the couple hesitated over an identification, he reflected that anyone could have come along and entered the house; according to Mary, the door wasn't kept locked. Defense counsel would make a lot of that. The kids, apparently, had been in a brightly lit window like the season's best attraction in Macy's.

He covered the mustache on the suspect's face, and the husband

and wife both recognized him. "And he wore glasses," the wife said. "He looked like a bank manager . . ."

When they left, they looked more cheerful. Danny called the First Precinct until he reached Pidusky. Keegan had told him about Danny's interest in the case, and Pidusky was a good cop and a nice guy. He checked with Merivale and called Danny back late that afternoon.

A statement had been taken from Lesska. It tallied with Alice and Mary Christopher's statements and was supported by Bartholomew Burgoyne. According to Burgoyne's statement, Lesska had returned to the Burgoyne house about 5:50 P.M., which left him twenty minutes for his drive, a quick run considering the slippery roads that night. He had gone to the main house instead of garaging the car, believing that Burgoyne needed him again, but Burgoyne had changed his mind. His guests had lingered after the concert and his sister was still directing the replacement of furniture in the music room.

So Lesska was out. But he *had* been there. Danny asked about the plastic-bag murders; they talked for a while and Pidusky had to leave. That night Danny had a drink with Matt Keegan at Callahan's on the West Side near the highway, one of the few Irish bars left in that part of town. Keegan liked the place, old and battered as it was, and didn't object to the pounding of traffic that shook the stools and tables. A dark Irishman, he didn't show the glow of liquor, but he was soon feeling mellow. He had also talked to Pidusky and was in the mood to be confidential.

"He says that Captain Bassett up there is going crazy, in a quiet Yankee sort of way. He believes the family are holding back evidence to avoid a scandal. He's sure they *know*. He's a real ferret, that guy. He's found something a bit spooky about the family trust. It should have been wound up, and it all goes to Mary, but the family are dragging their feet. She still gets the income, and she apparently isn't demanding the capital."

Danny shrugged. "It hasn't been that long. That kind of thing often gets dragged out. Mary Christopher's in no state to think of trusts or very much else."

Keegan nodded. "You're right there. When my wife inherited the condo in Florida from her folks, it took two years before it was settled. A mess if there ever was one."

Danny was still thinking of Bassett's assumption. "If the people up there really believe she did it, you'd think they'd want to turn her in. Then she couldn't benefit."

"Is that true?" Keegan said. "I mean with trusts. I know the law covers wills . . ."

Neither of them knew the answer.

"Besides, people aren't always reasonable," Keegan added reflectively. "That sort of reasonable. They are handling it their way. No trial, no publicity. They won't inform on her and she won't trouble them."

"Leave her out in the cold to freeze to death."

Keegan shrugged. "She gets her income. The money's well invested. She's not freezing."

"Don't bet on it," Danny said, soberly.

"What's the matter?" Keegan, amused, was teasing. "Got the hots for the Irish girl?"

Danny was irritated. The question was crude, he thought. But Keegan, a long-married man, had teased him about his women over the years, since Joan had died. Decent women, most of them, but Danny had never been tempted to marry again. And Keegan's cracks had never bothered him. You're getting pompous, he told himself. It was Mary Christopher. He had admired her since—that was four years ago. Joan nine years dead. Henry still living at home. A distant admiration. She was remote in her own world, the little boy, the baby.

That night, alone in his own bed, he had to admit he was strongly drawn to the desolate, bereaved woman. Those eyes . . . When he first saw her they had been laughing. Now they looked haunted in her hollow-cheeked face and as he drifted into sleep they drew him on some unknown journey.

As soon as he had free time, he went back to see Mary again. He needed more answers. Regina was in Mary's apartment with Connie Ferraro, but after the greetings they left him to speak to Mary alone. Her apartment seemed very bright compared with Aunt Regina's. It was uncluttered and airy, with comfortable chairs and a sofa and some nice old pieces—brought from Ireland perhaps. Or family stuff from Spenser. A photograph of a man on a tennis court: the husband. Good-looking guy. Preppy. A professor, Aunt Regina had told him. An egghead.

Mary still seemed sunk in the apathy he had noticed on his last
visit. There was dust on the top of the piano. He had seen Aunt
Regina's sharp eyes, observing. But Mary was roused enough to appear puzzled when he asked more questions about Lesska.

"Lesska wouldn't hurt the children. He's driven them since they
were babies. Why would he want to? It makes no sense."

"The reason I'm interested," Danny said patiently, "is that there
were just three people at the house with the children. You. Alice.
And Lesska."

"But I told you, he'd left."

She was wearing jeans and an old T-shirt, blue as her sad eyes. He
doubted that she was aware of what she had put on. The windows
were open and the room was cold; there were goose bumps on her
arms but she didn't seem to notice. He closed the window behind
her. Below, the branches of a dogwood tree looked black against the
snow. "Tell me about him anyway."

Mary wrinkled her forehead. "Well—he's Emil Lesska, but everyone just calls him Lesska. He's worked for Boy forever and he does a
super job—people all say they wish they could hire someone like
him."

"How long is forever?"

"Long before I married Quent. He's been with Boy since the end
of World War Two. They're both getting on. You see it more with
Boy because his hair turned white—he was a redhead—and he's gotten rather stout. But Lesska's one of those stringy, very fair men—of
course, his hair has silver in it but you wouldn't spot that. His face
isn't very lined; he doesn't get much sun. He's an indoor man. Always looks the same. Drab. He wears khaki chinos or some sort of
mud-colored jacket and pants and you just don't notice him."

"And he's the chauffeur?"

"Head cook and bottle washer, my mother would have said. Almost everything. Besides driving and taking care of the cars, he's a
marvelous mechanic and does some work for other people. Works on
the house, maintenance, repairs."

"Married?"

"Not that I ever heard about. Seemed like a born bachelor. But
really, he's the last person who would— I've never heard of any sex
molesters in Burgoyne or Spenser." Her face darkened at the
thought. "Or any talk about Lesska."

"What brought this Lesska to Burgoyne?"

"Boy. Quent told me. Boy was with the adjutant general's office or something like that in World War Two. He'd studied law before he decided that he wanted to be an architect and he got into— I think it had to do with the war crimes trials. He was in Vienna and he— Well, being Boy he became friendly with all the aristocracy there. Lesska is Polish, and he'd gotten into trouble with the Nazi occupation forces. Quent knew about him; he was quite a hero. He's a Catholic, but he helped a lot of Jews escape and then he was hunted himself. He ended up in a refugee camp in Vienna. There was a long wait for repatriation or resettlement and it was found that his family in Cracow had been killed.

"He could only speak Polish, but he managed to get a job with a Viennese countess as a handyman—illegal, but there was a lot of that, Quent said. That's where Boy met Lesska, at her house. After a while the local bureaucrats wanted to send poor old Lesska to another camp, more depressing than the Viennese one and the countess asked Boy if he could do something. Boy has never bothered much about rules and regulations and he just took him with the rest of his people when he went on to Paris. Civilian helper. No one was going to fuss because Lesska was so great to have around. Boy told Quent that Lesska serviced all their cars and when they couldn't get the right parts, he could usually adapt the wrong ones. Finally, when Boy came home, he brought Lesska with him as his personal servant—no one quite knew how."

Talking about her husband, and old times, brought back a little life, Danny saw. He'd seen that often, with old people.

"Boy gave him the apartment in back of the house, over the garage, and he's been there ever since. Alice always said she didn't know what the Burgoynes would do without him."

Her face looked pinched when she remembered her mother-in-law, and Danny tried to distract her. "Do you have a photograph?"

"Of Lesska? I would have to search. He never included himself when we were taking pictures. But I might have caught him—I took so many shots. She dug a small photograph from her wallet. "That's Boy, with Alice." They were a handsome older couple. "And the children."

The boy looked like Mary. The little girl was more like her father. Danny returned the photographs to her gently, and went on.

"Does Lesska have a lot of friends, acquaintances?"

"No, he's a loner," Mary replied. "He never really learned to speak much English. Not long before he died, Quent took a visiting professor from Warsaw up to Spenser for a few days and he tried to speak to Lesska, but the odd thing was, he didn't seem to remember an awful lot of Polish either. But he's very attached to the Burgoynes, especially Boy. Alice said—"

Mary Christopher couldn't talk very long without "Alice said," no matter how much pain it seemed to bring. He couldn't recall Joan quoting his mother that often. The two women had got along well enough, considering that one of them came from the city of the Mormons, and the other was a Catholic from Hell's Kitchen.

"Alice said that Boy was Lesska's Führer. Quent would explain that Lesska wasn't German and wasn't a Nazi, but she just giggled. He really does seem to worship Boy."

"Would you say he liked children?" Danny asked, his mind still running on the obvious. "Liked to be around them?"

"No," Mary answered, after a moment's reflection. "I wouldn't say so. Really, nothing kinky about him, if that's what you're implying. He seemed to think them rather a nuisance. Didn't especially want them in 'his car.' He never pulled a face, though, when Boy asked him to drive the children somewhere, but I always felt the face was there—behind the face."

Mary, he thought wryly, squelched any attempt to divert suspicion from herself with great decision and effectiveness. Yet he still felt a certain curiosity about Lesska. One, two, three, he thought. Alice could, theoretically, have done it, even in her weakened state, though that was arguable, but she had no conceivable motive. Mary? A guilty woman wouldn't have answered like that. Lesska—

In the next few days, he made inquiries through the Immigration and Naturalization Service. He was used to tracing people and had ways to get around the usual red tape. And Lesska was easy enough to trace, but what Danny learned by the end of the next week didn't please him. Everything Mary had told him was true. Lesska was now an American citizen. When he had entered the country in 1947 there had been strict quota restrictions, but a special exception had been obtained for the man who had worked so well with the U.S. Army and who before that had been a heroic resister of the Nazi tyranny. Documents had been obtained from the refugee camp, supporting his claim, and he had strong recommendations from the adjutant general's office in the person of the esteemed Major Burgoyne.

Regretfully, Danny had to put Lesska from his mind. There was nothing left but to consider other possible kidnappers. Two children had been scooped up, driven over thirty miles, and buried near Tony's Tavern. They could have been murdered anywhere along the route. But it was Mary's route. A lone pedophile, who just happened to be going that way, taking an opportunity, then frightened into murder, was a possibility. But it made no sense that he would have taken Mary's route. Someone had. Those bodies had been deliberately dumped in her tracks. The thought possessed his mind for a night, but the next morning a flood of work kept him fully occupied. An outbreak of flu left the squad seriously undermanned and he had little time to think of Mary, except to puzzle over the fact that only Lesska had been there, and that Boy Burgoyne had fixed his return to the house at 5:50. One, two, three. Out goes he. And only Mary left.

After a week, some of the flu victims returned and things quieted down. Danny had an early dinner in the Village and was ready to go home when he saw Connie Ferraro, plump and brisk, trotting along the street with Mary beside her. They had come from St. Vincent's Hospital, Connie explained, where she was a volunteer, and now Mary was working with her. Connie sounded very bright; most likely this was a therapy dreamed up by her and his aunt, but to his eye Mary, the once sturdy Irish girl, looked too frail. The dark circles under her eyes were now like bruises and her bones jutted from her face. Perhaps the women's medicine was too strong.

Connie was going on to a bingo game, so Danny walked with Mary. He asked her if she'd eaten dinner and she hastily said that she had. One of the recovered flu victims had been talking that morning with great relish about the complete revulsion he had felt from food while his fever lasted: "Everything was like shit, man." Danny fancied that Mary was enduring something like that. Despair—was it a kind of soul fever?

"Let's go in here," he said as they came to a café with a brightly striped awning. "At least you can have a cappuccino."

It was too cold to sit on the sidewalk, but they had a window seat and could watch the crowds of passersby. A very public place, but sheltered. Mary had followed his suggestion, but perhaps she would have followed anyone. She sipped her cappuccino and he let his espresso cool before him as he talked of pleasant, simple things— Aunt Regina's panettone; the soda bread baked by his Irish mother.

Mary looked up with the glimmer of a smile. "I loved soda bread," she told him. "We always had it at home. Mom didn't have much time for baking, but she always made that. She worked at nights, you see, down on Wall Street, cleaning offices."

Something in the atmosphere of the café calmed Mary and she told Danny about her father, Jim Rafferty, a firefighter. She spoke with warmth, with love. "He played with us like another kid and took us to the park. He was wonderful when we were little. Whenever he came home from his tour he would bring us each something, no matter how small. A candy bar, a plastic toy from the five and ten, chewing gum, funny little cards, barrettes for my hair . . . It drove Mom crazy. 'Foolish waste. Rubbish.' We loved it all." But Jim Rafferty had a problem that grew worse with the years.

"The other guys covered up for him, but Mom was always afraid he would injure himself, hurt somebody, get found out, lose his job and his pension. She thought we'd be penniless, on the streets. As it was, of course, a lot of money went . . . some with his drinking friends and . . ."

Danny knew all about it. It wasn't unknown in the Department, though nowadays it was more difficult to cover up. There were the treatment programs. Sometimes they helped.

"So she took the job. But it made her tired and angry and Pop stayed out more and . . ."

Danny remembered his days as a rookie, with two kids and Joan very edgy about his long hours on the job. He had stayed out a few times with the guys. Not so much for the booze. It was just easy to talk to them. Not that they'd talked much. Usually watched a game on the TV over the bar. But eventually he'd cut that down to size. For the kids. For Joan.

Mary had said, "He played with us." A brother? A sister? Regina had said she was quite alone. But he didn't disturb her with questions. He let her talk.

"When he died—I'd always thought Mom would be relieved, in a way. Start to enjoy life. But she was just worn out. And she wanted to go home, back to Ireland. She left to go and live with her sister, Aunt Kathy. It was after I met Quent but before we were married.

She didn't live long. Tom was three when she died. It was in the middle of the semester, so I went over with Tom for the funeral. I'd only been once before, when I was little. A small village, Linafry, near Dingle Bay. Very lovely"—her voice was musing—"and I started to remember things, places, from when I was small. But I was longing to come home, to Quent, our apartment—and Christopher country."

Mary told him about Christopher country. The children's paradise. The safe haven.

Having begun to talk, Mary found it hard to stop. She hadn't meant to speak of her last visit to Spenser, what Alice had said, what Alice had done. The look on her face—Mary's throat clenched as she remembered. "It didn't work out," was all she could utter, but she did tell him about Nutty Nell.

"I mean, I know she's crazy, but even so—that anyone could—especially up there."

Danny walked with her to her door and they spoke only of her hospital work. He left, wondering about the human way of shielding from the conscious mind what was screaming from the guts. Nutty Nell was saying only what she heard from everyone else. The crazy woman parroted what Christopher country was saying about Mary, but not to Mary herself. How long would she be deceived? And how long would this waiting go on?

As the days passed, it seemed as though it might go on a long time. The First Precinct didn't have much interest in Mary Christopher at the moment. The plastic-bag killer had not yet been found, though Homicide was almost certain the crimes were the work of one man. Mary had been asked to keep the precinct informed of her whereabouts, but as long as Merivale was quiescent, there was nothing for them to do.

Pidusky sent Danny an embarrassed professor from City College. He had been fleeced by a young woman with a charity racket. The charity, to benefit third-world children, was close to the professor's heart, and in his enthusiasm he had solicited contributions from his friends and students. The prof was hardly to be blamed, Danny thought when he heard the tale. The woman had a very solid-looking operation. But she had soon disappeared without trace. The prof couldn't recognize her picture in the mug book, but Danny had a good idea who it would be. She could change her looks to fool her mother.

He took the opportunity to call Pidusky and after they discussed the fraud, Danny asked what was keeping Bassett so quiet.

"He's a tight-lipped guy," Pidusky told him, "but I don't think he's got anything new. Not likely to get it now, except through luck. My guess is, he'd like the prosecutor to go ahead. But the big wheel with the Probyn Commission doesn't want egg on his face. Nobody's howling up there."

"I'd like a favor." Danny told him what he wanted.

"He doesn't have to," Pidusky said. "There's nothing we can do with it if we get it. It all happened up there. And we can't spare—"

"I know," Danny said. "But you could make helpful noises. Seeing the complete file might give you a line on something useful."

Pidusky swore, in English and Polish. It was impressive. "Think we've got nothing better to do than be gofers for Merivale?" he said bitterly. But a few days later Danny got a return call.

"I got that file for you. Come in and see it when you want. It was no sweat. Bassett must be stopped in his tracks."

Danny was pleased to hear it. He had seen Mary once since the evening at the café. There was a question that had to be asked; until then he hadn't been able to ask it. So he had stopped by her apartment and rung the bell. After a pause, Mary had let him in. She was working, she explained, at her desk in her bedroom. Quent's book. Still working for her husband, he thought. Dead four years. She looked reasonably composed and he decided to go ahead.

"I'm sorry—this might upset you, but there is a rumor. Perhaps you can tell me about it."

He told her of the report of her buying heroin. Years ago.

"About four years ago," Mary had answered calmly. "It's true. I hope you're not going to arrest me. Quent was released from the hospital for home care. He had spinal cancer, the most painful kind. After a while the morphine just didn't help. Quent couldn't stand the nurses and I did most of the nursing myself. They taught me 'pain management.' Management—it was a ghastly joke. The doctors wouldn't give him heroin, of course, and it was the only thing that could help. It's legal, for cases like his, in other countries. But he couldn't be moved. So I went and got it for him," she said. "Getting it was easy. Paying for it was something else. I couldn't ask Ernest. He wouldn't break the law. But he didn't see Quent when—" She broke off. "I'm not sorry I did it," she said. "I know it was wrong, but at least Quent died in some sort of peace."

So that was the reason for the debt. Mary, the librarian, going out into the street, to that scum, to buy horse. Quiet Mary. She had broken the law and taken her chances. Could a prosecutor drag it up? He wasn't sure. In any case, with a jury that could be a two-edged sword. It might arouse sympathy for the widow.

But when he saw the rest of the file from Merivale, he wasn't as sanguine. Bassett had questioned all the witnesses from Tony's Tavern a second time, and the added statements were very damaging. Jack Curlew, the man Mary had rebuffed, reported that when Mary left the tavern she had been staggering. That was confirmed by Mrs. Jarvis, who had been sitting by the window. "Too drunk to walk straight; you couldn't miss it. Took her coat off in the bar so the guys could see her ass wiggle in those tight pants. Got an eyeful when she was stumbling away."

Acute drunkenness—it might explain the folly of her going into the bar, then burying the children close by. All the witnesses in the bar said that Mary had been clean, but the stock boy in the supermarket in New York had seen her muddy and disheveled. He noticed another report, a statement taken by Pidusky at the precinct since Danny had last looked at the records. A Mrs. Carol Grafton, Mary's friend. Mary had told her on the night of the murder that the children were in Spenser. The statement had nothing in it that would damage Mary, except that Carol had noticed that her clothes were muddy and her hair blown by the wind. She and Mary had parted outside Fanelli's. Mary had been going back to the Corner Bar to pick up her car. Tony's Tavern, the Corner Bar, Fanelli's. Innocent enough, but prosecuting counsel would make it sound frivolous at least. The mother who had left her children for important business.

But there was more financial information. Bassett had been thorough. It wasn't a matter of a "mere" $270,000 trust fund. Alice Christopher's will was drawn up in the same form as the trust. Bassett must be very friendly with Alice's lawyer to have found that out. Now, when Alice died, everything would go to Mary. And Alice was rich.

Danny looked over the schedules that were attached to the report and rubbed his chin with his knuckles. An eye-opener. Joseph Christopher had left his widow an amount of money equal to that of the Christopher Trust and nine pieces of property, as well as the house she lived in. Joseph had been a good businessman. He had built houses and shops over the old Christopher farm, at modest cost no doubt, throughout his life. But the valuation now was considerable. It must have been fairly close to his death—Danny looked at the dates—when he entered on his last project. This schedule was complicated: a joint venture. Some of Joe's stores and businesses at a crossroads had been demolished and a shopping mall erected. Old Joe, as well as receiving a large sum of money, had retained a percentage of the new mall. It had been so successful that Alice's assets were now valued at five million dollars.

Danny wondered what a jury would make of that. It altered things. Millions. The word had a special effect. The question "Would a mother kill her own children?" became "Would a mother kill her own children for five million dollars?" The balance was changed. Danny, usually cheerful, felt gloomy and disturbed. He didn't like his own conclusions. Mary, he was certain, could not have murdered her children. But even without a witness to the children's presence in the car, Bassett had quite a case. Quite a case.

11

Boy Burgoyne was on his feet, his face radiant as, glass in hand, he finished up his after-dinner speech. The men around the long table in the private dining room of the Burgoyne Center for History and the Arts were laughing heartily. Boy was at his tiptop, peak, and crown on these occasions, his brother thought. Ernest had heard the speech before, or something like it; he and Boy belonged to the same societies and clubs, in Burgoyne and in the city, and Boy had always liked to amuse the members with tales of Burgoynes past. Of late, Ernest had given up attending most gatherings and never visited the city, but Boy still used his club there regularly.

"And so, gentlemen, my ancestor was not the Burgoyne who lost the battle in the field, he was the Burgoyne who won the battle of the marriage bed."

There was a general shout of laughter. The diners were local landowners and the top professional men in the area, and were familiar with the tale of Wilhelmina Van Vliet, heiress to one of the great patroons, who had married the first Burgoyne: her portrait was in the gallery. The diners had contributed generously to the Center, and were repaid with good food, fine wines, and old-fashioned service—a taste of the life of the rich as it had been lived a century earlier.

The atmosphere was heavy with the smell of food, mingling with the scent of the flowers that came from the greenhouses, still part of the Castle estate. And the smell of cigar smoke. For this one day the no-smoking rule was waived and several of the men had chosen to light a cigarette or a cigar, for pleasure and to re-create the old atmosphere. It made Ernest feel a little sick. The rich food had upset his stomach. One was not used to it anymore. His ulcer, he knew, would be acting up that night. He was sorry he had allowed Boy to persuade him; he should have sent a check as planned and he could have been comfortably in bed. "You can't let the Castle down," Boy had said. "This is a fund-raiser. The Burgoynes must show themselves. A chance to sit at the table with the family—that's what it is for the locals." Boy, the personification of Burgoyne to these men, always thought of himself as a cosmopolitan. Ernest looked at the glowing Boy with envy: *he* had a superb digestion. And on those occasions he was richly, splendidly, at home.

Boy sat down to a shout of applause; the bursar of the Center rose to reply. A lot of wine had been drunk and the bursar, indiscreet, alluded to an old rumor that the Burgoynes of Burgoyne were indeed descended from the British general, though not the general's wife. He became embarrassed, lost the thread, but the genial company laughed loudly and he went on with his oration. Boy had always liked the story and he waved his cigar and chortled.

While Boy was swallowing his brandy in great content, Ernest took the opportunity of broaching a delicate subject. Under the hubbub of talk and laughter he would not be overheard.

"Bassett latched on to me as I came in." He caught a glimpse of him, smiling politely at the bursar's speech, at the other end of the table. Bassett looked impressive in evening clothes, he thought, more like a judge than an investigator. "He wants to talk to Lesska again."

"I know. Let him." Boy was unperturbed. He waved his cigar in an airy gesture. "Lesska is all right. He won't drag the family in."

Ernest felt a twinge in his stomach.

"We can't go on with this," he said. *"We are involved."*

"Rubbish. I can't tell the man what to say. Bassett's job is to get information. Let him get on with it."

Ernest remembered Alice Christopher remarking, "Lesska would stand on his head in a bucket of mud if Boy suggested it." But the noise around them was dying down. The speeches were over; it was time to go.

They passed through the great studded doors of the Castle and

Ernest walked with Boy to his car. Not the Cadillac, he saw; Boy had driven himself tonight in a new toy he had acquired.

Boy, his hand on the car door, turned to face his brother.

"We can't do it, Ernest," he said, with a quiet gravity unusual in him. "A trial will kill Alice. Bristow knows that. Bring all that misery back again." He looked at his brother with the command a sixteen-year-old once had over a child of eight. "I'm not going to allow what little life Alice has left to be trashed by that—"

The last bitter words spat from his lips, but were drowned by an explosion of diners from the Castle, laughing, calling to each other, stamping their feet and slamming into their cars. They noticed Boy's acquisition: "What's that car?" "A DeLorean, I think." "One of Boy's fancies." "Could have trouble on the road." "Well, it looks pretty good around here." They watched the car, whining at a sudden start, peeling rubber as Boy shot away. The onlookers shouted after him in great camaraderie and they gave Ernest milder, though pleasant, farewells. They seemed to want to linger. He was longing for the quiet of his home and the soothing influence of his stomach pills.

Boy was decided, as usual. A good way to be. And Ernest, driving down to the highway more sedately, considered that though he himself was the lawyer, Boy had scored a good legal point. Neither he nor Boy had been at the Christopher house with Lesska. They had no direct knowledge of what occurred. The matter was between Bassett and Lesska. But Ernest's ulcer was troublesome that night. And the next morning.

On that same morning Danny had a visit from an elderly woman who had been sent to him from the Twentieth Precinct. Her name was Mrs. MacBride; she was eighty years old, neat, clean, and well spoken. She lived in a hotel for retired persons on the Upper West Side, and she told him she had been swindled by a woman pretending to be a social worker. "She said she came from the city. A nice young woman, but when she went I found my bank passbook was gone and my will."

"Your will?" Danny was surprised.

"Yes." She nodded and regarded him with a clear and candid gaze. "It's happened before. One of the maids who cleans the rooms, she stole my will and I had to get another . . ."

Danny quietly cursed the Twentieth Precinct, and asked for more information about the social worker. Mrs. MacBride carefully wrote down a name and a telephone number.

"I'll look into it, Mrs. MacBride," he promised.

She thanked him warmly, drew on her gloves, and trotted off.

Danny called the number. It was a social services office. A switchboard operator promised to have Ms. Samantha Jones call him back. Late that afternoon he heard from Ms. Jones.

"The precinct shouldn't have sent Mrs. MacBride to you," she said. "Must be some new blood over there." Her voice was pleasant, warm though resigned. "Look, she's really okay. She's a swell old lady, except she gets these ideas about her papers. I mean, like her passbook. She forgets that her bank doesn't issue passbooks anymore. They send her monthly statements. I checked up on her a couple of weeks ago and there were no other problems. I explain, but she forgets. She hides her money and her papers and she changes the place, so of course she thinks that the last person in her room took them.

"She has children and grandchildren," Ms. Jones went on, "but they live all over the country. She doesn't see them often. Pretty much alone, in that hotel."

Danny understood. He saw too much of it. Older people, so often alone, confused by the changes in the society around them. Surrounded by the noise and hustle of the squad room at that hour, he thought of the hotel apartments, carefully locked, the tenants with no one to talk to, no one to touch. A good thing about the Valentis, he reflected: they looked after their own. Of course, they had not dispersed. They were still in Little Italy and the Village. Then he remembered his two boys and gave a mental shrug. He'd put no strings on them.

"She'll find that will in a few days," Ms. Jones added. "But like I told her, she can just write another. It doesn't mean a thing until she's dead."

Danny thanked the pleasant Ms. Jones, but his mind leapt at once to Alice Christopher's will. Of course. His brain hadn't been working. He was too involved, too defensive, he thought wryly, about Mary. He took the time to speak to Mrs. MacBride. She was happy to hear that the bank would send her a statement. And she told him she was writing a new will. "I'm glad that Miss Jones is really with the department. She is such a nice girl. It must have been the switchboard operator."

Alice Christopher still lived. A will was just a piece of paper. Not so bad for Mary after all. With both of her grandchildren dead, Alice had probably drawn a new one. The prosecution would have to go with the trust. And he began to wonder, if the will was changed, who would benefit.

"Hello, Mary. It's Mildred." Even through the distorted sound of the intercom, Mary had recognized the voice at once, though it had been two years since she'd seen Mildred Christopher.

"Mildred!" It was a cry of welcome, of pleasure, and of some deep, unexamined relief. Mildred was Quent's favorite cousin, close to his own age. A stunning girl, he'd told Mary, laughing, sunny, "and the best girl in the world. Everyone loved her. I've always been a bit in love with her myself, but she married George." Mildred had married a Christopher cousin from Poughkeepsie, an archeologist, and had become an archeologist herself. Mary had always liked her, but with Mildred's long sojourns abroad, their meetings had been few. '

She was at the door. Mildred in a green wool coat and a small white hat, reaching out to her, was an echo of Christmases past. "Mary—I just heard, when I got back. About the children. There was a notice about the memorial in the mail. Oh, my dear."

Both women broke down and cried. After a while, Mildred wiped her eyes and became practical. "I've come to get you. You shouldn't be alone like this. We must talk."

Mary felt that the thing she most wanted in the world was to be with Mildred. But she couldn't go anywhere. She had hardly left the Village since— She had only gone when she'd had to go—up there.

"I have to be here," she said.

"Why?" Mildred asked. "Has anyone told you that you must?"

"No," Mary said slowly, "it's just that—the police—they might find out something."

"You can leave my phone number and address," Mildred said. Mildred could always make anything seem easy. She had accompanied George on many of his digs, brought up her children, gone back to college, "and all with no fuss," Quent had said. So how could she explain, Mary thought, even to Mildred, the sick, awful feeling that got worse at the thought of leaving the apartment, the Village streets?

"Mary," Mildred said, breaking in on her thoughts. "What is going on? I had a letter last year from Alice. She wrote that she had had a stroke, but made a full recovery. So as soon as I got back, I drove up to Spenser. Well, you know of course about her second stroke, but—I was surprised. The nurse, and Fiona Derwent being there."

"How did Alice look?" Mary asked.

"Very weak," Mildred said slowly. "Well, I would expect that. And the nurse. But I was surprised about Fiona. Alice never liked her, but things seemed to have changed . . . I've been away a long time, of course."

Mildred took it for granted that Mary would go with her. She helped pack Mary's bags, arranged with the super's wife to pick up her mail, and waited until Mary reached Pidusky and told him that she was going to Sag Harbor and at what number she could be reached. Then she looked up, puzzled.

"He wants to know how long I'll be gone," she said.

"At least a week," Mildred replied firmly.

"A week," Mary told the detective, without comment, but she wondered why he had asked.

Before they left, Mary tapped at Regina's door and told her that she was going away for a week to stay with her husband's cousin.

Regina gazed at Mildred and seemed to like what she saw. "Family," Regina said. "That's good. I am very glad that you have come, Mrs. Christopher. Very glad." Regina, ready to go out, was dressed in black furs and looked magnificent.

Mildred smiled as she opened her car door for Mary. "What an imposing old lady. Is she your chaperon, Mary?" She chuckled at the thought. "Old lady . . . Do you know I'm fifty-five this year? And Quent would have been fifty-three. Grown up at last?"

Mildred, teasing her cousin, had claimed that a professorship kept a man permanently juvenile. "Remember how he used to make fun of the fat old women who walked around the harbor in short shorts? The Sag ladies."

She had been shocked by Mary's looks and kept the conversation light on the long ride. It was dark when they reached her house and

Mary looked weary, so she gave her some soup and packed her off to bed.

Mary was wakened next morning by the squawk of seagulls. The room was full of the briny air off Shelter Island Bay. She stood at the window and gazed up and down the street of old houses with dark cedar shingles, each behind its white picket fence, just as she had stood, so many years before, on her first visit, with Quent. "I'm glad George kept this place," he'd said. It was a Christopher summer home. After George died, Mildred had sold the house in Poughkeepsie, and this house was her home, between her travels.

Mildred. She felt a great wave of gratitude for Mildred's very existence.

Downstairs, Mildred was smiling over the stove as she made pancakes for breakfast. She took Mary walking briskly around the harbor and for the next few days she kept her occupied. A fisherman she knew at Montauk owned a dragger and fished year-round. He was willing to take them out, but the *Phoebe II* was a working boat with just the pilot and a crew of two. The two women had to keep out of the way and fend for themselves, and on the choppy water, soaked with spray, Mary had her attention well fixed in the present. Some days they drove to Sag Harbor's long public beach, and to other beaches nearby, and walked along the water's edge. The weather had turned mild, very mild for the time of year; the sun shone and Mary's body responded to the good air, the exercise, and the food that Mildred provided. Little by little, Mary was able to talk about what had happened to the children, how nothing since had seemed real, in any way connected to the life she had known before.

Mildred could see that there were still things Mary couldn't speak of. Her eyes would darken; she would regain that curious, guarded look as though she were warding off a blow. There were questions that Mildred wanted to ask, but she waited for Mary to recover a little; she could give her time.

One afternoon they had been been shopping, but ended up by the shore. Mildred, tempted by the sun, rolled up the legs of her slacks and waded into the water. Mary was wearing pantyhose and hung back but Mildred pulled her along. "Okay, they'll get wet. They'll soon dry and they'll survive a dunking. Even a city woman might survive."

The rising wind was blowing them about. Mary smiled, held up her skirt, and splashed. The water was still ice-cold; she shrieked and almost laughed, Mildred thought. Soon the wind blew harder, and by the time they got home it was a boisterous, crackling storm.

Mildred had made clam chowder for dinner. After they had eaten the good food, they drank their coffee in the little parlor, listening to the rain on the window. Mary was leaving the next day; she felt she should be in the city, closer to the investigation. She told Mildred that she knew a police officer there, Regina's nephew, Danny Valenti, who was trying to help. "They must find the killer," Mary said, with a fierceness that surprised Mildred. "They must. There's no peace . . ."

Poor, sad Mary. She looked tormented as Alice had looked tormented. What a purgatory for those two women! Mildred shivered a little. The wind, colder now, penetrated the old house. She went to turn up the thermostat and thought with great thankfulness of her three children, healthy, happy, well married, and of her grandchild and the one on the way.

Mildred had wanted to ask Mary about Alice. Her own visit had been short; Alice was pleased to see her, but she had looked very tired. When Mildred asked how Mary was, Alice became very ill indeed, and the nurse said it was time for Alice to take her pill and go to bed. Aunt and niece had said goodbye affectionately but Mildred had been troubled. At the mention of Mary's name, Alice's eyes were strange. Revulsion, hostility? But that was absurd. The two women had been fond of each other in a way unusual for in-laws. Aunt Alice . . . She had always treated Mildred like the daughter she'd never had, and when Quent married Mary she had taken Mary to her heart in the same way.

Naturally, the death of the children and all the mystery around it had to disturb, profoundly, the mother and the grandmother. And Alice's illness—had it weakened her mind? She couldn't blame Mary for this tragedy; the children hadn't been left with a careless babysitter; they were with Alice herself. Mildred wished, as she so often did, that she could talk it over with George. George had studied psychology. He would have called it projection. The children were taken from Alice's house, so she must blame someone. And George could have believed that, but she knew Alice . . .

Mildred made up her mind to visit Alice again. She had to

straighten this out. It was intolerable for Mary. First, she would call and make an appointment, so that she would have enough time. For now, if ever, these two bereaved women should give each other comfort.

When Mary got back to the city she looked a little better, more rested. Her face was less drawn and a little color had returned to her cheeks. It was just as well, Danny thought; she would soon be needing all her strength.

"Bassett's decided to go for it," Pidusky had told him. "Pushing hard. The DA didn't want to know, but now he might be changing his tune; the Crenshaw case has got them all hopping up there. Media, of course, but the locals are really fired up. 'No more Lizzie Bordens.'"

The Crenshaw case had made the city papers. Crenshaw's wife and child had been killed by an ax seven years before. Crenshaw had claimed he was stuck in his car at the roadside; his battery was failing and he had been nursing it along in a thunderstorm. He couldn't prove where he'd been, but the police found no evidence that he had committed the crime. There was no prosecution.

Last year Crenshaw had married again. His wife got pregnant. And her body was found chopped to pieces. This time the police found blood on Crenshaw's clothes.

"So the public is talking about do-nothing prosecutors, and Kramer has his ear to the wind."

Mary's respite lasted three days. Danny was still at his desk, typing up reports at seven o'clock, when he had an impulse to stop by and see how she was. If Bassett had made his move, Danny was quite sure he would have heard. But he wanted to see her anyway.

He had been with her long enough to see that she still looked better, even though her dinner was a sandwich and a glass of milk. She had heard nothing from Merivale; nothing from anywhere, she told him. In the morning she worked on Quent's book. In the afternoon she helped out at St. Vincent's. It was a tranquil half-hour, and then the buzzer rang from downstairs. It was Mildred, returning from Spenser.

"Mary!" Mildred's color was high and she was sparking with indignation.

During the swift introductions, Danny observed that Mildred resembled the late Quentin. They were a good-looking family. Mildred was attractive, not young, and right now very excited.

"Mary," she repeated. "What is happening up there?"

Mary gazed at her without speaking.

Mildred removed her coat and scarf, her movements very deft and precise. "I've been up to Spenser," she told them. "I called—the morning you left, Mary. Alice's nurse answered and said that she was sleeping. I left a message that I was coming up—I arranged the time with her nurse, before Alice's afternoon nap.

"So I drove up—no ferries yet—but I got there in time. And there was nobody in the house but Fiona. Well, she did apologize. She said she had tried to get me in the morning but, of course, I had already left. Alice hadn't been doing well and the doctor had ordered her to go back to the hospital for tests. A bed came up yesterday and so she went in. 'I should have called you at once,' she told me, 'but it was a great bustle and I quite forgot until late last night—too late to call, I thought. I came over to explain . . .'"

"How is Alice?" Mary asked.

"She doesn't look well. But she didn't when I saw her last week. I had a heck of a job finding out, though. I asked Fiona which hospital and *she didn't want to tell me.* Said that Alice was weak and tired and needed a lot of rest. You know the way Fiona has of talking, as if everyone else is a half-witted child. So I told her as politely as I could that I intended to go to the hospital and check with the nurses. Then she had to give in, and she told me that Alice was in Slade Memorial. But, if you can believe it, she insisted on coming with me. She just followed me in her car."

She was sitting in one of Mary's armchairs, upright, leaning a little forward, with her hands on her knees like an eager girl. Her legs were as trim and shapely as a girl's, Danny noticed, with neat ankles. Her short, curling blond and silver hair and the light dust of freckles on her face added to the effect, but Mildred was a fully adult woman, with perception and judgment.

"When we got there, Alice was in a private room, and there was no trouble about visiting. In fact, when we went in to see her, Boy Burgoyne was sitting by the bed—taking up half the room, it looked like. You know Boy. Then Fiona slipped in and sat in the chair on the other side and I couldn't get near Alice. It—it was like a barricade."

Danny listened intently. He had heard what Mary had to say. Now the detective was hearing from a disinterested witness.

"I had no intention of letting those two stop me from talking to Alice," Mildred went on. "And I could see that Alice was happy to have me come, and everything else was fine except I practically had to shout from the foot of the bed. I asked Alice how she was and she told me that she hadn't wanted to come to the hospital, and it was just the doctor fussing. She couldn't wait to go home. Then I began to talk to her about you, Mary and—well, Fiona said Alice looked tired. Boy said we were wearing her out. Alice started to cry. Fiona spoke to a nurse who was passing by; Alice put her face in the pillow, and the nurse said perhaps we'd better let her rest. So I saw her for about five minutes.

"Those two," she said in disgust, "they could have let me have a little private time with Alice. They're not family. I was just so mad I drove straight here, though I have to get back tonight."

Mary listened in a turmoil of conflicting feelings. Oddly, her first emotion was relief, relief that someone besides herself thought that the Burgoynes were acting strangely, in a presumptuous and untoward fashion. And it was always good to see Mildred—Mildred, part of the old Christopher country—all that was left, for Mary. But there was pain. Mildred had seen what Mary already knew. Now it was confirmed. Alice couldn't bear to hear her name. Alice thought she had— In God's name, what did Alice think she had done?

Soon Mildred departed. She had traveled three hundred miles that day and she had another hundred to go. Danny, who had arranged a meeting that night with a witness in an upcoming trial, escorted her to her car.

"You're a friend of Mary's," Mildred said. It was only slightly a question, but Danny understood.

"Yes," he answered. "I have no involvement in the case; I'm in a special squad. Fraud. My aunt took Mary under her wing; she lives next door. I'd like to help her. It's a rotten deal."

Mildred nodded. "It's worse than that. It's unbelievable, but they seem to think that Mary— It's crazy. Boy and Fiona walked out of the hospital with me to my car. They started to say—all sorts of stuff. That Alice thinks— But how could she? I can't believe Alice would think such a thing. Alice isn't crazy; she sounded normal before—"

"Before you mentioned Mary," Danny said.

"Yes. Well, weak. She could be confused, but not *that* confused. I mean, she's known Mary for fourteen years. They've been like mother and daughter. Much closer than most in-laws. Does she think that Quent would have married a—a child killer? It's like some weird fantasy."

"You don't know what she might have heard," Danny said soberly. "Gossip. Stories. And when people are weak they can become suggestible."

"But who would gossip? About what?" Mildred was still puzzled. "I always thought the family was happy, united. Of course," she said, frowning, "George and I didn't get up to Spenser that often—we were away so much, and a lot of the Christophers have moved to the West and the South. Joe and Alice were the ones we were closest to, and Alice always kept in touch. Yet the Baileys were always warm and friendly; when George died they were all in Poughkeepsie at the funeral."

As they walked to Mildred's car, a man passed by, ragged and grimed with dirt. His eyes were red-rimmed and he was muttering and gesturing. At the end of the block, a husky boy of about eighteen was leaning against a wall eyeing a shiny bicycle that was fastened to a post by a tree. He looked as though he had all the time in the world. Catching Danny's gaze, he slowly, very nonchalantly, disappeared around the corner. Not like the family in Spenser and Burgoyne. Nice people. But he had read their statements. They had distanced themselves from Mary Christopher. They were willing to believe her guilty.

"And Boy," Mildred was saying, as she stepped into the car, "I always thought he liked Mary. Fiona—of course, Fiona doesn't like anyone except the Burgoynes and the Derwents. And sometimes she has doubts about the Derwents. But that's just her way. She couldn't think—"

Mildred drove off, a good woman, confronted with something she couldn't wish to see. That family was solid against Mary. Danny felt a measure of relief that she would have the comfort of Mildred's presence in the days to come.

12

The fragile peace that Mary had found at Sag Harbor was shattered. The night that Mildred left she dreamed she was in court, a prisoner, and the jurors were the Baileys, staring at her and muttering, "Guilty, guilty." Boy sat in the judge's seat, dressed in a wig as well as a splendid robe: Judge Burgoyne, the representative of the king. The court was filled with hostile strangers calling, "Death, death, death." Outside the court it was dark and in the lanes a child killer wandered, looking for his prey.

She woke sweating, but the dream did not leave her. Why, she thought, staring up at the ceiling, gray in the morning light, why was there no hue and cry for the murderer? Were they waiting for him to strike again, waiting to find another little corpse in the countryside?

That same night, Danny made two decisions. The first he acted on at once, dialing the number of Stephen Bostwick. He'd known Steve for many years, since Danny had assisted the Poughkeepsie police in a fraud case. Bostwick had represented the defendant, but the two men had come to like and trust each other. As an attorney, Bostwick was interested in the Christopher case; he listened carefully to Danny, asked some questions, and agreed to appear for Mary if she wished him to do so. "And the sooner I see her the better," he said.

"I agree." Danny was grim. "Up there, around Burgoyne, they're treating Mary like something unclean. The woman from Gomorrah-on-the-Hudson."

"Yes, well, Burgoyne is—different," Bostwick said thoughtfully. "I mean, it's not far from Poughkeepsie in distance, but it's a separate world. A long, perhaps unique history. Prosperous. Inbred. Clannish. Oak Avenue and the streets off it are just a small part. There are huge tracts of land up there, family owned, no developers wanted. There's a hunt. Shooting. All very private and quiet. Nothing in common with some of the valley towns that grew up around one millionaire family and sank into poverty when the family pulled out."

"What about the Burgoyne family?" Danny asked. "They are rich enough."

"That's old money. A historic family. They look down on the Vanderbilts and Rockefellers. Respected, but Burgoyne could survive well without them. It never had industry so it doesn't suffer from a post-industrial blight. Very NIMBY."

Not In My Backyard. Burgoyne, a strange place for Jim Rafferty's daughter, Danny thought. Then he remembered his Flanagan cousin, who had moved to a prosperous retreat in New Jersey. Golf courses, tennis courts, gatehouses: it was happening.

"So they don't take quickly to outsiders," Bostwick said. "But there are good people up there. I met Ernest Burgoyne at a county bar dinner and he seemed decent enough. Something about this case is weird."

Weird, that was for sure.

As soon as Danny arrived in the squad room the next morning, he acted on his second decision and filled out the standard leave form, the UF28. He had accumulated a lot of leave, planning to visit both of his sons. But the squad had been reduced since the last round of budget cuts and it never seemed a good time to go. And the kids were nearly always in the thick of their own affairs.

He turned in the completed form and waited for an explosion from the commander, Sweeney Hine, when he arrived. Hine was a dour man, a good commander, protective of the squad, but harsh in speech. There was nothing easy in his manner. The young guys called him Swine, but it was a joke; they respected him.

"Valenti!"

Danny went into the little cubicle in back of the squad room that was Hine's office. He was bent over the phone, his bald head shining under the fluorescents, but he replaced the receiver and looked at the form. The explosion didn't come.

"You might as well take off," Hine said somberly. "Nothing is going to get better. And Mitchell's coming back next week; he checked out okay."

Mitchell, the oldest man in the squad, had been out on sick leave. He'd been operated on for a stomach ulcer.

"Guess he'll soon be putting in his papers," Hine added. "I wonder if we'll be getting a replacement. Well, if we don't, maybe we'll have to raise the level again."

Certain fraud cases, checks and credit cards, came in to Special Frauds if the loss was ten thousand dollars or more. Until recently. Now, because of the lack of manpower in the squad, the level had been raised to fifty thousand.

"We'll just take care of the rich," Hine went on. "Nice work. And we'll get rid of bums like you."

"Get in some yuppie types," Danny agreed easily. "Wear better clothes. Fit in well, making a collar on Wall Street."

He called Mary and asked her to have dinner with him that night. "There are a couple of things we ought to talk about."

To Mary, the apartment, filled with mementos of Quent, the children, and the family, had always been her refuge. But that day she was feeling stifled; the apartment was a prison. Nevertheless, she could not decide to go out. She would put her coat on, go to the door, and then, with her hand on the latch, she would hesitate. The thought of the street outside was depressing. Why should she go? There was no purpose. When Danny's call came, she was quick to accept, thankful to have a reason to leave, an appointment at a certain time, a certain location.

The Italian restaurant where they met, a small, family place, was close by, but Mary had never been there before. Danny seemed to know everyone. None of the diners were especially well dressed; none of them were grubby or disheveled. Most of them were middle-aged or older. Village, not SoHo.

The lights were soft; the voices were not harsh; and the background music was familiar and muted. Danny, without asking, had ordered a drink for her—a bocce ball, he said. There was a lot of orange juice, a taste of almonds, and it didn't seem to be very strong; she found herself relaxing very quickly, and before the food came, she was pouring out all her bewilderment and pain.

Danny was very easy to talk to. Even in her anguish, with her mind hazy from the effects of the drink, she was aware of the quiet sympathy flowing from this man who was almost a stranger. Since her father died, there had been no one she could talk to in quite that way; her mother, like the Baileys and Christophers, had believed troubles should be locked inside and not displayed even to close friends. Mildred had lost her own mother and her husband within a few months, but all her mourning had been private. Quent, gallant Quent, had joked even in the worst of his illness. Between the bouts of unbearable pain he would tease the RN, referring to her as Sairey Gamp, and threatening, if she did not cease her painful ministrations, to produce a hideous, deformed infant. "And I will leave it," he'd said balefully, "on your doorstep."

Now Mary found she could eat the lasagna. It was delicious. Lasagna was the one dish she had always craved the most when she was dieting. Danny smiled when she told him that, and she thought it was a very attractive smile. Regina said that he was a widower and had been for many years. That was surprising. Carol had told her that any halfway decent man was snapped up before he could look around. He didn't seem gay, but then, of course, one couldn't tell. A great guy, anyway . . .

Danny, with satisfaction, watched her enjoy her dinner. "Good. Eat regularly, take care of yourself, and stop fretting about the family. In any family, a murder causes terrible confusion. Not knowing the truth, people get all kinds of wild suspicions, utterly crazy ideas, and behave in every way unlike themselves. For a time they're *not* themselves."

"But they know me!" The cry was pure anguish. Some of the other diners turned their heads and then looked away.

"They don't know what happened," he went on steadily. "And the police always think first of the people who are the closest, with the opportunity, some kind of motive. The family become aware of that. It's disturbing, too far from their normal lives. They don't want to think about it. You're a long way away, the city girl. It's easier to—to draw the wagons into a circle."

Clearly, Mary wasn't comforted. He had ordered red wine with the lasagna and she was gazing down at the glass in her hand, looking at pictures he could not see.

"Mary," he went on, "I have some leave coming. Starting on the first. I'm going up to Bathsheba and I'll talk to people there, people who've given statements, anyone else I can find with something to say."

"Can you do that?" Mary asked, and heard Quent's voice: "You can but you may not."

Danny was thinking much the same thing. He could, but Bassett wouldn't like it. He could raise a rumpus. Hine, who was a man for the book, with a mania for keeping the squad out of trouble, would go up like a rocket. Danny was touched that Mary, in all her grief, could pause to think of police problems. She seemed to understand. Some Rafferty relation, perhaps, had been on the job. With affectionate amusement, now, he could remember Joan's battle with the Department, which had lasted all their married life.

"It's okay," he said. "I'm doing it on my own time."

Assisting defense counsel. And that brought him to the point.

"Mary," he said, and hesitated. She was drinking her wine and looking more peaceful, and he hated to disturb that. But it had to be done. "I'm pretty sure they'll be summoning a grand jury. And you'll have to testify. I think you should be in touch with a lawyer. I know a good man up there, someone who can handle Kramer."

He avoided saying "a criminal lawyer." Mary didn't question him. "You gave Kramer a statement, remember?"

"Yes. It was going to be after I went up there—after I went to the morgue. But then they asked me to go back later."

"You should have had a lawyer with you, Mary."

"They said I could. But I didn't need a lawyer. I just told him what I told the police. There was nothing else I could say."

After the coffee, in the dim lamplight, he wrote out Bostwick's name and telephone number. Mary received the slip of paper calmly. She didn't seem to grasp all the implications, but there was time for that. Bostwick would handle her gently. Danny still remembered the case of Nancy Fallone, a Queens housewife who had been suspected of killing her husband, a wife beater. When she was summoned to appear before a grand jury, the terrified woman had committed suicide. And later it was found that the guy was mixed up in the rackets and it had been an ordinary mob rubout.

He took Mary home, and when he left he wished he could have stayed, to be with her when the effects of good food and drink and some companionship wore off and fear and suspicion crept in. Boy scout, he told himself. Who was he kidding?

That evening Captain Bassett dined early, with some formality, though he was alone in his house in Burgoyne. It was something he did often. He enjoyed the quiet and he loved the old Bassett house, which he had bought back from the family who had held it since the Twenties. It was not one of the large houses in Burgoyne, but it was one of the oldest and beautifully proportioned. He had restored it with care. Now he ate his meals at a long oak table under the original ceiling beams in the dining room, and in the summer he looked out across the rolling green hills of Burgoyne.

He liked to recall that it was from this house that his ancestor had ridden out to attend the Convention of Poughkeepsie. Those were the days, he often remarked, when politics was conducted by intelligent men in rational discourse. He was proud of his county's part in the founding of the republic.

And despite the present state of the nation, he had arranged his personal life well. Since his last promotion, his work at the Bureau of Criminal Investigation had been supervisory and administrative and he could, to a great extent, control his time. His investigators were competent men and it had been many years since he had taken physical charge of a case—until the disappearance of the Christopher children. His personal intervention there had been by his own choice and decision. Colonel Mayhew, his superior and an old friend, had not demurred.

Soon he would retire and everything was arranged. His domestic affairs were simple; a local woman came in to clean and did a thorough job, and she would come in an extra day a week to take care of the additional chores. He would run for mayor of Burgoyne; he would be next president of the local chapter of the Red Cross and when Boy Burgoyne stepped down as Master of the Hounds, as he constantly threatened to do, Gordon Bassett would take his place. He would not regret the end of his BCI career in the New York State Police. Honorable service, but after so many years it seemed a perpetual cleaning out of the Augean stables—nothing was better, only worse. Time to give place to a younger, ambitious man, willing to wade through the muck.

Coffee cup in hand, he stood at the window and gazed out, only half seeing the dun-colored grass of late winter, the twilight settling over the distant hills. The Pemberthy case had been the high point of his career, and he had prepared well for it. Solid work, meticulous investigation. It would be fitting if his last big case was the conviction of another murderer— Mary Christopher, perpetrator of a crime more heinous than that of Françoise Pemberthy. A woman who killed her own children. A cold-blooded monster who should not escape.

Kramer was still hanging back. The case, he said, was not complete. Bassett believed that the evidence he had would convince a jury, convince them from the opening of the trial. There had been no sign of violence in that house. Nothing to show the presence of an intruder. Yet someone had gone to the closet, gotten the children into their coats, and taken them out of the house, unprotesting, into the pouring rain. The boy was *nine*. The mother's story of an abduction by some unknown pedophile was trash.

Besides that, Bassett was convinced that the family was hiding something. Hayes, who'd helped in the taking of statements, had suspected the same thing. "But it might be just that they feel certain she did it, but don't want to say so. Quentin's wife. All that stuff."

Nevertheless, Bassett thought there was more. And once they were on trial, the truth would come out. People like the Baileys and the Christophers might be reluctant to come forward, but on the witness stand they would not lie. Kramer, if he wasn't such a wimp, would have had it out of them by now. But Kramer had ambitions to be a state senator and didn't want to put a foot wrong.

He had been against the arrest of Mary Christopher, then leaned toward it during the Crenshaw outcry, but now that the Crenshaw case was off the front pages, he was unsure again. Bassett looked at the morning paper, still on the side table where he had left it after breakfast. No mention of the Crenshaws from the first page to the last. A small accident at a nuclear plant had caught the public's attention and second to that was the exposure of a sex-abuse scandal in a large hospital.

From the first, Bassett thought, since the bodies of the Christopher children had been found, the newspaper coverage had been muted. He wondered how much that was due to the influence of the family and the Burgoynes. The *Burgoyne Register*, certainly. But the Poughkeepsie *Journal* was something else. He had always had a fairly good relationship with the police reporter on the *Journal*. He went into his study, settled himself in a comfortable leather chair, and picked up the telephone. Captain Bassett had a long, interesting conversation with the reporter, Leslie Shane.

The Leslie Shane article caused a stir not only in the Hudson Valley but down in New York City, where it was picked up by the newspapers and by both the local and the network television stations. Briefly, but enough to agitate the would-be senator, Morton Kramer. The article condemned the lack of vigilance, of vigorous prosecution and law enforcement, leading to such horrors as the Crenshaw case and the death of an abused child in New York City. Appended to this was a question: "And what has been done to bring the Bathsheba murderer to justice? A child killer, still free to prowl along the roads and lanes of villages and towns, with no youngster safe on its own doorstep."

It was a hard-hitting article that made every parent shudder. As Bassett had expected, the wave of agitation hit Kramer and at last provoked him into action.

Mary had seen a reference to the article in a city paper. She had felt a certain relief—the writer was saying what she had thought from the beginning. Why *had* there been no great manhunt for the killer? It was wrong, terribly wrong, and she felt gratitude to Shane for urging on the police to do their duty. It was not her only relief. Mildred telephoned.

Her bright, cheerful voice always lifted Mary's spirits and she brought good news as well. "Mary, I spoke to William and Isobel. She's been home from the hospital awhile now and she's almost completely recovered. They're going to call you. Isobel feels so dreadful about the children—William didn't dare tell her at first. Mary, I told them what was happening and William had a lot to say.

"Of course, William could never believe that you— And neither could Isobel when she heard about it. But they are puzzled, very puzzled. They can't understand why Alice believes it."

Mary's heart gave a great thump. It was the first time that someone had said— But she saw Alice, her head bent, cowering in the aisle of the church; Alice, in the house at Spenser, her face twisted with revulsion, her hand up as if she were trying to protect herself from something abominable— It hadn't been said but she, Mary, had known. She had been exhausting herself, trying not to know.

"William said that Alice isn't crazy," Mildred told her. "Ill, but not feeble in her mind. And she wouldn't lie. But Alice told them there is absolute proof."

Mary and Mildred talked longer, puzzling over the mystery. And soon afterward William and Isobel called, warm and affectionate as they had always been, offering sympathy and help.

"It must be too awful for you in the apartment now," Isobel said. Her well-remembered voice was a little husky but full of welcome. "Why don't you come up and stay? I'm really better now and . . ."

Mary, her heart full, thanked her, promising that she would, sometime soon. "A dainty piece of porcelain," Quent had said, but Isobel was much more. She kept one of the most beautiful houses in Merivale; she was a noted hostess; she ran a local charity and the social life of her church; and she did it all in a seemingly effortless manner. Beside Isobel, Mary had always felt rather untidy, and re-membered with guilt any mess she and the children had left behind at home, but she had always admired and respected her. Now she was almost overwhelmed that Isobel, the invalid, was reaching out to help her.

William repeated her invitation. He was kind and thoughtful and Alice had said he had the best brain in the Bailey family. Mary saw him in her mind's eye, a fine-looking man, much more impressive, she had thought secretly, than the blustering, flamboyant Boy Bur-goyne. William owned some of the Bailey land that was still being farmed, but he was also an inventor and over the years had been quietly successful.

Later, when she told Danny about her great relief in finding the William Baileys unchanged, he nodded. "William Bailey. A guy who has to use his head. It figures."

He decided to talk to William and Isobel. He would see them as soon as his leave began. But before that the news came from Pough-keepsie. A grand jury was being summoned.

Danny was held up for a few days, testifying in court on a collar he had made months before. Mary went alone to keep the appointment

he had made for her with Bostwick. Driving along the familiar gran-
deurs of the Taconic Parkway, she felt the return of sick apprehension, as though the comfort she had found in Mildred, in William
and Isobel, had never been. She wished Danny could have come
with her. It was silly; he was a stranger, but somehow she felt better
when he was there. Of course, he had his own life. He did what he
could: Regina Valenti's nephew who was kind to her neighbor. Mary
hadn't wanted to see a lawyer, but he thought she should go. Almost
certainly, he said, she would be called to testify before the grand
jury. And although the lawyer could not be with her in the
courtroom, she should have his advice and support.

She was muddled in her mind about grand juries. Had Captain
Bassett found a suspect? Then surely someone would have told Alice,
to clear her sick fancies from her mind. Besides, Danny would have
known. If no suspect had been found, then it was all just a cha-
rade—perhaps to quiet the newspapers. As she entered Poughkeepsie, she wished she hadn't come. It brought back vividly her visit to
the hospital morgue, the bodies— She closed her eyes for a second
and a driver who wanted to pass honked his horn angrily.

Bostwick and Gaither was on the first floor of an old clapboard
house, set on a grassy plot in a street of two-story buildings, not a
threatening place. But once she was inside, she was surprised to find
herself in a crowd of clients, mostly very young men, many of them
teenagers. The only women were the receptionists and secretaries,
who were taking names, finding seats, and keeping the boys in some
kind of order.

"Mr. Gaither will see you soon."

They said the same to each person who entered, and the boys,
restless, would laugh and jump up to talk to each other, lean against
the walls, and pull out cigarettes despite NO SMOKING signs. Petty
criminals, she thought, though they all seemed amiable enough
now. It seemed strange to be waiting with them. But she didn't wait
long. Steve Bostwick, a man in his late thirties or early forties, with
a loping stride, a pleasant smile, and a hank of hair falling over his
forehead, came out to greet her and ushered her into his office.

"Sorry you had to wait, Mrs. Christopher," he said. "A phone call
that had to be dealt with."

His telephone rang again, but he pushed a button and the room
was quiet.

"Now, you tell me everything that's happened."

Later that day Danny had a call from Steve Bostwick.

"Listen, that lady is not in good shape. I couldn't just lay it on her all at once that Kramer will go for an indictment and that there's nobody to indict but Mommy. Not that he'll get anywhere. Oh, the grand jury will probably go for it, but when it goes to trial he'll fall on his face. I got one of my sources to find out if he has anything you haven't seen. But he's got plenty of nothing. The case against Mary is shit. Not one witness to place the kids in the car. I'd be happy to try this case. Especially if Kramer tries it himself. But she'll have to cooperate, put up a fight. Damn it, she looks frightened and guilty. What happened to the old Irish spirit?"

Lose a husband, lose two kids, lose the bonds with a family, and see, Danny thought. The "nice" woman who had gone into the streets to buy heroin for her dying husband had spirit. He wished he could fire that spirit now.

But that night Mary dreamed again. She was Medea, standing, with her hands dripping blood, over the bodies of her children while Quent, draped in a shroud, writhed with agony on his deathbed.

Once more, Danny's leave was postponed. Ed Mitchell, convalescent, had developed a viral infection, and Danny was caught up in another investigation. When Mary was summoned to testify, the William Baileys insisted that she go to them and they drove her over to Poughkeepsie for the two days of her testimony. Bostwick had already talked to William. "He's okay," he told Danny. "He'll be a great witness at the trial. The others have tried to get to him, but he's used to making his own decisions and he just doesn't buy it. I told him what's going to happen and they're keeping Mary until the indictment comes down. I'll be there; don't worry."

But Danny worried. After four days of testimony, two indictments were returned against Mary, charging her with second-degree murder. Bostwick was with her when she was booked and arraigned; William Bailey posted her bail. Bostwick, William, and Isobel had prepared Mary as much as possible for the events, and Bostwick reported that she seemed at least no worse than she had before, but still quiet, apathetic, sick—"as though she could vomit up the world," Bostwick added.

The New York tabloids had the story. The plastic-bag killer had found another victim, so Mary was spared the front page, but it was bad enough.

YUPPIE MOM INDICTED IN BATHSHEBA MURDERS.

MEDEA MOMMY was the worst: a full-length photograph of Mary on the courthouse steps. Kramer had gotten in the picture, his short, plump frame making Mary look taller. In her dark coat, with her long black hair framing her stark white face, she was a somber, dominant figure. The striking beauty of her facial bones only served to make her more remote: the dragon lady.

Parker, a young guy, the newest man on the squad, looked over his coffee cup at the story.

"Medea?" he asked. "What's that?"

Like most of the young, he was untroubled by the classics.

"An old goddess type," Danny said. "Murdered her kids when her husband took off."

"Like the Bloggs woman in Queens," Parker answered, still staring at the paper. "Nothing on that girl-chopper from your neck of the woods," he added, but he was wrong. There was an arrest that afternoon, so that took care of most of the network coverage that night. Mary appeared briefly on Channel 9 walking away from the court in Poughkeepsie—"A Village mother was indicted today in the Bathsheba killings"—but a shootout on Fifty-fourth Street between drug dealers in which three bystanders were killed, caught live on camera, was the big story.

It could have been worse.

William and Isobel wanted to keep Mary, but she longed to go back to the city. She explained to Danny that they were kind, heartwarming, and wonderful in every way—"I don't know how I could have got through that court business without them; they were both at my side everywhere they were allowed to go." And she loved their house: "It's so beautiful. But it's in Merivale, not so far from Burgoyne. Susan is very close, and— It's all part of up there," she said, wretched. "And just to think about it— I had to come back."

Danny sat with her for a little while in her apartment. In a few days he would be free and he was going "up there." He had talked to William about Mary's return. William had asked if Mary would be allowed to leave the county, and Bostwick told him that Kramer was making no difficulty as long as Mary didn't attempt to leave the state. And William was concerned about the effects of the publicity.

"We can keep her protected up here," he'd said. "But in the city . . . ?"

"I don't think people here will trouble her too much," Danny said, hoping he wasn't making a mistake. "It's a big place and people have a lot on their minds."

Aunt Regina and Connie Ferraro would look after her. Their network of friends and relations all over the Village would be helpful and so would the members of the two local churches. She might have to give up her hospital work—Danny had already had a word with her editor, a bright guy, to suggest that he ask her to hurry along with the book.

"Got it," Meyer had said at once. "I can tell her that we need it for the autumn list. Will do. We're behind her."

"No one scared off?" Danny asked.

"Well, a few are cautious. We're a conservative house; a good part of our list is academic books. But we don't like lynchings."

Danny had smiled a little. Meyer would see it that way. So often guys like him would bug the police to distraction; every collar was a lynching. But right now he felt grateful to Meyer. All the Meyers. Yet there was no lynch mob upstate. The family and the Burgoynes thought her guilty, but they hadn't wanted Mary to be punished. Bassett had wanted the arrest, but only as any police officer wanted a collar when he was sure he had the perpetrator. And in the absence of any other suspect, Danny knew that many police officers would have believed Mary guilty. The only question would have been, as it was now: Can we present sufficient evidence for conviction? And yet, though it made no sense, this time he was sniffing at the same stench that assaulted Meyer. The sweaty, foul stench of a lynch mob.

13

Mary felt she was trapped in an endless nightmare. The fear and horror that had possessed her when the children were missing, and after they were found, had never entirely subsided. Now they returned in full force. Bostwick's calm assurances and William and Isobel's warmth and affection had kept her from breaking down, but after Danny left that night she was desolate. She hadn't slept for two nights and at last, exhausted, she fell into a restless sleep. At two in the morning she woke up, full of rage, shouting, "It's all wrong; it's all wrong."

Sobbing with harsh tears, she called Danny.

The detective was used to sudden awakenings. He listened to Mary, relieved to hear her angry at last. Early next morning, after he had checked in with the squad, he met Mary in a coffee shop downtown. It was a big, rather drab place, serving the workers from local businesses: doormen and drivers, salesclerks, deliverymen, messengers, people in a hurry who wouldn't be likely to stare at and perhaps recognize the woman with a scarf around her head, tinted glasses, and no makeup.

Danny had suggested the change in her appearance; she had obeyed. Her fire was gone. As he saw her waiting patiently, she seemed subdued again. But this time he questioned her hard, as he would any other witness, point by point. Events. Relationships. Especially Lesska and Burgoyne. Burgoyne had been called before the grand jury. Bostwick had sent Danny the photographs from the

Poughkeepsie *Journal*. A lion-headed aristocrat, standing in front of the courthouse as if he owned it. There was something familiar about his face, yet Danny knew he had never seen him before. A teasing resemblance to—someone. The identity was elusive.

Lesska had not appeared. He had been in the hospital—an appendectomy, Bostwick had learned. Danny thought it very convenient. Elective surgery? An appendix could grumble for years. Lesska, the hero. Burgoyne's man.

Mary spoke of Boy Burgoyne, respected widower, landowner, citizen.

"So that's all you know about that big showoff?" Danny questioned.

"Well, showoff—" She hesitated. "He just naturally looks like that. Larger than life. Impressive. And his voice—Alice calls him Roaring Boy."

"Why didn't they marry?"

"I think they liked things just the way they were. Boy seemed happy as a widower. Alice—she loved Joe, but after he died I think she enjoyed, in a way, being master as well as mistress in her own house. And Boy, she said, used up a lot of air. But she's fond of him. Flattered, a little—people admire him, up there. Master of the hounds. A crack shot. A good sailor. He keeps a yacht, downriver, the *Emma III*."

People around them were coming and going. No one stopped in here to linger at this hour of the morning. Everyone hustling for a buck, Danny thought. A world away from a place like Burgoyne.

"And he has the devoted Lesska," Danny said dryly. "Wearing himself out in his old age for his kind master."

Mary was not observing the flux around them, and her attention was only in very small part on their conversation. The hand holding her thick coffee cup was trembling, and her blue gaze was clouded with introspection.

"Lesska's healthy enough," she said. "Of course, you haven't met him. Although he's thin and not tall he's strong. I've seen him lift heavy tools and equipment alone with those big hands of his when he's working on cars in the Burgoynes' garage. Though he's timid, in a way. I remember"—the tone of her voice changed as she recalled a time before the murders; he had heard that same change before; it belonged to a world she could live in, dream in—"years ago, Boy was taking Alice and me to the Burgoyne Playhouse. His father had put up some of the money for the building when the theater got started. So it's always been a bit special, arriving with Boy. When we got there a white dog with tan patches was running along the sidewalk, off the leash. We knew that dog, a Jack Russell terrier, and it was nasty tempered. A woman on Maple Road complained that it had bitten her child, but she hadn't actually seen it and the child couldn't describe the dog well enough for anyone to be sure. But the owner had been told to keep it on the leash in town.

"Lesska opened the car door—I think it startled the dog because it jumped up at Lesska as Boy was getting out. Lesska howled and kind of ran backward—it looked funny, although he was hurt. Boy just leaned over and cuffed the dog and it ran off. He was wearing a beautiful pearl gray suit and there wasn't a mark on it. Boy was totally unruffled. Lesska's clothes were ripped and his hand was bleeding, so I suggested we take him to a doctor, but Lesska stared with those pale eyes and didn't answer.

"Boy just said, 'Don't worry about Lesska; he'll take care of himself. No puff pastry, eh, Lesska?'

"And Boy smiled that radiant smile and swept into the theater with Alice on one arm and me on the other in full glory.

"So there's nothing unusual, really, about Boy and Lesska. They suit each other. But I always thought more of Lesska after that. When you think of him, risking his life over and over—and he a timid man. Noble, really. I asked Alice, afterward, if the dog had been tested for rabies. He was okay, I guess. Alice said, 'Oh, Lesska was bitten by a sane dog.' And she giggled."

"I thought you said she liked him."

"She always spoke well of him. But with Alice—well, laughs just bubble up. When things strike her as funny. The same as Quent."

She spoke as though her husband were still alive. Perhaps, Danny thought, for her he was. How long had it been for Danny Valenti before he was drawn to a woman after Joan died? Not four years . . .

Suddenly, Mary turned her full gaze upon him. "They'll never find the murderer now, will they? No one will search anymore. Steve Bostwick said Kramer had to do something, so this grand jury is what he did. That means the investigation is over, doesn't it?"

"No," he told her, "it isn't. Bassett's not looking for anyone else at the moment but I'll make my own investigation and Bostwick has his ear to the ground. Whoever did it will be feeling pretty confident right now," he added. "That's the time when these characters make mistakes."

Mary stammered through her thanks. She looked grateful, puzzled, worn. *Miss Valenti's nephew who was so kind.* Did she guess how he felt? Probably. She wouldn't want to think about it. It was over forty degrees that morning and the sun was shining, but it was still hard winter for Mary.

Unthinking, she had pushed the scarf back from her face. A pulse was beating in her throat and she seemed so very vulnerable. "I got something in the mail," she told him. "An envelope, with a piece cut from a newspaper in it. About me."

Danny was seized with a desire to find whoever had sent the article and kick him or her in the teeth. Anonymous correspondents, stabbing at the walking wounded. It was just a few short paragraphs in a Poughkeepsie paper, next to a photograph of Mary in her wedding gown on the arm of her bridegroom. Mary's background: parents deceased; her father, Jim Rafferty, a firefighter with an alcohol problem; her mother, an office cleaner; her brother, killed in a gang fight at age eighteen.

"True? About your brother?"

Mary nodded. "I didn't think to tell you. It was so long ago, before I married Quent. Poor Richie. He wasn't really bad," she said hopelessly. "Pop was . . . not much of a help there. And Mom was too strict. The neighborhood was getting run down and there were street gangs. A lot of it was just dressing up, strutting about—a bunch of showoffs. If Richie had lived to be a bit older—but he didn't. He and the other kid were both hurt. The other kid survived; Richie died. Mom never got over that. I think that's why she went back to Ireland, after Pop died."

The article went on to say that Mary had married Quentin Christopher, only son of the Christopher family of Spenser, long established in the area. It gave the ages of the couple when they married. Nothing but the truth. But the people who read it and saw the photograph would think that Quentin Christopher had married a woman much younger than himself, a very good-looking woman, from a trashy family. Much younger.

Some of the people who read that paper would be among those

summoned as jurors at the trial. But it would all have come out anyway. No privacy for defendants in a murder case.

Danny took her out of the coffee shop and called a taxi to take
her home. She was bundled up again, and as he helped her inside
she was stooped like an old woman. Last night she'd cried, "It's all
wrong." The indictment had forced her to see what she had refused
to believe. Now she had withdrawn again, but the knowledge was
still there. He wondered if she would ever recover.

The next morning Danny drove upstate, following a plan he had
been working on for some time. He retraced Mary's route in reverse,
stopping and asking questions. Almost everyone he spoke to had
been interrogated and reinterrogated by Bassett and his investigators, but Danny's questions were different. He was inquiring not
about Mary's car but about Boy Burgoyne's Cadillac.

After Brewster, he stayed on the highway, bypassing Bathsheba,
to take in the gas station where Mary had changed the windshield
wipers. It wasn't too busy. He was lucky that the mechanic who had
put them on was still working there. "These guys come and go," the
owner told him. "Charlie!"

Charlie, a blond, hefty guy, nearer forty than thirty, by this time
was sick of giving statements. He'd taken a lot of razzing, it seemed,
for his gawping at the Christopher woman and not noticing two kids
bouncing around. After testifying before the grand jury, he was obviously sorry he remembered her at all. He certainly didn't remember anything about a black Cadillac. "Look, it was a busy night.
Real heavy rain. Two guys out on breakdowns. Sure, I remember the
looker in the white car. But for the rest—Caddys, Chevys, Fords—
you name it. We probably had them all. But I wouldn't remember."

And nothing could shake him. Danny looped back to Bathsheba,
but that didn't turn out to be a whole lot of help. He found Tony's
Tavern, and its owner, Jerry Crump, who lived on the place. It was
late in the morning, but he was red-eyed and unshaven. He was
surly about talking to a detective from New York who was working
for the defense, but Jerry Crump was a talker and eventually he
talked. But he said nothing he hadn't said in his previous statements.
He was the only bartender and had no time to look out at passing
cars on the road.

Danny sympathized. A bartender's hours, he remarked, were as bad as a detective's. "No time for yourself. And the women don't like it."

He had opened a floodgate. But nothing came out about a black Cadillac on the evening of the murders.

"Try Jack Curlew," Crump advised him. "He's out of a job right now, so you should catch him at home. He's the one who saw the white car. See, any other cars that were parked would be from folks around here and Jack would know them. If there was a big, new Caddy he would spot it."

Bathsheba was the kind of town, or maybe it was a village, that no sooner were you in it, you were out of it. A short row of stores, traffic lights, and you were on your way to another place much like it. Houses were scattered through the surrounding scrub. As Crump had predicted, he found Jack Curlew at home. He lived with his mother, a woman in her sixties, who looked as though she didn't expect much of anybody. She let Danny in with a resigned air that made him wonder if she was accustomed to detectives coming and asking for her son. The house was neat and clean, but it appeared run down. Jack Curlew wasn't too active about the place.

When his mother called him, he looked in at the door, dressed in undershorts and a T-shirt. He slouched away, and came back covered by a short bathrobe. In his mother's house, Curlew wasn't as quick with the sexual allusions. He had noticed Mary's car when she went out. There were a few cars in the parking lot, two Chevys, a Ford Escort, a station wagon, a Nissan—he knew them all. The white car was parked not far away, near the stretch of bushes where the bodies were found. He hadn't seen any other car, nothing on the road or parked by it.

"If there'd been another car, I would have seen the headlights, but there wasn't nothing."

Unless they were out, Danny thought.

"Where was your car?"

"I didn't bring my car. It was in the garage at Rattinger's Corner, getting the wheel alignment checked for inspection. I met Amy Jarvis coming out of the drugstore and we went to Tony's together in her Toyota."

Danny made the rounds of the houses close to the road by the tavern, but no one remembered seeing a black Cadillac that night or

the plate number BBB100. Amy Jarvis, who had made the acid remarks about Mary, looked sick in the morning. Puffy feet, puffy
eyes. Her hair was too brightly dyed and she was haggard. Danny,
who had learned to be as winning as the best con man, got her to
talk in a friendly way.

Her husband had left her, ten years after their marriage. She had
worked as a nurse's aide to bring up her children. It was lonely for a
woman in the country. To Amy, who had driven Jack Curlew to
Tony's Tavern for an evening of entertainment, the vision of Mary,
young, vital, beautiful, with the local men buzzing around her, must
have been a cold slap in the face. Amy's shoulders were stooped and
her knuckles swollen, and Danny felt an unwanted surge of sympathy. She was very willing to linger in talk with him, but she had
nothing useful to add. Yes, she had seen Mary fall, but after that she
was out of sight. She hadn't noticed any cars. "This place is strictly
nowhere," she told him, shrugging. "My ex—he took off for L.A.
Doing well for himself, I hear. Got married again. Some young
chick."

"Mary Christopher is a widow," he told her. "Her husband died of
cancer."

She gave him a keen look. He had been up front, telling her he
was working for defense counsel. "Well, it ain't easy. A woman
alone."

Bostwick could do something with her, Danny noted. Take the
edge off her as a prosecution witness. But it didn't help him, looking
for one Caddy on the road so many weeks later. A pity Lesska hadn't
used the de Lorean. Mary said Boy liked to drive that himself.

Danny made the rest of the journey to Spenser. There was no gas
station attendant on the route with any memory of a black Cadillac
driven by someone resembling Lesska. Mary had found a snapshot of
Alice with Lesska in the background, by the car. Danny had circled
Lesska and shown it, but it hadn't helped. The responses were similar.

"The police were here before. But that was about a white car."

"This the same case? The kids?"

He drove slowly around Spenser. The Christopher house, he saw,
was isolated on the tree-lined lane. There was no other house and on
the other side there was a long stretch of orchard. Part of the
Johnson farm, Mary had told him, but the farmhouse was too far off

for anyone there to catch even a glimpse of what went on in that lane, even in the daytime. Behind the Christopher house was the garage, and then the tennis court, set in a stretch of woods.

He turned back to the Johnson land and rang the farmhouse doorbell. Jane Johnson came to greet him. An angular, fresh-faced woman in her sixties, she was baking for a family get-together. But she was pleased to talk to someone from the defense, and took him into her kitchen. "They must be mad down there in Poughkeepsie," she said, slapping the dough with floury hands. "What mother would do such a thing? Certainly not a girl like Mary Christopher. Quentin was a fine man and they were a good family. I would have kept Linda and Tom here as long as Mary wanted, she knew that, but we all thought Alice was much better. It was some stranger got hold of those poor mites while Alice was poking around in the garage."

She rolled out piecrust with an easy, deft motion, her hands seeming to work of their own accord while she gave him her attention. Savory smells came from a huge pot on the stove and Danny remembered he had left without breakfast that morning.

"I'll tell you, I blame Boy Burgoyne some for what happened," she said. "Getting Alice to fuss around looking for those old maps. Why, he's right in Burgoyne and they have copies of all that stuff at the town hall if he wanted to make a search. Just like him, to get someone else to do his work for him. People around here think the earth of the Burgoynes," she added, "but I've always figured Boy for a lazy man."

She was relieved to learn that Mary had a police officer working for her and she insisted that he drink a cup of coffee and sample her apple turnovers. "The last of our own apples until the fall."

Danny was thoughtful when he left Jane and drove along the road to Burgoyne. He was driving slowly, looking about him, when he caught a glimpse of a large three-story house, well set back from the road, surrounded by tall trees. From Mary's description, it must be the Burgoyne house. She had spoken of it as if it were in the town, but it was physically separate, on the western approach. He stopped at the side of the road and looked through the trees. Handsome. A lot of house for one man. Many houses of that size were turned into nursing homes; it was too expensive to keep them privately. The drive was on the side, leading to the back of the house. Walking around, Danny could see the garage, and the floor above it where

Lesska lived. The housekeeper, Mary had said, didn't live in. No one but Boy would have known when Lesska drove up that night. Unless someone was passing, just by chance.

As he got back into his car, Danny was speculating just who might have been passing that evening, that night. A shopkeeper, closing up after the help had gone? A doctor on a call? Any resident of Burgoyne who had decided to drive somewhere else for dinner?

He had as much chance of success as a ticket buyer in a lottery, but he made inquiries anyway. They were not well received in Burgoyne. Nor was Danny Valenti. When he told the shopkeepers that he was inquiring about a black Cadillac, license plate number BBB100, they stiffened at once. All of them said, in their various ways, that they saw the car frequently but could not remember seeing it on that day or night in particular. He tried several houses, but the owners were reluctant to speak to him at all. Danny remembered the old days in Little Italy. *Omertà*, Anglo-style.

His last attempt was the one doctor with a brass plate on the main street, Marcus Bristow, M.D. Bristow was a man of about his own age, comfortable in a good suit and a well-furnished office. A Persian rug on the floor, a desk that was a fine old piece, and an unobtrusive telephone. The professions were doing well these days and Dr. Bristow in Burgoyne was enjoying the good life.

His manner was courteous until Danny began his questions on the Burgoyne car. Dr. Bristow froze, stared, and thawed only enough to remember an appointment at the hospital. "I do know the car, of course. Not too many chauffeur-driven vehicles these days. But I wouldn't remember any particular time or place. And on December 28"—he took a diary from his desk drawer—"Yes. I was at a meeting in Highland Falls, the gerontology group. An association of physicians in the area who find that much of their work is with the aged. An exchange of information and views . . . I'm sorry I can't help you further."

When Danny left, Dr. Bristow, flushed, a little agitated, picked up the phone. He didn't buzz his secretary; instead he found himself calling Ernest Burgoyne directly. His actions irritated him, because he felt compelled to make them. But why? he asked himself. Why should he bother? It was natural enough that everyone concerned would be investigated. Why should he feel an obligation—?

Ernest answered personally. And Dr. Bristow told him what had happened. "A detective. A sandy-haired fellow from the city."

Danny drove away, slowly, reluctantly. Burgoyne was a citadel. Boy's town. If anyone here knew anything, it would take a battle to get it out. He gave a mental shrug at the irony. The questions he had asked were merely to clear the ground. If someone disinterested had reported seeing Lesska and the car at 5:50, as Boy claimed, then the two of them were telling the truth and Lesska was cleared. But Danny didn't believe it was the truth. And now there was only one way left to find out. As it so often happened, it was the long way. He turned back toward Bathsheba and checked into the nearest motel.

It was a routine procedure. Just a matter of going to every house in the area, making sure he met the people who had been around on the evening of the murder, and questioning each and every one about the black Cadillac. He didn't limit himself to the town; he took in a ring of homes and villages around it.

A lot of people did remember that night: the news of the missing children and the later discovery had imprinted it on their minds. But except for the people who lived in the town, none of them had gone near the place. It wasn't on any good roads and there was nothing in Bathsheba to draw visitors. Not even Tony's Tavern. "A dump. Rotten food. People go to the Red Rooster or Gurney's Inn."

One man had gone to visit his in-laws there, but he only remembered seeing a trailer truck that crowded him on the road. And Danny had no success with Bathsheba's residents. "Round here you see more pickup trucks, station wagons, Chevys, small cars. Not many Caddys and that's the truth."

One of the last men he spoke to admitted to having seen a black Cadillac, though not in Bathsheba itself. Dick Krantz was a man in his fifties, turning gray, with a few pounds too many under his belt, an office man, a supervisor for the telephone company. He looked sharp enough, alert, and he had a quick temper.

"I was on the road coming home from Schuyler's Junction," he said. "Sheets of rain and I was stuck in a line behind a crawling truck. When the car in front of me finally got a chance to pass I tried to follow, but this damned big black Caddy came roaring up from behind and cut me off. If I hadn't been quick as all hell he would have sideswiped me—the bastard. I was so damned mad . . ."

Danny's spirits were sky high. If he could place Lesska near the scene, even if the guy hadn't seen the kids—"

"Did you see his license plate?" Danny asked in his official voice that betrayed none of his excitement.

"Did I? I tell you, I was so het up I meant to do something. But when it comes to it—what can you do? But I looked. I still remember. It was LAN718."

Chagrin came like a blow. Well, Danny thought, he couldn't expect to get so lucky. It was on Mary's route after she left Brewster. And Krantz would have been a good witness. But the number was not Burgoyne's, just a passing motorist's.

Before Danny returned to the city, he stopped at Merivale for a visit with William and Isobel. Their house, more than a century old, had dignity and charm, as did its owners. Isobel was an attractive woman, slender, but not bony; her pretty face, lightly made up, was graced with a frame of silver curls. William was a distinguished, handsome man, and that was the least to be said about this couple. They had brains and character and their support of Mary was solid and unwavering.

Danny lunched with them in the dining room that overlooked the Bailey land. They spoke of their outrage at Mary's indictment and their astonishment at the family's silent acquiescence.

"Even Susan," Isobel said unhappily. "She was always a favorite with us and a friend of Mary's."

Danny remembered the statement given by Susan Bailey Taylor. "Of course, the family was surprised when Quent married Mary. A city girl." No need to tell them that. Instead he told them of Jane Johnson's remark about Boy Burgoyne.

"Boy Burgoyne," William said with disgust. "Involved in this from start to finish. Why did he have to testify before the grand jury? He wasn't there when it happened."

"But Lesska was," Danny pointed out. "And he wasn't subpoenaed because he was in the hospital. I suppose Boy testified about the time he sent him to Spenser and the time he returned."

Isobel had gone to get the coffee. The two men looked at each other in silence. Then William spoke about the business of the trial.

He was prepared to take care of Mary's legal fees. "I doubt that the Christopher Trust will cover it." He inquired about Bostwick as trial counsel and whether he would need any assistance.

"If only Alice would testify for Mary—"

"But she won't." Isobel was pouring the coffee. A pleasant scent came from her wrist, a small pleasure that softened, for a moment, the harsh truth. "William and I went over, to make one last try. She wouldn't talk to us, Danny. She looked so ill we could hardly finish. Boy and Fiona were with her and they looked furious, but we didn't care about them. They were very rude to Mildred—I expect you heard."

Despite the pleasure of meeting William and Isobel, Danny, on his way back to the city, had a familiar, unpleasant sensation: the feel of an investigation that had not worked out. The case was still clear in his mind. Three people at the scene of the abduction. Two of them could not have committed the crime. But he couldn't lay a glove on Lesska. Lesska, the hero. The timid hero.

That night he didn't see Mary. He had returned to New York in time to get an unwelcome message: Ed Mitchell had died. Without warning, he had suffered a major heart attack and was dead when he reached the hospital. A service was being held that evening at a church in Queens. Danny drove out to meet other men from the squad and some of the other elite squads who had known Mitchell. In the front pews were men from the local precinct where Ed had worked as a young patrolman, and all his family and friends. It was a moving service and afterward, when Danny had paid his respects to Ed's wife, whom he had met before, Hine got him alone.

"I know you've got a lot more time coming, Valenti, but—"

"I got you. Okay."

Hine looked relieved. "We're really up the creek. I don't know when we'll get a replacement. I'll do my best. Maybe you can take a few days."

"Don't worry about it."

The case was in Bostwick's hands now. And Bostwick wasn't worried. "I wouldn't be surprised," he had told Danny, "after the excitement dies down, if the charges were dropped." But Danny wasn't satisfied. What then? Unless the killer was found, people would always whisper. "Well, lack of evidence, you know. But who else could it have been?" Not the way that Mary should have to live. If that black Caddy had been the one Lesska was driving— But it wasn't. Krantz had been all too clear about that. Still, Danny determined to find out more about Lesska.

Leaving the church, he saw a few guys from Missing Persons and Keegan among them. Keegan lived in Queens and they went to a neighborhood restaurant for dinner, a steak and lobster place. "You'll like it. Cheaper than Manhattan," Keegan said, and he was right. That was about the only agreement they had over dinner except that Mitchell was a good guy and would be missed.

"You've got that Lesska on the brain," Keegan told him. "Why are you knocking yourself out with him?" Danny noticed that Keegan didn't ask why he was knocking himself out for Mary Christopher. It didn't take a great mind to guess.

"He had no motive for killing those kids. Slapping them, maybe, for fooling around in the car, pulling their seat belts off—"

Keegan had been off the case once the bodies were discovered, but that hadn't ended his interest. There weren't that many kids missing and found murdered.

"Busting the cervical vertebrae like that, on both of them—it couldn't have been an accident. You've got two deliberate killings."

"The boy was nine," Danny said thoughtfully. "Not exactly a chicken's neck. If his mother was trying to break his spine, wouldn't he have fought back?"

Keegan gazed at him in exasperation. "Look, at first that case wasn't even a Missing Persons. Just an old lady fussing about the telephone. Nobody took Mary Christopher in to see if she had bruises or scratches. Nothing. The kid could have fought like the devil and she might have had marks all over and no one the wiser."

Danny had to make an effort to consider a suspect, not Mary, just a suspect. "The autopsy didn't mention marks on the kids, either, except in the cervical area. And the breaks were clean. More like a pro's work than a housewife's."

Keegan wasn't impressed. "People think medical examiners are gods. Show me one report, and I can get another coroner to swear to the opposite. The kids were frozen for two weeks and then roughed up by the dog that found them."

But Keegan didn't know Mary. Everyone was impressed with Lesska, the hero. While Danny was up in Burgoyne he'd asked a few questions about Emil Lesska. People were as unwilling to discuss Boy

Burgoyne's chauffeur as they were to identify his car. "A fine man," was all he'd heard. "Wonderful with cars. Been with the Burgoynes for years."

Yet there had been one guy, he remembered, who hadn't been part of the chorus. When he stopped for gas at the station in Spenser, he had had a few words with the owner. A smiling, pleasant countryman, not too busy to pass the time of day with a customer, he hadn't become edgy when the city man asked about Boy's Cadillac. But on the night Tom and Linda had disappeared, he had not been at the station. "Took a few days off around Christmas. The kid was here, Johnny. Captain Bassett had him in and asked about cars but he didn't even remember seeing Mary Christopher go by. Raining like all get-out that night and Johnny, he would stay inside unless someone hollered. Loud."

Danny had asked about Lesska.

"Been with the Burgoynes one hell of a long time. They say he's a great mechanic. Works on cars for a lot of folks in town, on his own time." He looked up from the hose connection and glanced at Danny. "Harder than hell to get a decent mechanic these days, even with wages what they are. Beats me why a guy like that tails after the Burgoynes; Boy don't pay nobody more than he has to."

He had taken Danny's money and smiled. "Mary Christopher, she's a nice lady. Damned shame about the kids."

A shrewd guy, behind the easy manner.

As he drove back into Manhattan, Danny was wondering why Lesska hadn't wanted to testify. Or why the Burgoynes hadn't wanted him to testify. Something to do with the "missing piece of evidence" that Bassett dreamed about, evidence that the family were gallantly suppressing?

The next day, he arranged for a check on Slade Memorial about Lesska's hospitalization. Hospitals were stubborn about releasing information, but he had his ways. Word came back, not straightforward but bent a little, like so much that came from Burgoyne. Lesska had suffered from pain in the area of the appendix for some time. X rays had not revealed any inflammation, but the pain had become acute and his physician, Dr. Bristow, had decided on immediate surgery. He had made a good recovery.

Inconclusive, Danny thought, and then he was caught up in the press of work. He had had an unexpected piece of luck. Two years ago he had arrested an evasive woman who worked a new version of the old handkerchief switch, but to his disgust, the case had been thrown out of court. Recently she had pulled another job and vanished. She had gotten clean away with the money and could not have been traced, but she was a devoted New Yorker. After a cautious interval, she took advantage of modern technology and wired the money from Florida to a New York City bank. That electronic transfer made it a federal case and the FBI were ready to move in. Danny was needed only to identify the suspect and that was a simple job, a stakeout in the lobby of a new hotel.

When it was over, Danny finished typing up his report in the squad room and then he looked over the notes on Lesska, after his talks in Burgoyne. "Such a hard-working man. You always see him working on something." . . . "Never has time for social get-togethers. Maybe once or twice a year at the church supper. He tends to business."

"Such a sweet woman," the victims had said of the swindler. "We couldn't believe . . ."

"A good organizer," one of the shopkeepers said wistfully. "Handles the upkeep of the big house, and helps out at Ernest's and Mrs. Derwent's. Yet he's never one minute late if Mr. Burgoyne wants to go here or there. I wish I could hire a man like that, I can tell you. But he's loyal to the family."

Lesska could have done well in the United States. Yet he'd chosen to be Burgoyne's servant. The guy at the garage had put his finger on it. Something didn't fit. But Danny was drawn out of his rumination by Sweeney Hine, who shouted for him to come into his room. "Get over here!" Gratitude for the postponed leave was forgotten. Hine was in a black rage.

"What the hell have you been doing upstate?" The commander soon made it clear he didn't know where Burgoyne was and didn't want to know. "A Captain Bassett from Merivale has been hollering plenty over the phone. Claims you're interfering with witnesses in a Dutchess County case, hindering his investigation; threatens to go to the commissioner, and a lot more besides. What the hell is going on here? Tell me the truth and get it over."

I'm in love with the accused woman, and I'm going to get her cleared, no matter who's in the way. And how would Sweeney Hine like that truth? Yet he was right to be mad, Danny thought, after a surge of anger of his own. Doing his job. Protecting the squad.

"A little job on my vacation. A bit of investigating for defense counsel. All strictly on the up and up. Bassett's making noises because he's got a rotten case. He needs to have something to complain about."

Hine was still frowning. "It's a gray area, you know that. Too easy to go over the line. We've got enough manpower problems without you getting in fights in other jurisdictions. Christ, don't we have enough grief down here without you looking for it in the boondocks?"

He looked at Danny thoughtfully for a moment.

"Wasn't that Matt Keegan's case? Missing Persons? Two kids?"

Danny nodded.

"Rotten business," Hine remarked. "But it's got nothing to do with you. Stay out of it. Keep your nose clean. I mean it. Remember, you've got a lot to lose."

Danny knew what he had to lose. And he knew Hine meant what he said. But Danny also knew that he couldn't stay out of it. Even if he ended up in uniform. Somewhere in the Bronx.

14

There was silence from Poughkeepsie. Aunt Regina, talking to her nephew, was astringent. "And what are all you police officers doing? That girl will go into a deep depression and she will never recover. I have seen such cases."

Danny doubted that Regina had known any women indicted for murder, but nevertheless, he agreed. Mary had stopped her work at the hospital. She rarely went out; she ordered food by telephone. Her doctor prescribed tranquilizers, but she refused them—they interfered with her work on Quent's book.

The writing seemed to be her only grasp on reality. A strange reality—he had seen some of the manuscript. Ancient gods and goddesses, tormenting each other, trifling with mankind. At one time a parish priest would have forbidden such labors to a good Catholic girl. But Mary had long since left the Church and if the tricks of Hermes and the loves of Aphrodite calmed her mind, he was glad of them. Even if they tied her to the memory of Professor Christopher. In his photograph he looked like a middle-aged preppy, a Burgoyne man. But he had married Mary Rafferty from Queens, Danny reminded himself. He wasn't a jerk, jealous of the dead, like Danny Valenti.

Despite his return to the squad, Danny had been investigating Lesska. "Chauffeur on the brain," Keegan said. "Or the butler did it."

Lesska, the Catholic who had saved many Jews. Sacrificed himself and his own family. It didn't fit in with the misogynist who was a bootlicker for the Burgoynes. Like the old handkerchief switch, the cover was similar but this was the wrong bundle.

The INS had accepted Lesska. But they would have been interested only in whether or not he was entitled to a special exemption from quota restrictions: a matter of identity papers and recommendations. Recommendations that, in this case, were instigated by Boy Burgoyne. There could be more information available. Mary said that he had been in a refugee camp near Vienna. Probably most of the refugees were Jews and some Jewish organization would have been there.

He telephoned an acquaintance, Seymour Roth, a fund-raiser for the United Jewish Appeal, and asked for his suggestion. "HIAS deals with immigrants," Roth told him. "I know some HIAS people. Emil Lesska, you say. And he's not Jewish. I'll see what I can get on him, if anything, and I'll be in touch."

While Danny waited to hear from Roth, he made more inquiries about Boy Burgoyne, architect. He went to the major architectural firms in New York and inquired at the architectural schools of the universities. The result was interesting. No one had any knowledge of a single building of note designed by Bartholomew Beaulieu Burgoyne. He was dismissed with a word. "Derivative. He does adaptations of colonial houses for the new burghers of Dutchess County."

So, Danny thought. He was just a big fish in a small pond. A big blowhard. An odd choice for a woman like Alice, who, according to Mary, was, or had been, sharp and bright. But he *had* been the local eminence.

The response from the HIAS was less to his taste. HIAS was enthusiastic about Lesska. No doubt about who and what he was. He had saved many women, children. "A true hero. In a small way, as a private person, he was a Raoul Wallenberg, one who escaped, thank God. He should have been given some award. Years, decades, ago, he was invited to be guest of honor at a dinner, but he declined. Said that he liked to live quietly and to put those days behind him. The memory of his lost family . . . Of course, the committee understood."

He hadn't been hero enough to testify. And Mary said he had no liking for children. Yet in the episode with the dog in Burgoyne that she had described, Lesska, though frightened, had been stoical about his wounds. "No puff pastry," Boy had said. Boy, who knew him well. But for all that, Danny just couldn't buy it. Not that creep. Raoul Wallenberg!

He called Seymour Roth again. "You're absolutely certain?" he asked. "People have given themselves good cover stories since Adam. The guy wanted to jump the quota."

Roth laughed. "HIAS has been watching these stories since Adam. The serpent was authenticated; it's Scripture. And Lesska—there were so many people who remembered him. The children of those he saved revere his name. There are documents, proof of all kinds. Lesska is impeccable."

Danny was gloomy and puzzled. Nothing worked out. The whole case was out of shape. He could find no useful evidence. Bassett, on his side, believed the family had evidence but were holding back. And Mildred said that Alice was convinced of Mary's guilt. *By what evidence?* No witness had come forward to say that the children were in the car with Mary, because they hadn't been in the car with Mary. By her first frantic phone calls, Alice had demonstrated that she didn't know whether or not the children were in the car. Lesska said Mary's car was dark. He didn't know if the children were there or not; he hadn't seen them. But perhaps he had told Alice something different. That must be it. Ninety-nine percent sure. Anything else was too far-fetched, some Bailey or Christopher or someone part of their tight little clan claiming that they had seen Mary on the road that night, returning to the city, and that they had seen the children. Perhaps imagining that they had. No, it was too unlikely. Those people would not care to lie under oath or present doubtful suppositions to public scrutiny.

He was still stuck with Lesska.

Meeting Keegan in the elevator riding down to the lobby, he told him of the frustration. "Doesn't fit? Doesn't fit your theory, you mean. You've got all the true faith, you jerk, of a middle-aged guy nuts about some young chicky-poo."

Keegan was laughing. Danny wished he'd kept his damned mouth shut.

A few days later, Danny was once again booking Handsome Harry. Harry had been out on bail and had made a quick pitch to a visiting widow from Columbus, Ohio. A lazy man, he had taken her to a pleasant small restaurant where he had courted his last victim and had been spotted by that lady, the very angry paralegal. The only difficulty had been persuading the new victim to make a complaint. Obviously she cared more for the man than her money, but the paralegal, backed up by some friends active in the women's movement and supported by Danny, convinced her.

Danny, stuck with a mound of paperwork, cursed both himself and Harry for diligence. And the widow might yet pull back when she got to court. It had happened before. He looked thoughtfully at the records of her depleted bank account. She had been looking for a co-op in the Big Apple and had left Columbus well heeled. And there were her hotel bills: she had entertained Harry in the bar and in her suite. Beds and bank accounts. The answer to most of the mysteries. Harry's hair might be getting a bit thin but he still had his smile and his swagger.

Sweeney Hine kept his depleted squad busy. Danny had meant to see Mary, but he didn't have the chance. He knew she wouldn't feel neglected, or feel that he had lost interest in her troubles. She knew about the job. Or perhaps she simply didn't care.

Mary called him early one morning before he left for work. She had heard from Isobel. "Bad news," she said, her voice faltering. "Alice is—is dead."

He arranged to meet her that night. He was delayed and she arrived first at the restaurant. From the doorway he caught an unexpected glimpse: for a moment she was a stranger, a wan, desolate creature, sick, feeble, her head resting on the wood panels of the wall.

There were no arrangements for a funeral, she told him. Isobel had said it would be a private burial, like the children's. Nor had any plans been made for a memorial service. "I expect there will be one. Isobel didn't tell me, but I can guess. The family don't want me there. It doesn't matter."

Her fingers crumbled some bread. Crumbs dropped to the tablecloth, but Mary didn't notice. Alice was gone. There would be no reconciliation. She was alone. He longed to take those hands, to press them, give her comfort. But he knew that he was the one who would be comforted. As for Mary . . . He knew she found some solace in his presence, a friendly police officer, an ally. Could there be more? It seemed indecent to think of love, of passion, in connection with that frail wraith of a woman. She trusted him. Was that close to affection? He put the foolish thought from his mind.

That night, in the interval of a troubled sleep, it came to him whom Boy Burgoyne resembled. Of course. Handsome Harry. Bartholomew Burgoyne of Burgoyne, descendant of an old English family of considerable wealth and distinction. And alone, in the darkness of his bedroom, Danny laughed.

The laughter did not survive the night. By morning, the resemblance of Boy to a common swindler—the air, the attitude more than anything else—was an oddity, without significance. Aunt Regina called him early in the squad room and asked him to pay her a visit. She gave him dinner, with some formality, but over the coffee she unburdened her mind and it was no sweet dessert. Regina was disappointed in Danny's failure to solve Mary's problem. Her expression was much like Sweeney Hine's when an extensive investigation came up with zilch.

"Mary, of course, says nothing. Whatever happens, she bears it. And now this." A small enameled spoon tinkled against the tiny porcelain coffee cup, evidence of her perturbation. She was talking of the death of Alice Christopher.

"It is very bad," she went on, "because Mary is a woman who pretends. But there is nothing she can pretend anymore."

Danny was startled. He also found himself angry. Surely Aunt Regina had not come to believe . . .

"She has lived a long time in pretense. Her husband died, but she lived like a woman with a husband; the children, the grandmother, they were the family. She went on just as she had before, caring for the children, visiting the grandmother as though her husband had gone away for a little while."

"Mary moved. She left the apartment where they had lived together," Danny remarked.

"She had to. In that place you can't stay if you are not connected to the university. But she did nothing else. Made no new life. She kept to her enclosed little world, the children, the family upstate. But she was not their blood, not even their own kind."

Danny remembered. Christopher country.

"Then the children were gone. She couldn't believe they were harmed till the bodies were found. And still their room in the apartment is the same, nothing cleared, nothing given to charity. What has she wanted all this time? To run to the mother. To be back in the old dream. But that mother is no longer her mother—and now she can't pretend it will ever be different."

Danny listened. What Aunt Regina said was true. She saw clearly. He went away more troubled than he had been before. Mary. She had clung to a vision, a mirage that turned to sand at the last, barren, empty desert. The daughter of Jim and Eileen Rafferty had never, herself, been part of "Christopher country," that human Disneyland of her imagining. Even the warmth and strength she had found in Mildred, and William and Isobel, came not from the family tie but from their essential decency and integrity, a refusal to see the unfortunate hounded. Rare qualities, the policeman knew, the salt of the earth. But could Mildred's buoyant compassion, William and Isobel's anxious care, save Mary, or would she retreat into sickness, melancholia, madness?

Very early next morning, he put through a call to Ireland. Mary had talked of her Aunt Kathy Riordan and mentioned the village in Kerry where she still lived. Perhaps she could help. But Aunt Katherine was salty.

"Well, it's not much I know of the girl. I've only seen Mary twice in her whole life." Her voice came clear over the line; it might have come from any Irish neighborhood in the city. "Eileen brought her to visit when she was five years old. A pretty little thing; she had the looks of her no-good father. After that there was no time or money for visits, with Eileen working like a donkey. For all she got from America, she would have done better to stay home. There were boys who liked Eileen, boys a lot better than Jim Rafferty. And then Mary came again for her mother's funeral, with the little boy, Tommy. It's a sad thing. A terrible country where children are kidnapped. And a bad-luck family."

Katherine was an angry woman, but she was very willing to talk. She hadn't heard, it seemed, that Mary had been indicted for murder. "My sister went to America to marry a drunkard. Then her son was murdered. And her daughter, Mary, my sister told me before she died, her Mary loved the father and would never admit what he was, although she saw what she saw, all through the years. Rubbish, that was Jim Rafferty, a man who breaks his wife's heart, and her back besides. The girl didn't cry for all her mother went through."

Aunt Katherine would be no help to Mary. Her judgment was

severe, but there was truth in it. Mary had to cling to her dreams. Not the worst of sins. But it left her in a hard place now.

The first man in the squad room, he drank his coffee and glanced at the morning paper. A multimillionaire had died earlier that week. Now the content of his will was causing citywide interest. He remembered Alice Christopher's will. That five million dollars. What would it mean to the jury? He called Bostwick to ask him to check the will in the court in Spenser as soon as it was filed.

"The court's in Burgoyne," Bostwick told him. "I've had an associate over there checking. The will was filed yesterday. You were right about one thing," he said thoughtfully. "Alice cut Mary out. That's a plus for our side. The greedy, cold-fish mother that Kramer will try to show would surely have thought about that five mil. Worth waiting for. Maybe Kramer will turn tail now."

"Who gets the estate?" Danny asked.

"You'll love this," Bostwick told him. "Every penny, every stick and stone, goes to Boy Burgoyne."

Danny was quiet for just a moment. "Did Ernest draw up the new will?"

"Franklin Lacey. Usually does trial work. Shares offices with Burgoyne and Thrale."

"The stench rises." Danny felt a growing excitement. Five million dollars. All for Boy Burgoyne.

"I've got you. But it won't faze bloodhound Bassett."

Danny got Pidusky to make inquiries. While he waited for a reply, he talked to William. "I always thought it," William said instantly. "There was no other reason for the Burgoynes to behave as they did. Now the truth is out."

Yet Bostwick had been right: Bassett was certain that the change in the will made no difference to his case. Because Mary Christopher was greedy, it didn't mean she was smart. To his mind, the Burgoyne inheritance strengthened the prosecution. Mary had seen Alice's growing dependence on Boy and her deepening affection for him. Perhaps she had feared a marriage, the inheritance lost, and nothing left but the trust, which must be hers alone. Like so many murderers, she had not dreamed that she would be suspected. All her stories, all her statements were pointed toward an unknown killer-pedophile.

Danny got a few days off from Sweeney Hine, who warned him to stay away from Poughkeepsie and Burgoyne. That he couldn't do, but he had no intention of making a noise in Bassett's backyard. Instead, as Bostwick's associate, he dug discreetly through old court records and found the will of Philip Burgoyne, father of Bartholomew, Ernest, and Fiona. The chief heirs were Boy and Ernest—presumably Fiona had got something at the time of her marriage. There was no great fortune. By the time the estate had reached Boy and Ernest, it was considerably diminished from its past glories. The financial assets alone would be peanuts to modern plutocrats and not significant in the world of old money. But there still was land: not the vast tracts of the past, but a good inheritance. Perhaps the old belief in primogeniture lingered in the Burgoynes, as Boy had received the lion's share.

That was the simple part. Then Danny dug through the land registry, looking at the parcels Boy had received. Many had been sold over the years, to provide income, no doubt, to maintain Boy's lifestyle. A steady drain.

Next he visited the historical society at the Castle. The history of the Burgoyne family was well preserved in two volumes bound in dark red leather. It came down to the present generations: Bartholomew, granted degrees by Harvard Law School and the Beaux Arts in Paris; performed military service at the end of World War II; profession, architect; m. Emma Dryforth (d. 1975); one son, Beaulieu, and a daughter, Phyllida. Another entry dealt more fully with the son, a Harvard man working for the State Department, and others with Ernest and Fiona.

The librarian had been helpful and Danny thanked her. It was quiet in the library. "We're outside the town; people don't come as much as they might," she said regretfully, "but of course, if we were in town we could never get quarters like this."

"This" was a room as large as a ballroom. With its elaborately plastered and gilded ceiling, rich carpets, and gleaming mahogany tables, it seemed to overwhelm the small, plump woman in the neat navy blue jacket and skirt, and the plain white blouse. She tried to hide her feet, in blue and white running shoes, under the seat of her chair, and then she looked up at him in apology.

"I wear heels to come in. But I run around so much all day . . ."

Danny conjectured what Chinese women might have said when they first removed their foot bandages. She laughed and then they talked in a friendly way. "You're interested in the history of the town?"

"It's an unusual place. Not much Dutch influence. Still traces of the British. The old Brits."

She agreed. Then he remarked on the Burgoyne family. "That's unusual, too, in America anyway, for a family to stay put so long."

"Well, the young ones have gone. Bewley—that's how they pronounce the name—Bartholomew's son, and his wife live in Virginia, though now they're in Paris with the embassy. Ernest's daughters are still here, though, Margaret and Jane. Not that they are really young anymore—grown, with their children growing up, too."

"I suppose the town is always interested in the Burgoyne family," Danny said, with a graciousness that the librarian appreciated. There weren't many city people who came to the library; a quick walk through the art gallery was enough for them. Only students came, and they weren't interested in the personal life of the town. Just the historical bits they could pick up to fatten a thesis.

"Oh, yes. People still watch for the *Emma*—now it's the *Emma III*— in the yacht races, and they look for the Burgoynes on opening nights. But my mother says there hasn't been a great Burgoyne splash since Boy—that's Bartholomew—married Emma Dryforth. The Dryforths were a very important family in Dutchess County then. They owned the Dryforth Company—farm equipment. The biggest manufacturers in the state, I believe, until they were bought out by some national company. The Burgoynes gave a picnic for the whole town. We have a sketch of it here; I'll show you."

She padded across the shining floor under a great chandelier and Danny had a sudden vision of Mary, dressed in blue, in that room. Then he fixed his attention on a short wall by the door where sketches of local scenes were mounted. The picnic looked very formal. The women wore dresses, the men slacks and shirts, and some had light jackets. Hats were still to be seen. 1947. Boy had returned from Europe and Lesska with him. The bride and groom were shown in two oval portraits beside the sketch, Boy's vivid with his flaming hair.

"And so your lucky Mr. Burgoyne got not only a pretty wife," he said gallantly, for Emma had a thin face and a somewhat commanding expression, "but a rich one."

The librarian giggled. "Well, I wouldn't know about that. My mother always said that Mrs. Burgoyne's father was very rich, but then the poor lady died before her father, and the money eventually went to the grandchildren. But you're not interested in local gossip," she said, reproaching herself, and made her way back to her chair with a little sigh of relief.

"It's delightful to meet a librarian with such a real interest in the locality," Danny said, in perfect truth. "Not just a provider of guide books . . . Mrs. Phelps," he added, noticing the name on the desk plate.

"Mona," she said. "Everybody calls me Mona. Well, I hope you come in again, when you are visiting Burgoyne, Mr. . . . ?"

He smiled as he took his leave. "Everybody calls me Danny. Goodbye, Mona, and thanks." As he went back into the town on the clear, sunlit afternoon, he could imagine the picnic with Boy Burgoyne and his sour-faced wife, who was to bring him the riches he desired, though they were to elude him at last.

The next morning Danny saw Bostwick in his office. "I see where you're going," the lawyer remarked. "But even if you can prove he had the shorts—and it would take some doing; the guy's no Rockefeller, but he's not exactly ready to join the homeless—so what? There were nearly a dozen people who stuck around after that concert, hanging out with our Boy, having one for the road. If you're looking for some sort of conspiracy, that's just too many people. You have to give it to Bassett, he's thorough. He's got statements from every one."

Bostwick was a lawyer, looking first for proof. But Danny remembered Ed Mitchell, who could look across a crowded street at a strange guy and know he was a perp. And he was never wrong. Proving it came later. Poor Ed. His talents, he'd complained, were wasted under the new regulations. Ed had been Danny's first partner in Special Frauds, and he'd learned a lot from him. Among other things he'd learned to be thorough in his work, even in the dullest part, like searching through municipal records. So he went to the tax assessor's office, to see what had happened to the Burgoyne land that Boy still held.

It was quite a search. Back to the land registry and a look at papers in a bankruptcy proceeding. It would have been a pain to get through the bureaucracy, but Bostwick put him on to a local man, who, for a stiff price, was willing to lend his assistance. Danny got not only the recorded facts, but the local businessmen's gossip as well.

Burgoyne, who had failed to distinguish himself as an architect, had acquired another ambition. Occasional commissions to design single houses in reproductions, carefully modernized, of old New York styles were hardly rewarding by his standards, and he had looked with envy on the great property developers whom he heard so much about on his visits to the city.

He owned land and he would develop it. Dutchess County was not the city, but money was being made there. Investors weren't easy to come by, however, and for the most part he used his own money and his family's money, as well as his own land, to build several small projects. While some were moderately successful, others were not, and he lost more money than he could afford. Then he had been hit by the crash of '87.

Bostwick listened but he still said, "Red herring. Suspicious, but that's not enough. And we don't need it. All we have to do is sit tight and let them try to prove something. And they can't."

Before he left the county, Danny was determined to get a look at Burgoyne and Lesska in the flesh. His new acquaintance, a retired police officer from the area, told him it would be easy to catch Boy.

"The Manahatta Yacht Club's dinner is in Burgoyne this Friday. They have it at this time every year, a get-together before the boats go into the water. Your man will be there. At the Van Vliet Inn. A good dinner there, but pricy. Maybe you'll catch the chauffeur, too."

The Van Vliet Inn was not the best place in the world to keep under observation without being conspicuous. On one side there was a dress shop, closed at seven o'clock, and on the other a hairdresser's, where fortunately patrons were still coming and going. Danny was wearing a dark blue suit, which seemed to be the usual outfit for a restaurant dinner in Burgoyne, and he waited by the hairdresser's like a patient escort.

The dinner was a stag affair—not frowned on here, as yet. The men who drove up looked relaxed and ready for a good evening and the snatches of talk he heard were cheerful. If they noticed the lone male on a leash outside the hairdresser's, it might have increased their enjoyment. Some of them had arrived early; Danny had watched them when he took his post at 6:45. Cocktails at seven, dinner at eight, he had learned, but by 7:45 it looked as though the place must be full, and there was no sign of Boy. Sounds of voices, men unrestrained and enjoying a good blast, penetrated the door to the street. Perhaps his informant had been mistaken. Danny felt a sharp disappointment. He hadn't been certain of seeing Lesska—Boy might very well have driven himself the short distance—but he had been sure of seeing Boy. And he wanted a good look at him, the guy who was getting the money.

By 7:50 he was wondering if it was worthwhile staying longer. Then a gleaming black Cadillac glided along and Danny glimpsed a thin face over narrow shoulders behind the wheel. The driver double-parked and stepped out to open the door for his employer. Lesska was as Mary had described him: a no-color man. In the twilight he was drab in khaki pants and jacket, his hair like a layer of dust on his narrow head. But he was no ghost. There was vigor and strength in his movements that belied the fine lines on his face.

Then Boy stepped out and Lesska was invisible. Boy wore the Yacht Club blazer, and on him it shone with splendor. He really was a magnificent creature; the photographs hardly did him justice. Larger than life were the white mane, the majestic shoulders, the rich laugh that echoed through the evening as the door of the restaurant opened and his friends came out to greet him. Boy, cigar in hand, stood on the sidewalk for a moment while his friends were paying court. There was no other word to describe it, Danny thought. He had seen the same thing when a powerful politician appeared, to be surrounded by toadies.

As he waved his cigar in acknowledgment of the greetings, Boy caught sight of the stranger on the sidewalk, waiting for someone to come from the hairdresser's as the lights went out. Danny, curious, broke the first rule of observation—he met Boy's gaze. He had an odd feeling that Boy recognized him. But he didn't look disturbed; rather, he seemed amused. His full lips puckered a little and his eyes were bright. Then Boy plunged ahead through the open door, and the others followed in his train.

Lesska, turning the car, might have noticed the stranger also, for the two women who left the shop didn't greet him, but Danny walked off with them as if they had and soon Lesska was shooting past. The license plate—BBB100—gleamed up at Danny as though it mocked him. If it had been LAN718, then Bostwick couldn't say he was wasting his time.

Boy had seemed to enjoy their encounter, Danny thought suddenly. *Could* he have recognized him? Of course. Bristow. The Burgoynes had probably gotten a full description as soon as he left the doctor's office. And so to Bassett. And Sweeney Hine. Unlike Boy Burgoyne and his friends, Danny had nothing but a nasty taste in his mouth. Sweeney Hine was going to go up like a rocket. Danny wished he'd never gone back after starting his leave. He was in for a nasty half-hour.

Then he thought of Mary, her eyes dark-ringed, enormous in her thin face. Her head had rested wearily against the wood paneling in the Village restaurant, as though she no longer had the strength to hold herself upright. His own troubles seemed very small.

15

Getting back to New York brought some joy as well as grief. Predictably, as soon as he got in, Sweeney Hine was on his tail. He was blistering, and Danny hadn't had his coffee.

"Who pays Bassett, anyway?" Danny said irritably. "Boy Burgoyne? Maybe I should complain of police harassment."

"Wise guy." Hine's face was an unhealthy crimson.

"Look, I haven't approached one of his witnesses since we talked about it. I was upstate and I passed one of them on the street. I wasn't even jaywalking."

"Why can't you stay away from the damned place?" Hine was growling, but he'd cooled off.

"I was looking into a real estate deal. But maybe that big frog didn't like me splashing in his pond because he could find himself a bit muddy. His chauffeur was driving him, the guy who couldn't appear before the grand jury in Poughkeepsie because he was recovering from surgery. Seems he recovered pretty quick after the indictment came down."

Hine wasn't fooled. And the Christopher case wasn't his case and he didn't go shopping for trouble. Nevertheless, he was the Special Frauds commander and he was beginning to get a familiar whiff. He would stand by his man, unless Danny went right over the line. Of course, First-Grade Detective Daniel Valenti might have to do just that.

And then the good stuff came. He got a cryptic call from Pidusky.

"I've got no time to talk to you guys. We're not an elite squad and I can tell you, I'm dragging my ass."

"Maybe you'd like to park it on a bar stool. Tonight, maybe? Callahan's? Eight o'clock?"

"Seven-thirty," Pidusky said. "If I get off at all, I'd like to get back, look at my wife and kids, if they're still home."

Pidusky wasn't making a social call. "I'll be there," Danny said.

He had to wait awhile at Callahan's. Danny had chosen it for convenience and because the guys in the First Precinct liked the place. He wondered why. It was shabby, it smelled of stale beer, and you couldn't hear yourself talk from the noise of the trucks. Maybe that's what they liked.

Pidusky came in, looking as though he could use a good night's sleep. "The fire-escape rapist. We don't have a lead."

The New York nightmare, especially in areas with old, small buildings. Every woman would shake in her bed and jump if the wind touched the window. Except Mary, who was beyond normal fears. He must really have been out of it not to have remembered. He should go up and make certain her windows were secure—and Aunt Regina's. Those maniacs cared nothing for age.

"I was going to call you before all this came down. Just something I heard when I was working with some guys from Manhattan North, on the plastic-bag killer. We'd been running a check on a lot of young girls who'd reported threats at one time or another, trying to get a lead. They'd talked to models and actresses and they gave names of other models and actresses, show-business types who'd had nasty fights with boyfriends—we were scraping at anything. A lot of work with nothing to show for it, but Arthur Kelly, who used to be Sixth Precinct, was telling me about some of the young chicks he'd come across, actresses with their own social security he calls them— a rich old man in the background."

He sipped his beer moodily. No vodka tonight; the First Precinct was working flat out.

"Same as twenty years ago, fifty years ago, nothing new," Danny said, waiting.

"Yeah. But what got Kelly— He's a good man. Wish we had him— It was one of those little darlings on the subsidy. She hadn't been threatened at all but the inquiry made her nervous. She took to wondering about her big daddy; that was a joke. Kelly remembered the name from the Bathsheba story. One Mr. Bartholomew Burgoyne. Thought you might want it," Pidusky said, yawning. He finished his beer.

"Here's Kelly's number. I'm going to catch a few hours in the sack. I think it's been two days. We're all wiped out. I wish he'd fall off the fire escape and smash into jelly. Every house needs a floodlight . . ."

Danny got through to Arthur Kelly the next morning.

"I thought Pidusky might be interested since he caught the case in the beginning," Kelly said. "I got quite a stable of lovelies, I can tell you, out of the plastic-bag killings. If it wasn't for AIDS, I'd be sorry I'm a married man. Are you involved with the Bathsheba thing?"

There was no point in holding back. "The mother's a friend of mine."

"Tough luck. Well, you might like to know, from what I've heard, the present girlfriend is far from the first. It seems that Mr. Burgoyne of Burgoyne likes his ladies very young and very pretty. Out of work, of course, to make them more amenable. He 'helps them with their careers,' according to Elaine Harcourt. Also known as Greta Hoechner from Pennsylvania."

"Interesting," Danny said.

"But not criminal. Not yet anyway. Well, lots of luck." He gave Danny Elaine's telephone number. "But I think she's afraid of talking to strange men."

Kelly was laughing as he hung up.

Danny wasn't ready to call Elaine. No sense tipping Burgoyne off on exactly how much information he had. Boy Burgoyne, the squire of the elderly charmers of Burgoyne and surrounding territories. A taste for very young women. It meant an apartment as well as his club in the city, an expensive taste. His "long devotion to Alice." What garbage.

Bostwick always had to see both sides. He laughed at the news, but said, "Doesn't mean he couldn't have had a sentimental feeling for an old sweetheart. Enough to look after her, even if he didn't want to sleep with her. But the guy sure spends money. I figured out what it cost him to run that yacht. He's not exactly a do-it-yourself type."

To Danny it was all plain as day. *Cui bono?* Who benefits? The first question in the history of detection. It was Boy who stood to benefit from the death of Alice's grandchildren and their mother's disgrace. It was Boy who had the motive, a five-million-dollar motive. Boy, who was Lesska's employer. And it was Boy and his sister who had kept Alice surrounded after the children's kidnapping so that the only voices she heard were their voices.

That afternoon, he had to go to Penn Station to collar a swindler on his way from Washington. The man had skipped town before the warrant could be served on him, but someone who didn't love him had called to give the time and place of his return. Danny was there early with the youngest guy on the squad as his partner and, as they waited at the gate, Danny told him about the elaborate three-card-monte type of swindle that this smart bastard had got away with. So far.

The train was late, and while he waited Danny reflected that the Spenser crime was something like a three-card-monte game. Now you see it, now you don't. It must be there, but it isn't. Mary saw the children on the porch. She knew, when she left, that they were there. But when Alice came in, the children were gone. Someone had switched them. And it had to be Lesska.

He could see, in his mind's eye, exactly how it had been done. Mary saw Lesska go, but she couldn't know how far he went. He could have driven the short distance to the end of the lane, turned left at the corner, switched his lights off, and waited for her to drive up and turn right, seeing nothing of him. He could have been back at the house in moments, even on foot. And then gone in by the porch door, telling the children that their mother had changed her mind and that they were to go back with her that night. Probably he promised they would be back for the party—he wouldn't want an argument. But they must hurry. He grabbed their coats, hustled them into his car—probably he killed them there and then as they got in. The boy first—it would have been easy; they trusted him. And then into the trunk, the tarp ready and waiting. Easy enough to catch up with Mary, who was afraid to make time on the icy road.

The crowd of people jostling at the gate brought Danny back to the present. All that was easy enough, but the problem remained. No judge or jury in the United States would believe that a handyman, however devoted to his employer, would oblige him one rainy evening by murdering two children. Not even an ordinary handyman, let alone the hero of Cracow. And Boy Burgoyne was no Mafia don, to order an execution. Danny sighed in exasperation.

Then his train came in; the passengers burst out of the cars and rushed up to the gate, and he and his partner became a rough sieve to lift their man from the rest. To Danny's annoyance, it was the kid who spotted him first.

Ernest left Captain Bassett's office in Merivale, his usual, precious calm shattered, and drove nervously back to Burgoyne. Instead of returning to his office, he went to Boy's house and found him in his studio on the first floor, a large, pleasant room. The filing cabinets were unobtrusive; the drafting tables bore sketches of various projects; there was a conference table for meetings with clients and a set of comfortable chairs; at the end was Boy's desk, a massively handsome piece of furniture, and Boy, behind it, dominated the room.

"So Bassett had at you again? You look very ruffled, Ernest. Let me give you a drink."

It was too early for a drink, but Ernest took the brandy that Boy produced; perhaps it would settle his nerves.

"He's concentrating on you," Boy said thoughtfully, "because he believes you're the weak sister. Not Fiona. He's not interested in talking to her again. Fiona can get very duchessy when she chooses."

Ernest ignored his remarks.

"Bassett is very keen to proceed," he told Boy, "and he thinks we're holding back. He as good as said so. Not in an unpleasant way. He said that he's a family man himself and he understands how hard it can be. That people withhold evidence from the best motives. And he said, Boy, that now that poor Alice has gone, she won't have to suffer from the trial. He *knows*, you see. But more or less, in a very decent sort of way, he made it clear that we have a duty to come forward."

"When isn't he anxious to proceed?" Boy scoffed. "Nothing new there. It's Kramer who doesn't want egg on his face."

"Well, Kramer seems to be veering again. The governor was asked a question about the Bathsheba case by some newshound up in Albany. Maybe Kramer got a call from the mansion."

Boy studied the tip of his cigar. "I don't think we can make Lesska testify, Ernest. He really is very reluctant. You know his English isn't good; he hates the idea of an interpreter, and he's really a bit of a recluse. Leave him in the garage with some cars to play around with and he's happy. It would be cruel to push him into open court with some sharpie lawyer trying to make a goat of him."

Ernest couldn't disagree. He knew very well it was true. He wished with all his heart that Lesska had never told Boy about the Christmas-tree ball in the car and he wished that Boy hadn't told him. But it made no difference. If the case went to trial, Lesska must testify. Boy had to know that, although he argued. And if he testified, he must tell the truth. All the truth.

"We can't encourage perjury, Boy."

Boy still looked less than convinced. He was standing by the drafting tables, looking at some sketches. They were the sketches for the Wadsworth townhouses, Ernest saw. No draftsmen were working on them now; it looked as though the project was stalled. The financing had not worked out. Boy had had bad luck. And so had Fiona and himself, junior partners in the venture.

"Lesska's testimony is necessary, essential to prove the case. He must testify. If Mary is not convicted after the trial, Boy, there will be a certain awkwardness. After all, Alice changed her will because of Mary's guilt. Mary could challenge it, I believe."

Boy turned away from the Wadsworth sketches, his lips pursed. His gaze was blank and Ernest wasn't sure that he had his brother's attention. Then Boy thrust his fingers through his hair, restored to his usual vigor and resonant speech. "Ernest," he said, "I'll do what I can. I'll talk to that stubborn old Polack. But you know how he is."

Ernest did know. But he had never known Lesska to reject Boy's wishes. He didn't look forward to the trial; nevertheless, he felt a great relief.

Danny was late back in the squad room and he was the last man there writing up his report. Usually he liked the talk in the place but lately, with his mind intent on Mary, he valued the quiet. And in the quiet, as he finished his work, he knew there was only one answer. And only one way to go. He sat, drumming his fingers on his desk, and then looked up the home number of Seymour Roth, in Westchester.

The fund-raiser for the UJA left the dinner table to take Danny's call. Danny had never called him at home before; their acquaintance was a working one. But he heard Danny out and when the story ended, he sounded thoughtful. "It seems crazy," he replied. "Between Vienna and the INS—all the documentation. There is no way—" He was silent for a moment. Then he spoke again, in a different tone, the usual cheerful, confident, after-dinner-speaker's manner gone. His voice was lower, harder-edged. "Look, HIAS has checked every-where there is to check, but— I'll give you a name. A name I've heard, someone I don't know. He's in Tel Aviv. The name is Simon Mordecai. Legally, his group was disbanded by the Israeli govern-ment a long time ago, but he goes back a long way and he might know something no one else remembers. It's all I can tell you."

It took a few days for Danny to reach Mordecai. But when he did there was no waste of time. Danny mentioned Seymour Roth from the UJA and heard a grunt for a reply. He told his story concisely and Mordecai answered without hesitation, "You got a photograph?"

"I have a snapshot."

"Send it to me. I'm coming to New York to visit my daughter. If I've got anything, I'll be in touch."

The squad was so busy that Sweeney Hine posted a schedule of one day off in ten. Then Bostwick called with the news. The DA was preparing to go to trial.

"It's a whole new ballgame," Bostwick said. He sounded like a very worried defense lawyer. "Kramer's cocky. There was no reach. No offer of a deal—though that might come. But they've got new evi-dence, that's for sure. Well, we'll get it. We'll soon know the worst. But I don't feel good about it."

Bostwick soon learned about Lesska's new statement. He gave the details to Danny when he caught him in his apartment at one A.M. Danny had got in, showered, and was just feeling the comfort of the sheets when the telephone rang, but his mind was alert enough to take it all in.

"So he doesn't come right out and say he saw them."

"No. But it's almost as good, for them. He saw that ornament flashing. And it was found in Linda's hand."

"You can make him look like an idiot. A flashing light—inside the car, outside the car, moonbeams, spots before his eyes . . ."

"Sure. I can make him flunk in perception and logic. Call in expert witnesses to help. Maybe satisfy a shrink and a professor. But what about the jury? Even if his testimony was struck, the jury will have heard it. And it will make up their minds. That ball was in the kid's hand. The kids were in the car. Why the hell would he come up with this tale now?"

"Because someone wants to push Kramer," Danny said shortly. "Listen." He told Bostwick about Simon Mordecai.

"Well, if he can find anything, it'd better be soon. In three weeks it's plea day. You're not going to want to hear this, Danny, but maybe you should talk to Mary. Perhaps something could still be worked out. She's facing Murder Two."

"Hang tough," Danny said. "The ballgame's not over."

"It's Mary's game, Danny," Bostwick said. He sounded depressed. "I'll have to advise my client."

Danny lay awake until morning. Was Bostwick seriously thinking of a confession to a lesser charge? Mary would never do it. Bostwick had been taken by surprise. Sweating about things that hadn't bothered him before—the heroin buys, which he could probably keep out; the debts, which he probably couldn't. Mary Christopher, the greedy young woman who couldn't wait to get her hands on the Christopher money. He could bet that Bassett had spent a lot of hours trying to find the lover who was to share it with her, as he had found Françoise Pemberthy's. Probably all he'd come up with was Detective Daniel Valenti of the Special Frauds squad. Or perhaps, in the four years of her widowhood, there had been somebody. She'd never mentioned anyone. But why should she?

He tossed and turned. Lesska would not have come forward unless he was prodded. Why had Boy Burgoyne decided to push for a trial? What had changed? Alice had died. But Boy had never spared her feelings—the greater her anguish, the more certain his gain. And how had he persuaded Lesska to change his testimony? He remembered Boy on the sidewalk in Burgoyne regarding him with a serene amusement, an amusement that held a hint of mischief. Danny remembered his son Mark when he was about five years old. He would look at his father in just that way, from the security of his mother's lap, when he was convinced he had got away with something.

Almost at once, the city became too much for Mary. All the newspapers and the networks were running stories on the Bathsheba murders. They had learned about Mary's contracted book, and the name "Medea Mommy" was used often. And it seemed as though the entire population of the tri-state area would have to know that Mary's father had been an alcoholic, and that her brother had died in a gang fight. Mary's neighbors were still kind, but she feared going in the streets to meet the cameras and the stares. She had had to get a new unlisted number; the telephone had never ceased to ring, and many of the calls had been obscene and vicious, as though the whole outside world had gone mad.

Danny remembered the Poughkeepsie paper that had first broken the story about Mary's family, her father, her brother. He soon discovered the source. The friendly informant was Boy Burgoyne.

He discussed it with Mary at Sag Harbor, where she had taken refuge. Mildred had collected her. "I'm working over my notes and diaries," she had said to Mary. "You bring your work and we'll hunker down together."

Mildred showed Mary a smiling disregard for all the notoriety, but she confided her anger to Danny. Her house was a safe haven, but it couldn't shield Mary entirely from the public furor and private betrayals. Now Danny saw the tears on Mary's cheeks.

"Alice must have told Boy about my father and Richie. Before you, she was the only one I ever told. Quent knew, of course."

She looked lost, bereft. She and Danny were sitting on the white railing at the end of Long Wharf. Well wrapped up, in the sunshine, they could have had an illusion of spring, but a sharp March wind reminded them that winter was still lingering.

"Alice was so sympathetic when I told her about Richie. She thanked God they had no gangs in Spenser. She wanted us all to go and live there."

Alice had given her little secrets away to Roaring Boy.

"Of course she was sympathetic," Danny told her. "Telling Boy doesn't mean she wasn't. It happens. Two people, so much together. There is a whole ocean of time to be filled up. Everything is said, at last. And no one knows, unless some big event brings in the newspapers. A run for political office. A murder."

"I used to think Boy liked me," Mary said reflectively. "I think he was often glad to see me."

"We've found out that Boy goes for young women."

"He only went out with the older women in Burgoyne. Old friends, of course. I didn't think it was physical, especially. I always thought it was because he got easily bored in Spenser and Burgoyne. Alice, of course, was mostly interested in local matters. He liked it when we talked of the city. The gossip. Well, he'll be able to spend more time in the city now. And travel abroad—he loves that."

Her words were bitter. He had told her of Boy's inheritance. But still, Mary could not suspect. Unlike William, who was deeply suspicious and full of healthy rancor. He had called Danny to tell him that Boy had left for a short visit to the West Coast. "He told an acquaintance of mine that he needed a rest—he'd been looking after a sick old woman until she died."

But Mary knew that Boy had descended on Alice when she was feeble and kept herself at arm's length, and all the things that implied. But still, not murder. And to almost everyone who knew him, the idea of Boy Burgoyne dirtying his hands with the brutal killing of two children was absurd.

Detective Valenti was getting nowhere. He had gone to see Elaine Harcourt, as a colleague of Arthur Kelly's. But she had nothing more to tell than the usual story. From her looks, Boy might have been in trouble for statutory rape, but in fact she was nineteen. Small, pale blond, with a pretty pout, she had received him at the door of her apartment on West Fifty-seventh Street at noon in a short silk dressing gown. Now that the plastic-bag killer was in custody, she was no longer keen to discuss Boy Burgoyne.

"Well, I guess I shouldn't have blown my stack. I mean, he's really an okay guy. Real cool. No weird stuff, if you know what I mean."

She looked up through pale eyelashes: her face wasn't made up yet and it looked clean and healthy. He knew what she meant. "Only he's so damned heavy," she added, as Danny was leaving.

Elaine had made him laugh, though he hadn't been in much of a mood for laughing lately. When he left her he had known that for all his certainty, he had not one scrap of evidence against Boy Burgoyne. Sitting beside Mary, who was still ravaged by grief, he thought that life was good to Boy. He had had the affection of Alice Christopher and the charms of Elaine. And now it seemed his financial problems were over. And nothing to stop him—

"Danny," Mary said suddenly, breaking into their private silence, which had seemed intensified by the cries of the gulls and the slap of water against the pilings, "I've become very selfish. I didn't know until last night, about Mildred. She only told me because she had an appointment today at the hospital for a checkup. The last time she came home, she had surgery. Cancer. She's been all through that and I never knew. And now she laughs if I say anything. The post-op treatments were miserable, she told me, but as soon as they were over, she'd gone back to the dig. Now she's perfectly all right, she says. Mildred. She's so *brave*. The way she was when George died. She never came to cry on my shoulder. If Mildred can bear that . . ."

Mary was looking not at him but out across the choppy water, under the smudged gray sky. "One should be able to accept pain. Offer it up, my mother would have said. She must have known a lot about it."

The wind lifted her black hair from her shoulders and it blew like a pennant. Her sad face, in profile, had a noble look. Perversely, he would rather she had wept in his arms. Selfish bastard, he thought.

That night he told Aunt Regina about his visit.

"Christian resignation," his Aunt Regina said. For a pious Catholic woman, she didn't sound pleased. "Ready to be thrown to the lions. You have to fight her lions for her."

"Not exactly the modern woman," Danny observed.

"A woman." Regina looked at him in exasperation. "She has received a wound so deep she cannot fight. She is heartbroken."

Aunt Regina, a woman who still wore gloves whenever she went out on the street, was a tough battler. She bullied her brothers about family business and in her dealings with the rest of the world she kept her lawyers busy. Yet she could understand Mary.

He called Bostwick in Poughkeepsie. There was no move from Kramer. "Mary won't take a deal," Danny told him. "I know," Bostwick said, "but I'd feel better if they were offering. I have an ear to the ground, by the way. The Burgoynes aren't overjoyed about testifying in a show trial—there's talk of television cameras. But there's real pressure for a strong prosecution. People remember that big case in the city—two kids abused, one died, but nobody got the max. Senator Crosley was hooting away at a Bar dinner that an upstate jury would have done better. Kramer was all ears, you bet."

Bostwick was *really* depressed. "I was wondering if I should call Kramer. Maybe—"

"Forget it," Danny said. "You think Mary will perjure herself and confess to a crime she knows nothing about?"

"Yeah. Yeah. It's just that you can never tell, with a jury. A city woman. She doesn't live far from the place where that other kid died, does she? It was all over the front page up here yesterday. You're right. We should win. There's still no hard evidence that the kids were in the car. Only an assumption. But . . ."

Danny hung up, feeling depressed himself. It was the worst moment since he'd taken Aunt Regina's first call. Because Bostwick was right, and Mary was right. She could only plead not guilty, but she was facing what? Thirty years? She could face it, maybe. He couldn't.

In the morning, he felt no better. For the first time since Daniel Valenti had been a rookie cop, he didn't want to go on the job and he felt no interest in his latest assignment. He would have liked, he thought, to go upstate and beat up Bassett and Kramer. And then he'd like to shoot Burgoyne and Lesska. But in real life there was nothing he could do up there to help. Nothing at all. He was at a dead end, unless he heard from Mordecai. Mordecai, who was coming over sometime to visit his daughter.

The first call he made when he got into the squad room was to Tel Aviv. Three P.M. there. No surprise—Mordecai was out. Through the day he called as often as he checked in with the squad room, but he got no reply. And there was no reply the next day, or the next. Mary had just ten days left to plead when he received a message. Mordecai. The telephone exchange was in Brooklyn. Mordecai had nothing to say on the phone. He arranged a meeting at Danny's apartment that night. It was a tough day, and Danny had to help his new young partner in making up his report. When he got home Mordecai was on his doorstep.

It couldn't have been anyone else.

16

Simon Mordecai was nothing like Seymour Roth. The man who gave his time to work for the United Jewish Appeal was a good-looking, well-dressed businessman. He and his wife were patrons of the Metropolitan Opera and she belonged to the Society for Ethical Culture. Simon was a short man with a large head that poked forward aggressively. His hair was a few white strands stretched over the brown-spotted scalp and his face was a collection of wrinkles. He carried a large, battered briefcase. His suit was shabby and creased—he had slept in it on the flight from Israel and he had just arrived that day.

He spoke English with a heavy accent. His eyes were set in dark hollows, but as they gazed at Danny they were sharp. He accepted a glass of beer, but he was ready to talk business as soon as he wiped the froth from his lips. Taking a folder from his briefcase, he began a monologue. He spoke swiftly, in even tones, a recitation of facts. Occasionally, he glanced down at the cluster of pages.

"There was a man named Gregor Brodki. Chief foreman at a big munitions factory in Czestochowa, Poland. Young, but a good mechanic and capable of instructing and directing the workmen, well respected. When the Occupation began, the Germans respected him also. And he respected them. Nazis, men after his own heart. Brodki kept up output better than most of the factory foremen; too many workers had gone to the army and been killed. And so the district was supplied with slave labor."

Danny was listening intently, resisting the urge to jump in with a barrage of questions. The man sitting in his armchair, in his living room—a neat but rather dull and shabby place, for he'd done little to it since Joan died—was talking of a time just before Danny's birth, but he spoke as if it were yesterday.

"Brodki was not pleased to get the slaves instead of his former workers. The slaves were men, women, and children; they knew nothing of machines; they were mostly Jews; they were thin, underfed, unhealthy. And filthy. They did not live in neat homes. They were bedded down in the factory yards by the railroad with no sanitation except a ditch that overflowed. He resented having these vermin in his factory, though they were anxious to fulfill their work quotas, for when they failed they were marked for death. It was he who decided when a slave had outlived his usefulness, and his new power pleased him as much as his extra food rations and the light truck allotted for his personal use.

"He soon found other pleasures, little games. Some of the work involved bathing the machine parts in acid. His Polish workers had worn protective gloves and masks; the slaves got none. Brodki enjoyed hearing them choke and watching their agonies as the acid ate their hands. Once they were useless—or before, if they annoyed him—he killed them himself. His German masters were indulgent: he continued to keep production high and they liked the man. The *Untermenschen* had to be disposed of and Brodki had the slaves pile the bodies in railroad cars to make the short journey to the burial fields.

"The men he shot. He had various games with the women." Mordecai looked up. "It is said he did not enjoy sex much, in the usual way. But he had his own ways. And the women died. As for the children, their necks were broken."

Danny was quite still.

"Brodki had been brought up on a farm and he had enjoyed killing animals. We have been looking for him for a long time," Mordecai said softly. "When I got your call, it stirred something in my mind. And when you sent the photograph—"

"You believe—?"

"It's more than forty years later. The picture you sent—it could be." He was looking at the snapshot, a clear shot of Alice, with Lesska in the background by the car. Danny went to his desk in the room that used to be his boys' bedroom. In the last week he hadn't given all his time to the squad. He had bugged the hell out of the INS and gotten a copy of the photograph on Lesska's naturalization papers. He showed it to Mordecai, who gave an appreciative grunt. "Much better. From this, I think, an identification can be made."

Danny, despite the sickening nature of the story, could not help feeling relief and joy. He insisted that Mordecai join him at a restaurant for dinner, though Mordecai grumbled that his daughter would be expecting him, and it was soon obvious to Danny that he had very little interest in food or drink.

Mostly he talked while Danny ate, though Danny told him he felt he owed very special thanks to Seymour Roth of the UJA for getting them together.

"Hmm." Mordecai's wrinkles became a grimace. "The best present you can give perhaps is not to mention my name. I am not a person exactly in good standing these days. I live in Israel as a retired person. Officially."

Danny listened as Mordecai told him of the birth of Nakam, the vengeance group, which had begun even before World War II. Mordecai had been an early member and had had, it seemed, as many adventures as James Bond, though not of an amorous sort. He was a family man. When the State of Israel had outlawed Nakam, Mordecai and a few others had not been compliant. They continued to work, against the laws of their own land and every other country. The risks were enormous; achievement was their only reward. "Very few left," Mordecai said thoughtfully. "Just a few old, useless men."

For the first time that evening, he grinned. Suddenly Danny saw another face, with youth, humor, behind the mask of age.

"Did you see this Brodki yourself?"

"No. I knew the camp in Vienna, but I never saw this man. I saw his photograph in the Nakam file. It was a photograph from a Polish newspaper, published when Brodki had received an award for outstanding service to the war effort. Someone had turned it in to the authorities after the war ended, but it was too late. Brodki had disappeared."

They talked long that night, until the restaurant was closing, and Danny drove Mordecai back over the bridge to Brooklyn. Mordecai knew of Emil Lesska, a quiet man and a true hero. He had made his way to the refugee camp, but he was shot by a border guard on his escape route and never completely recovered from the wound. The hardships of the journey were too much. Mordecai believed that Lesska had died in the camp, though no death certificate was found.

"His papers—probably they were sold by a secretary. Such things happened. At that time, papers meant everything and they commanded a price. Two old men who had been at the documentation center had remembered the arrival of Lesska, but now they are dead. All of Lesska's family were murdered after his escape.

"Young man, I have to tell you." Mordecai's manner changed. He had been eager to impart information, but now he was sober with warning. "You are in a great hurry. But it can be years, decades, before your Emil Lesska can be proved to be Brodki. Courts do not move fast. Officials, government departments, are not quick to admit that they have been careless, wrong. And you say this man has support. You must prepare for a long battle."

They had entered a part of Brooklyn with long rows of fine old houses, some kept up, some in the process of restoration, and others in various stages of decay from run down to ruined. The detective's eye spotted young men lingering in dark spaces on no apparent business, and noted the heavy gates and bars on every storefront.

"My daughter has lived here since she came to the United States," Mordecai said. "I have asked her to come to Israel, but she will never leave, although she is a widow now."

The Mordecais, Danny thought, had a stubborn streak. His luck.

Mordecai's assessment of the judicial process was, Danny knew, correct. But he refused to be discouraged, not now, when the truth that had been so real to him had acquired legs and could walk into the world. Instead he told Mordecai of Lesska—he still thought of him as Lesska—and his employment with a Viennese countess.

The old man listened carefully. "It could be true. It was a bad time for the Viennese aristocracy, though the American sector was the best to be in. A good handyman who worked cheap would have been very useful. And they wouldn't have checked his papers too closely. Nazi or not, it made little difference to them."

"Major Burgoyne, as he was then, must he have known?" Danny had drawn up at the spot Mordecai indicated and the two men sat in the car outside a house with a neat hedge and a fine flight of steps leading up to the front door. A lamp was lit in an upstairs room.

"If he made inquiries. The adjutant general's office dealt with prosecutions, but they had to work with people who brought information. And even without that he must have suspected the truth. The real Emil Lesska came from Cracow. He was an educated man, the owner of a bookstore, who spoke several languages. It was no doubt convenient for the major," he said dryly, "not to inquire too far."

"He was sure early on," Danny said, "because he blackmailed him all these years. Friendly suggestion, maybe, at first. And at the last, he got him to commit murder."

"With freedom as the price? And some money, perhaps. Your Lesska wouldn't have shrunk from the job."

He got out of the car with a vigor that belied his age, clutching his briefcase, lighter now; he had given Danny a file of papers. "Copies," he had said, "but where an original exists, the place it can be found is noted."

For a moment he lingered, with a last word for Danny. "You have to watch. If the major takes fright, he might send him out of the country." In the light of the phosphorescent lamp, his wrinkled face looked harsh, stern, strange. "In the old days," he said, "we wouldn't have let it happen."

Then he clattered up the steps, a senior citizen going home. Danny waited until the front door was opened and closed before he left. On the way back to Manhattan his right hand would reach down to touch the papers beside him. He was right; he would prove it, and Mary would be safe.

He had driven home fast through the quiet streets to call Mary. But when he picked up the telephone, he paused. How much should he tell? It would be a great relief to her to know that the real murderer had been discovered. Would she be devastated to know that it would not, at once, set her free? Under the law, Lesska was Lesska until he was proved to be an imposter. Mordecai had talked of years. Danny would not allow it to be years, but could Mary, in her precarious state of mind, endure the violent swings of emotion she was about to suffer?

His fingers dialed the Sag Harbor number anyway. It was Mildred who answered, and he apologized for disturbing her.

"Oh, don't worry, Danny. I can always get back to sleep, even in a tent in a rainstorm. But I don't think I should try to wake Mary. She's been having such trouble sleeping, she's taken two sleeping pills and—"

"No, don't," he said, contrite. "Perhaps it's just as well. I was on a high and I don't want her to have to face a letdown. Mildred—"

Mildred had a cool head along with a sunny disposition. He told her, briefly, what he had learned. Both coolness and sun vanished for a moment. Mildred was a flash of anger. "Horrible man. I never liked him. I did think—one had to think—but everyone else was so sure about Lesska. The children—"

When she recovered, they spoke about Boy Burgoyne. At last, Mildred grew calm from the relief she felt about Mary.

"We're not out of the woods," Danny cautioned.

It was settled that Mildred would tell Mary that Danny was making excellent progress with his investigation. The next morning Danny would arrange an appointment with Bostwick and he would meet Mary in Bostwick's office.

"I wish I could be there," Mildred said with regret. "But I'll be a few hours at the hospital. Mary will be okay, though. When she knows you have a line on the killer. My God!"

Bostwick had a full schedule that morning, but after he heard Danny, he promised to see them at noon. Danny had checked in at the squad room and had a word with Sweeney Hine. When his partner arrived, their schedule was juggled to give Danny some free time. The morning was bright, though cool, with only wispy white clouds trailing over the spire of the Municipal Building. He made good time upstate and was in Bostwick's office before Mary.

The waiting room was already crowded, mostly with young defendants. The receptionist saw his glance. "Mr. Gaither's clients. Mr. Bostwick's on the telephone. He asked me to take you to the conference room and give you and Mrs. Christopher coffee."

Danny went into the book-lined room with the large table and Bostwick joined him in a moment. He looked over Mordecai's papers and the newspaper photographs, while Danny drank coffee and talked. They were so intent, Bostwick didn't notice the light flashing on his telephone and the receptionist had to come and tell him that Mrs. Christopher had arrived.

Danny and Bostwick both went out to greet her. Among the young toughs, Mary looked out of place, very clean and fresh in light blue denim pants, a chambray shirt, and a navy blue windbreaker, but she didn't seem to notice them. Her eyes—eyes still dark with shadow—were on Danny. Mary had driven for four hours, but the weariness in her face spoke of more than the journey. She looked frail and she was paler than she had been on the wharf at Sag Harbor.

What had he expected, he asked himself. Joy, effervescence? Mildred had told her very little. She drank coffee, her expression watchful. She listened quietly while Bostwick put Danny's discoveries before her, explaining how they could, and could not, affect her position.

Mary had never suspected Lesska; Danny had looked forward to astonishment, rage—but Mary wasn't Mildred. Perhaps, he thought, she had been through too much to feel anything except her enduring grief and misery. And Bostwick was only cautiously optimistic.

"This should help," he told Mary. "The problem is, we need time." He said essentially what Mordecai had told Danny. "It can take a very long time to prove that the Burgoyne Lesska, citizen of the United States, is actually the Gregor Brodki who disappeared from Czestochowa in 1945. I will do everything to keep the case from coming to trial, but the prosecution will push to go forward. They'll say 'red herring,' usual defense delaying tactics, and so forth. If they succeed, they may be able to exclude the whole Brodki story at this stage. And if we get something in, they can rely on jurors who for the most part have no recollection of World War Two. And this 'fishing through history'—which is what they'll call it—will be termed irrelevant, because there is nothing to place Lesska near the children at the time of their deaths. Boy Burgoyne places him in the house at 5:50."

"Burgoyne's unsupported word," Danny broke in. "The five-million-dollar baby."

"We're not sure of that. Someone might come forward."

Fiona, Danny thought.

"There is one possibility," Bostwick said, looking more cheerful. "Perhaps this will start cutting too near the bone. Bartholomew Burgoyne, king of the Castle, will have a little surprise when he comes back from vacation. He might want to pull back while there's still time. He can have Lesska discover that he's not sure about that ornament after all. He had come forward with his idea because he thought he should, but perhaps, after all, it was just a trick of the light. And Mrs. Christopher is such a nice lady . . . Kramer would get scared and just drop the charge, quietly."

It wasn't the ideal conclusion. Though they could go on with the search. But Danny had a vision of Boy on Oak Avenue, totally aware of his opponent, unafraid, amused, mocking. Boy Burgoyne, like Handsome Harry, too blithely confident to feel normal fear. Boy, he was certain, believed himself invincible.

"It won't happen," he said. "We have to hurry the other business up."

"Let's hope," Bostwick retorted. "Remember, you're talking of a conspiracy. The hardest damned thing to prove."

"So we get started."

Bostwick gave him a look. "I tell you what. There's a guy I knew in college. He's in the Justice Department now. Maybe he can help. I'll see if I can get him before he goes to lunch."

The two men had been talking to each other. They were still talking as Mary stood and hung her bag over her shoulder.

"You two don't need me," she said. "I've heard." She put a hand on Danny's, the lightest of touches. "I'd like to leave now. Take it easy and miss the rush on the Long Island Expressway."

What she said was true and made good sense.

"I'll call you tonight and keep you up to date," Danny said and the door closed behind her.

The friend in the Justice Department was not so easily tracked down. Bostwick was tied up on the telephone, while Danny was contemplating the usefulness of visiting Czestochowa and Cracow.

Mary, leaving the parking lot after a short delay, didn't take the route she had used that morning. Instead she turned the car east. Her foot was on the gas; her hands moved the wheel; her eyes checked the road, but in her mind there was just one picture.

Bostwick was still on the telephone. "Will you tell Mr. Cordweiler that Stephen Bostwick of Poughkeepsie called and ask him to get back to me as soon as possible?"

He grimaced at Danny in despair. "Talk about bankers' hours . . ."

The door to the conference room burst open. The neat, calm receptionist was flushed, panting, and her hair was bobbing around her face.

"Mr. Bostwick—it's Mrs. Christopher."

"What—?" Danny was on his feet.

"Those boys," she said. Her hands were locked and jiggling up and down. "They were huddled together in the hall, laughing. As though they were up to something. So I went to see what was going on. And they told me. They said that Mrs. Christopher had talked to them. Tried to buy a gun . . ."

Bostwick and Danny were out of the conference room in seconds, grabbing the boys who were ambling out of the building. They protested virtuously.

"We don't know about no guns."

"We told her we didn't have no guns."

"The lady, she cut out like she was crazy, see, hot to make a buy."

Bostwick and Danny stared at the parking lot. Mary's white car was not to be seen.

"They wouldn't have brought in a weapon," Bostwick said, wretched. "But it's conceivable they might have told her where to go."

"We can't play games," Danny said. "The only thing to do is to get there first."

His car was at a nearby parking meter. It had more power than Mary's.

"Take Route Forty-four," Bostwick said. "Mary will, and then she'll take 343. It's the most direct way and it comes out on the west side of Burgoyne. But one lane on 343 is closed for construction; I came that way last Thursday. You can get into a slow crawl. We should take the back road off 343 that loops around to the east; we'll make time on that."

There should be no trouble getting there first. No trouble, Danny told himself.

"Unless we get pulled in by the troopers," Bostwick added. "It's a thirty-five-mile-an-hour limit, in town."

Danny swore. A patrol car would have been useful. How long would it take Mary to get a weapon? The heat wasn't on in the car, but he was sweating.

Mary met no traffic jams. It was as though the road had been cleared for her. She rolled her window down and let the cool air whip her hair back from her face as she leaned urgently forward, pressing her foot on the gas. She might have been flying, propelled by a favoring wind. Effortlessly, she consumed the miles. Soon she was approaching the township of Burgoyne. Then it came together, the picture in her mind and the picture-postcard house, the Burgoyne house, white against dark branches under the blue sky.

Danny and Bostwick were quiet on the journey. Danny's eyes searched out every small car on the road, but none of them was Mary's.

"She's probably behind us," Bostwick said.

Bostwick was being reasonable. It had been reasonable to take this turnoff and avoid the construction, but they were poking along in a no-passing zone behind an old man in no hurry. Danny swung over the double line and shot past the crawling car, failing to register the driver's indignant shout and Bostwick's raised eyebrows. Because Danny knew in his guts that Mary was ahead. And he was frantic. His sleeping beauty had been awakened not by any loving kiss but by a searing jolt of truth. Propelling her to what? Vengeance? Death?

The Burgoyne house was quiet, still. A faint echo sounded in Mary's mind. Danny's voice: "Boy Burgoyne has flown to California." The echo died away. She parked her car and walked to the back of the house, where the drive led to the garage. Behind the screen of trees were four cars—not Boy's. Fords, Chevys—Lesska's personal jobs. Outside steps led to his apartment, and she went up, silent in her canvas shoes. She tried the door. It was unlatched. Her hand groped inside her jacket.

Danny, barreling into the east end of Oak Avenue, was stopped by a traffic squeeze. He cursed and hollered.

"Don't go crazy," Bostwick said. "It won't help anything. You don't know that she's here. Or if she intends . . ."

Danny computed the time it would take to run the length of Oak Avenue to the Burgoyne house on the outskirts. Too long. He eyed the sidewalk, thronged with shoppers. Mary. He couldn't reach her; he had failed. He was pierced with anguish; she had slipped from his grasp. The sidewalk cleared for a moment; he rammed the car up on the curb. As the shoppers scattered he looped around the stopped traffic and drove through a red light toward the Burgoyne house.

Mary was in a narrow entranceway. The heat was stifling; she threw her windbreaker down. On one side was an open kitchen. Everything that could be painted was painted a dull khaki color, matched by a few straw rugs. The place looked like Lesska, neat, drab, efficient. A row of knives hung, shining, along the wall, but she didn't need them. The young men had not been able to sell her a gun, but one of them had followed her to her car and offered this very serviceable knife. She pushed the next door open, a bare barracks of a room, and there, bending over a workbench, was the man who had killed her children.

Lesska turned, his eyes widening a little as he saw Mary. Grabbing a heavy wrench, he lunged toward her. Mary flung herself at him with all her force. Caught off balance, he toppled backward, his arm hitting a chair, and he dropped the wrench as the two bodies crashed to the floor. Mary was on top, the knife still in her fist. His hands reached up and snatched her wrists in a deft and vicious twist. The knife fell, clattering, as Mary gasped in pain. For a moment she thought her wrists were broken, but while she thought she raised herself and kneed his testicles. He howled, but his body writhed and the side of his hand sliced into her neck and knocked her on her back, with the knife out of sight. Now he was on top and reaching for her throat. She smashed his chin up with a quick painful thrust of her injured hand and sank her teeth into his neck. His fingers slid around her head and caught her hair; she jerked away and smashed her elbow across his nose. He moaned, but once again those fingers tried to grasp her neck.

Mary felt all the strength of his wiry body as she twisted and turned to evade his grasp; from under the dark workbench she saw a glimmer and stretched her right hand toward it. His fingers squeezed and she slashed the nails of her left hand across his eyes; as he flinched she grabbed the knife, rolled over, and put the steel on Lesska's pale throat. Then the door behind her opened and a man was on her back, ripping the knife from her hand.

17

The state troopers from the substation at Hastings Wood arrived within four minutes. There were no problems. The woman had already been subdued and neatly tied to a chair. A doctor had been called for the victim. His throat was bloody from a knife scratch, his eyelids were red and puffy from her fingernails, his nose was a mess, and he was in pain from getting her knee in his groin. But he would survive.

"It's Mary Christopher," Ernest Burgoyne told the troopers, in case they didn't recognize the scarlet-faced, furious woman. Her shirt was ripped, her brassiere exposed, but she seemed to care nothing about it, just struggling and shrieking nonsense.

"I came in and found her attempting to kill Mr. Lesska. Another few seconds and I would have been too late. And it's just luck that I came in," he added. "I stopped by to ask Lesska if he'd look over my car; it stalled this morning at a traffic light."

The state troopers listened. They knew Mr. Ernest Burgoyne; he was a well-respected man and an attorney, and on that day he had an air of real authority. His cheeks were pink. He'd struggled with a killer and he'd saved a guy's life. They had the knife, short enough to conceal, sharp enough to kill. A city street weapon.

"Mr. Lesska is going to be a vital witness at the trial," Ernest said. "She was trying to silence him. And she very nearly did."

They took the ropes off the woman and put the cuffs on her, everything by the book, although her wrists were red. They tried to give her the usual warning, but she wasn't listening. She hadn't stopped hollering since they came in, screaming that the man was called Brodki; he was a killer and they mustn't let him get away. One of the troopers knew Lesska; he had worked on the trooper's car. And done a good job at a fair price. Lesska wasn't squawking, just sitting there listening, as quietly as if nothing had happened.

The trooper asked if he could do something before the doctor came. Lesska shook his head. "Just get that crazy woman out of here."

Despite his pain, Lesska was calm, even happy. He enjoyed seeing Mary in handcuffs. He had always despised the Irish wife. He knew what the Burgoynes thought: Amercans didn't name it, but the Germans had called such people *untermenschen*. Also she was a soft, weak woman, no possible threat. She had let him take her children and kill them. He had been sure he could lie right before her in court and she would not suspect him, stupid as she was, stupid as all these people were. Then suddenly she had turned, with all the violence of a vengeful Jew and the strength of a young man. But luck, which always followed him, appeared again and Ernest came.

Lesska watched with keen interest as the officers tried to hold Mary still. Her thin shirt ripped further. Although she had got skinny, the woman still had a good bosom; he had been aware of it as they struggled. Despite his pain and soreness, he was flicked by a certain excitement, a pleasure half forgotten.

A crash broke up his musing, a thud of running feet. The workroom door burst open and two tall men with big shoulders came in and just took over. The freckle-faced one grabbed the woman and held her, muttering idiotically, "It's okay, Mary; it's okay," while the other one announced that he was Mrs. Christopher's attorney. They should both have been arrested for trespassing, damaging property, and interfering with the officers in the performance of their duty. Instead these undisciplined Americans listened to the lawyer, while the other man soothed the woman.

The troopers knew Bostwick from frequent meetings in criminal court in Poughkeepsie. He was shrewd and knew his business, and if a trooper was a hairsbreadth out of line, Bostwick would get his hide. He introduced himself to Ernest Burgoyne and Ernest's pink flush soon changed to two high spots of red on his cheekbones.

Bostwick pointed out that Ernest had seen two people fighting.

He had no actual knowledge of who had attacked whom. If his client had brought a knife, as Mr. Lesska had alleged, it could have been for her defense. Matters had come to light that would certainly make the mother feel in danger, as her children had been. He commented on the wrench, still on the floor, which could have smashed the woman's skull.

Dr. Bristow arrived, looking unhappy. He checked over Lesska, cleaned his scratches, and gave him prescriptions for his pain and for an eye lotion. Bostwick insisted that he also look at Mary. There was a red streak on her neck, and her wrists were already swelling; Bostwick suggested X rays and the doctor nodded. "You'd better get those cuffs off," Bostwick admonished the troopers. Lesska could see that the woman was being transformed from prisoner to patient. Bostwick was quick to point out that any lasting injury to his client would be the direct responsibility of the troopers and that any arrest was unnecessary and premature. He painted a picture of a woman desperate to solve the mystery of her children's death, brutally battered in her search for information. He was hardly helped in all this, Danny thought, by Mary herself.

The pitiful, stunned creature he had seen so long had vanished. Mary, her face flushed, her eyes blazing, panting hard, was an Amazon, straining to charge. His embrace was not merely an expression of love, he was holding her still. "Let Bostwick handle it," he said quietly. "Trust him." His mouth was close to her ear. "My darling," he added, without intending to, and thought afterward that he was an idiot.

Ernest was arguing; the troopers looked puzzled. One of them called in to Hastings Wood, and the substation transferred the call to Merivale. But Captain Bassett was at a meeting in Poughkeepsie. The trooper waited for a connection to Lieutenant Hayes.

Danny was certain that Mary would not be arrested. On a point of criminal law, Bostwick could eat Ernest for breakfast. But they would not arrest Lesska either. There was still no evidence.

His mind, which consciously had been filled with pictures of Mary, had also gone along with its usual function, collecting images of the road, the scattering pedestrians, the look on the driver's face when Danny only just avoided his car after running the red light. He had hardly been aware of the images as he plunged to the end of Oak Avenue, to the white house, the drive, the screen of trees, and the cars in the yard. He had run through the yard in great haste, but now he saw, sharply, a light blue car, a late-model Chevy, nothing to have caught his notice except—

The troopers were removing Mary's handcuffs. Bostwick was having his way. Even Mary seemed under control, held by his watchful eyes. Danny, suppressing his own desire to grab Lesska—whose smug and gratified expression had been replaced by a scowl—and do a job on him personally, quietly retreated and made his way downstairs.

The sun was shining in a cloudless sky. The blue car, recently waxed, sparkled like a child's toy. Danny, with an odd, choking excitement, walked around to the back. The license plate was clean also, clear for all to see: a New York plate, LAN718.

Afterward Danny told Pidusky, "If there's one thing that always gets a con man, it's his overconfidence."

The precinct detective thought about it. "Hmph. And that bigshot leaving everything to the handyman. Not so smart. Switching plates, okay. But just changing them back and—"

"The owner of the Chevy would have been very surprised if he hadn't. Lesska could hardly expect it would be in for service when we made our call. After all, we didn't write. We didn't phone," Danny said blissfully.

There was still plenty of trouble. Bostwick told him it was all he could do to prevent Mary from admitting she had tried to kill Lesska. Bostwick's friend in the Justice Department could only confirm what Mordecai had told him: it would be many years before Lesska could be established as Brodki, if ever. And, as Bostwick said dolefully, they would still have to prove that Boy Burgoyne had known the truth. "They must be tied together in some dance of death," he said grimly, "or we might not get either of them."

At the beginning of the case Danny had taken a strong dislike to Spenser, Burgoyne, and Bathsheba. To Christopher country. Up there. But things had started to break. Dick Krantz of Bathsheba had turned out to be a firm witness. He was not going to be shaken about that license number. He had seen what he had seen; he remembered. Bostwick tested his visual recall of figures; it was excellent. Kept sharp, no doubt, by his work for the telephone company.

"I've talked to Kramer," Bostwick told Danny. "They know they will have to drop the charges against Mary. The pool is much too murky now. But he's not ready for a new grand jury. He says Krantz alone isn't enough."

They had met, with William, Isobel, and Mary, at an old restaurant in Merivale. Isobel was sparkling with pleasure at Mary's liberation and William glowed with solid satisfaction. A great wrong was being righted and they had helped to make that come about. Some people "up there," Danny thought thankfully, were really great. But Mary—Mary was restored to life. She wore a bright red dress; her eyes were clear; she was leaning forward and banging her fist on the table at Bostwick's words. The frail victim was quite gone. Nor was she the quiet, pleasant young mother he had first met. In the Burgoyne garage he had seen his wild girl and now he saw a fiery, indomitable woman.

"And Bassett?" Danny asked. "Was old Bloodhound in on your conference? Still after Mary's blood?"

"Bassett was there," Bostwick replied soberly. "You've never been fair to him, Danny. He does his job. This time he just got stuck in the Pemberthy case. The Brodki story shook him although he knows what it's worth at this point. But he had to look again at Boy as the new heir, and at his financial condition. He's not a happy man, but—"

"I'll cry later," Danny said. "If he goes gung ho after Boy and Brodki I might even think he's a good guy. But we can't rest just because the charges are dropped—"

"I know," Bostwick said, soberly. "We just have to hope for a break."

Bostwick was already engaged with the Justice Department, the State Department, and the INS. The lawyers' route, a long one. On a fine Sunday in April, Danny drove upstate and called on Bassett at his house in Burgoyne.

Pink-cheeked, silver-haired, Bassett was a frosty man, but in the setting of his own home he was courteous. Danny hadn't called in advance; he didn't choose to risk refusal. But all went well. The two police officers sat down together in the study and Danny gave Bassett every scrap of information, every idea, every possible line of inquiry he could think to suggest.

"I'll have them both in," Bassett said. "They'll be questioned again." Danny felt that he meant business. His manner had changed while he looked at Danny's notes on his investigation. Elaine Harcourt, the young girl. Boy and his actresses—that had flicked a raw spot. The old Puritan. Bassett was thinking of Alice, weak, dying. Boy Burgoyne was his friend but— Had Boy tormented Alice on her deathbed to pay for his young actresses? Murdered her grandchildren to ensure his comforts? Every feeling denied the possibility, but reason and duty left him only one course.

Bostwick called Danny with exciting news. Boy's love of name-dropping had made it easy to establish the identity of the Viennese countess. She still lived in Vienna and was soon traced.

"I got a guy who does work for the consular office to go and see her. The old lady just wants to keep her hands clean; she's not looking for any trouble. She remembers Burgoyne, all right, but she didn't want to talk too much about Lesska. Then she said she remembered something, an odd bit of gossip. Major Burgoyne enjoyed gossip and she had written to him about it while he was in Paris. She had met someone at a dinner who had known Lesska in Cracow. He had been surprised that Lesska was working as a mechanic and handyman, though the times were difficult. He was a cultured man, quite 'salonfähig,' her acquaintance had said. 'Hardly *our* Lesska,' the countess said. 'His blood is pure motor oil, that useful little man.'"

"So Boy should have been suspicious, and yet—"

"Enough?" Danny wanted to know.

"Well, one step forward."

Danny had been sweating because he couldn't interrogate Burgoyne and Brodki himself. As he had feared, Bassett got nowhere with Boy Burgoyne, rosy from the California sun. Prudently, Ernest had engaged a competent lawyer to accompany Boy to Merivale, but Boy, for the most part, overrode his counsel's objections and answered every question serenely. Boy was still the *grand seigneur* amused at any hint that someone would question his actions. He had taken losses in the real estate market—who hadn't? As for the legacy—that had been Alice's idea, no one else's. He had believed the money would go to her family. He had no notion of her disposition until after her death. Women . . . He implied, without actually saying, that Alice was in love with him and that no one could have prevented her from doing whatever she wished to do. He reiterated that Lesska was a model employee, always had been, and that was all he knew of him.

But "Lesska" was different.

Lesska had gone to Merivale well represented and well instructed. He was told to answer the questions but to say as little as possible. He did as he was told, but he went home worried. Bassett had looked at him and he had not believed him. The police knew the truth. Gregor Brodki feared Captain Bassett—he was hand-in-glove with the New York detective who had watched for him outside the Van Vliet Inn. The New York City police would be tough. Worse than Captain Bassett.

Major Burgoyne had laughed and told him to forget it. But he didn't forget it. The Major had once been the rich, all-powerful American, a godsend to a fugitive in the hellish mess that was Europe, but that was a long time ago. Men far less able than Gregor Brodki became rich men in the United States, yet he had never felt it wise to separate himself from the Major. Major Burgoyne smiled and was gracious, but he was a nobleman at heart. Behind the smile, there was the same contempt that Polish noblemen had always felt for their inferiors. The Major had his knowledge of his servant's true identity to take the place of the whip and the boot.

The killing of the children had been nothing—he had rather enjoyed it—but he had been aware of the risk. Well aware. That time, too, the Major had just laughed. Nothing could go wrong, he had said. But things had gone wrong. The Major had told him to follow the woman on the highway and to get rid of the bodies in some dark fields or woods along her route, far away from Spenser, near the city. The Major hadn't known she meant to take the train. Brodki had been surprised when she took the road to Hastings Wood instead of making for the Taconic; he had had to hang back while she fooled around at the gas station and then, after she had gotten to the railroad station, she had pulled out again. He didn't know what the hell she was doing; he was afraid she was going to meet a lover—the Major had never thought of that.

He had sweated when the woman dragged him through the town of Brewster; he was determined to get rid of the bodies at the first opportunity, but there was no opportunity. Then he nearly lost her.

He had been keeping a car or so behind her on a road where traffic had slowed to a crawl. Suddenly she revved up and passed a big damned truck in front of her and was out of sight. He had panicked and almost sideswiped the car in front of him, trying to get ahead. The driver had been honking his horn loud enough to alert all the troopers on the road. That had been the worst moment. After that, she'd led him to the tavern where she met whoever it was—he didn't care. It was a perfect spot, dark, no houses, no one on the road. He'd dropped the bodies in a hollow by a bush, scraped some mud over them, and gotten out of there. And he'd been damned glad he'd gotten back without being spotted. And the Major had said, "Perfect, perfect. I knew you'd have no trouble."

Neither of them could possibly be suspected, according to the Major. He would handle everything. As he always had. And that part was true. Brodki was aware that the Major had a way of commanding people. Certainly he had had those two stupid women jumping through hoops. So when the Major had made the opportunity, he had taken it. This was an order from a master to his man. Even after all those years, he hadn't dared refuse.

The Major had spoken of benefits to come: a house of his own, greater pay, his own business if he wanted it. But the Major would still have his knowledge and his proofs. When, in front of the police, the woman had called him by his real name, he had been shocked, terrified; yet soon he calmed down, for he realized, in the next moment, that he was free at last of the Major.

Nobody came to his door from the Immigration Service, telling him to pack his things. His first fear receded. Sense returned. Through the years he had followed the stories of suspected war criminals. Men who had done far more than Gregor Brodki. The cases were hard to prove. None of his victims had lived to identify him—he had made sure of that before he escaped. Sitting by his workbench in the quiet of his apartment behind the big house, he decided that his fear, born in Vienna, should have died long ago. He owed the Major nothing.

There was another thing he had learned, living in the United States. If two or more people commit a crime, one of them can make a deal with the authorities: immunity from prosecution if he testifies against his partner or partners for the government. When he was called back to be questioned by Bassett and Kramer, he astounded his lawyer, so carefully selected by Ernest, when he told the law officers simply, "The Major made me do it."

Of course, it was Bostwick who got the news from Kramer that charges against Mary had been dropped and a new grand jury was being summoned. Lesska was being held. "There was some question about Boy Burgoyne being arrested at this point," Bostwick told Mary, "but he made Kramer's mind up for him. Bassett was having Boy watched. The *Emma III* had been moved to a harbor on Long Island Sound, and when Boy tried to board, the police grabbed him. That yacht was equipped for a long voyage. A very long voyage."

To Danny, Bostwick was jubilant. "What a break. They've got both of them cold. Kramer's beginning to see the glory of it. 'Fearless DA pursues the last of the patroons. The killer-handyman— former war criminal?' The TV crews are up here already."

Danny was concerned that Mary would be hounded, but Mary, he learned, could handle it. After a visit to Sag Harbor in the warm May weather, she was returning to the city with Mildred, in good health—her own woman. He was glad and a trifle melancholy. He would have liked to give her the news himself, but that was childish. On the day of her return he stood in front of the bathroom mirror, shaving. The bright sun showed up the cracking paint, the rather threadbare towels, and the blood on his cheek where he'd nicked himself. He swore. In truth, he told himself, what he was suffering from was regret. Aunt Regina had summoned him to help a lady in distress. And now it was all over. His job was done.

It was of no use to telephone Mary; although she had the unlisted number, her line was constantly busy. Perhaps she had left the receiver off the hook. So he walked around. Just to say welcome back.

He had no trouble seeing her. Mary, with Mildred, was on the front steps of her building, caught by the newshounds. On the sidewalk, under the flowering dogwood tree, the super's wife watched, smiling. Mildred in green, Mary in blue, they made an attractive sight. Mary was beautiful, serene, competent. The deep shadows had gone from her eyes, and the color had returned to her cheeks. She answered a reporter's questions with sense and good taste and managed to slip away while Mildred held their attention: plainspoken Mildred, who had no qualms about saying what she thought of "the Burgoyne gang."

Mary hadn't seen him, but Mildred did, and hailed him as the camera crew packed up.

"Danny! I'm glad you're here. I wouldn't have left without seeing you. We've just got in. Mary wanted to be home. She's okay now."

Her face was bright, though her anger was not all gone. "All that rat's nest dug out and shown up for what it is. All the dirt that they threw at her cleared away. I wish they could all get the chair."

He walked her to her car. Mildred had business to do around town.

"Do you think Mary has really got a grip on things? The trials will be messy. And the children . . ."

"The children. The poor darlings." Mildred was sobered. "I don't suppose any woman could ever get over that. All that's gone."

She thought of her own three, grown now. Her grandchild and the one on the way. "But now she can admit to herself that they are dead. Accept it at last. And she's young enough to begin again. She's working on her book, you know. That's why I feel free to leave," she added. "I've been asked to join a group who are starting a dig at Tenochtitlán, but I wouldn't leave the country with things as they were. Let's be sure to meet again before I go."

She looked up at him and spoke quietly. "I don't know what we'd have done without you. God bless." Then she smiled. "Mary thinks so much of you. She's always telling me, 'Danny said this. Danny said that.' Are you going up now? Mary must want to thank you."

Danny felt a strong aversion to being thanked by Mary. The kind police officer. Regina Valenti's nephew. In any event, it was Mordecai who had cracked the case. Danny had called the old man with the good news. Mordecai received it with grim pleasure. "One more marked off. A pity you have no death penalty. At some time, I expect, Israel will try to extradite him for his war crimes." He gave a bark of laughter. "He is a rat, Brodki. And he acts like a rat."

Mordecai understood "Lesska" as Boy Burgoyne never had. To his cost.

Before Mildred got into her car, she turned to Danny and gave him a big hug and a kiss. Warm, sweet, it was a sister's embrace. Mildred, he thought, was one hell of a woman.

In the hallway, he rang Aunt Regina's bell. He would give Mary time to collect herself. Perhaps he would see her tomorrow.

Aunt Regina had watched the scene from her front window. She greeted Danny with a sigh of satisfaction. "Irish," she said. "Just like your mother. They have spirit. They fight back."

He wondered whom his mother had had to fight. Among others, Aunt Regina, no doubt. He remembered the talk in his grandmother's apartment, hushed at his arrival. "Hell's Kitchen. Not a dollar saved in the whole family . . . Giovanni gives money to her mother."

"A rich Irishwoman," he said gloomily. "Do you realize that eventually all that five million dollars will come to Mary? Burgoyne can't inherit. He was an accomplice to the murder."

Danny thought of his pay, after taxes and pension deduction; of his own funds, after the cost of his sons' education. Beside Mary's new wealth, his assets were beggarly.

Aunt Regina pursed her lips. "You still don't know that young woman. We have talked. She is not one, I would say, who should have the handling of family money. Too generous, too impulsive. But her idea on this is good. Some part of that money will go to a fund for sick and homeless children. Connie and I will help her to see it is well arranged. But in any event, Daniele, you must be more with the times. You think like that loudmouth up in the country. Today five million dollars is not great wealth. Your Uncle Paul bought a few buildings in this neighborhood many years ago. And last year he sold two of them for over four million dollars.

"I, too, have made some good investments over the years," she said, regarding him sharply. Aunt Regina was not known to discuss her affairs with anyone, except her brother. "And you will some day receive a substantial inheritance. I loved your father," she said, in a gentle voice that he had never heard before. "Giovanni was not the shrewdest man in the family, but he was a good man, a good heart."

Her gaze was still upon him, a mixture of affection and perplexity. "But he would not have wanted you to become a policeman. Still—" she shrugged—"it has its uses."

Danny would have been amused, as well as grateful, but he still had less than cheerful thoughts.

"Thanks, Zia Regina. But I'm afraid Mary has too much spirit now for an old cop. Forty-six. And Mary thirty-something and stunning."

Regina gave up on English and expressed herself forcefully in Italian. His aunt, the grand lady, the pillar of her church, rapidly descended to the language of the streets. In the swift flood of abuse that passed her lips, he caught a well-known word. Aunt Regina was deploring his lack of virility.

Suddenly, he laughed, a buoyant laugh that was a release from old anxiety and a heady ride to joy. As Regina stood by, smiling, he went next door to tell the tale to Mary. Mary, who was standing on a stepladder hanging up fresh light curtains, had seen him entering the building and had left her door ajar. As he came in, she turned, saw him, jumped down from the ladder, and ran into his arms.

"Danny," she murmured in his ear, "I thought you were never coming."

When he released her from their first real embrace, they stood for a moment, holding hands, smiling, and then drew close again. Outside the dogwood tree spread its burden of white blossoms wide to the glowing sun.